MYSTERIES OF COBBLE HILL FARM

Borrowed Trouble

SHAEN LAYLE

A Gift from Guideposts

Thank you for your purchase! We want to express our gratitude for your support with a special gift just for you.

Dive into *Spirit Lifters*, a complimentary e-book that will fortify your faith, offering solace during challenging moments. Its 31 carefully selected scripture verses will soothe and uplift your soul.

Please use the QR code or go to **guideposts.org/spiritlifters** to download.

Mysteries of Cobble Hill Farm is a trademark of Guideposts.

Published by Guideposts
100 Reserve Road, Suite E200
Danbury, CT 06810
Guideposts.org

Copyright © 2025 by Guideposts. All rights reserved. This book, or parts thereof, may not be reproduced, stored in a retrieval system, or transmitted in any form or by any means, electronic, mechanical, photocopying, recording, or otherwise, without the written permission of the publisher.

This is a work of fiction. While the setting of Mysteries of Cobble Hill Farm as presented in this series is fictional, the location of Yorkshire, England, actually exists, and some places and characters may be based on actual places and people whose identities have been used with permission or fictionalized to protect their privacy. Apart from the actual people, events, and locales that figure into the fiction narrative, all other names, characters, businesses, and events are the creation of the author's imagination and any resemblance to actual persons or events is coincidental. Every attempt has been made to credit the sources of copyrighted material used in this book. If any such acknowledgment has been inadvertently omitted or miscredited, receipt of such information would be appreciated.

Scripture references are from the following sources: *The Holy Bible, King James Version* (KJV). *The Holy Bible, New International Version* (NIV). Copyright © 1973, 1978, 1984, 2011 by Biblica, Inc. Used by permission of Zondervan. All rights reserved worldwide. www.zondervan.com.

Cover and interior design by Müllerhaus
Cover illustration by Bob Kayganich at Illustration Online LLC.
Typeset by Aptara, Inc.

ISBN 978-1-961442-46-7 (hardcover)
ISBN 978-1-961442-47-4 (softcover)
ISBN 978-1-961442-48-1 (epub)

Printed and bound in the United States of America

MYSTERIES OF COBBLE HILL FARM

Borrowed Trouble

GLOSSARY OF UK TERMS

aye • yes

brilliant • fantastic

biscuit • cookie

chap • man

chuffed • very pleased

cuppa • cup of

fancy • like

goggle • look at

innit • isn't it

lift • elevator

loo • restroom

mate • friend

peaky • ill

proper donkey's years • a very long time

rubbish • bad

YRO • Youth Rehabilitation Order

CHAPTER ONE

H arriet, we have a problem."

It was midafternoon on Saturday, and August light poured through the back church window where Harriet Bailey and her wedding party had set up a dressing space. Harriet turned from the mirror, where her mother had been carefully pinning her veil into place, and faced her matron of honor, Polly Worthington, and bridesmaid, Ashley Fiske.

Polly lived in White Church Bay and was Harriet's right-hand woman at the veterinary clinic that Harriet ran, while Ashley had flown to England from the States with her preteen son, Trevor. The last time Ashley was in town, she had helped Harriet solve a decades-old mystery. Today was all about celebration though. So why did both of her friends wear matching expressions of concern?

"Uh oh. What's wrong?"

Harriet's stomach tightened as her thoughts ran ahead. Had something gone wrong with the flowers? Or the music? What if Will had taken sick at the last minute? She had waited so long to find the love of her life. She certainly didn't relish the thought of a delay in their wedding ceremony.

"It may not be a big deal at all," Ashley rushed to explain. "The hotel staff assured us they're taking care of things."

Harriet and Will had planned to have their reception at Ravenscroft, a lovely historic castle-turned-B&B on the outskirts of White Church Bay. It was romantic, historic, and large enough to comfortably seat all those invited. But if Ashley's vagueness about the reception hall was meant to ease Harriet's worry, it wasn't working.

Harriet braced herself before continuing. "Details, please?"

"They're having some issues with birds in the main hall." Polly picked up where Ashley had left off. "They think they got in during renovations."

Harriet had been thrilled when the hotel manager informed her of the venue's upcoming renovations. Things would be in tip-top shape for the reception. But then when the renovations dragged out, stretching closer and closer to their booking date, she'd gotten jittery. Maybe she'd been right to feel so.

Harriet's mother chimed in as the voice of reason. "If the staff said they would take care of it, I'm sure we have no reason to worry. I'll call them after the ceremony, Harriet, while you're getting pictures with Will. We'll have it straightened out in no time. The worst thing that could happen is the reception starts a few minutes late."

Aunt Jinny smiled reassuringly. "Every wedding must have a hiccup or two. It makes for a fun story later."

Polly and Ashley echoed their reassurances and hurried from the room to get in line for the processional. Harriet's mother returned to smoothing the filmy, translucent folds of Harriet's veil over her shoulders. "Sweetheart, you look lovely."

Harriet reached back to place her hand over her mother's, which rested on her shoulder. It was so good to have her here. Since

Harriet had moved to England a year and a half ago, in-person visits with her parents had been few and far between, and video calls just weren't the same. Having her mother and father close at hand for her special day meant so much. Of course, she enjoyed having her White Church Bay family close at hand too. Today represented not only Will and her joining together in marriage but also the melding of Harriet's American and English lives. Had she really been in Yorkshire running Grandad's veterinary practice for only the past year and a half? The place and people now felt so familiar to her, it seemed she had been in White Church Bay forever.

"You're prettier than a picture, lass." Aunt Jinny echoed her sister-in-law's sentiment.

Harriet squared to face the mirror again. She normally shrugged off compliments, but today she believed her mother and aunt's words. She couldn't help but feel beautiful on her wedding day. Radiant happiness had a way of painting the world in sunshine, and that was how it felt to finally be marrying Pastor Fitzwilliam Knight.

She smoothed the front of her dress, and its pearl-encrusted fabric glimmered in the glass. Within the hour, she would walk down the aisle of White Church and recite her vows before God and all her nearest and dearest friends and family. Some brides got cold feet, but she wouldn't. How could she doubt that God had brought Will and her together?

"All right, final touches." Her mother handed her the bouquet of English roses mixed with aromatic lavender. "It's almost time to go. Are you ready?"

Harriet nodded but paused when Aunt Jinny held up a finger.

"Wait, I have one more thing for you." Aunt Jinny riffled through the handbag that she'd plopped down on a nearby chair. She removed a small jewelry box tied with a ribbon and handed it to Harriet. "Consider this as your something old."

Harriet untied the ribbon and opened the box. Nestled inside on a bed of wispy cotton was a gemstone brooch. It had a gold underplate, and its top was set with vibrant emerald stones and fashioned in the shape of a heart.

"It's beautiful," Harriet breathed. She turned the brooch over in her hands. It was heavy and showcased the craftsmanship of a bygone era. "Did it belong to a family member?"

Aunt Jinny nodded. "Yes, though I don't know who first owned it. It's called an endearment brooch, and it's quite old. Mum is the one who passed it down to me, but she didn't know the details of its history. I suspect, however, that this"—she reached over to unhinge a tiny clasp that had escaped Harriet's attention, and the front of the brooch swung open—"is the original owner."

"How clever. It's like a locket." Harriet peered at the picture that occupied the brooch's hollow space. It was of a young man and woman dressed in opulent clothing. Whoever the couple were, they appeared completely in love. They sat next to each other on a velvet settee with clasped hands and tender expressions. Were these some of her relatives from generations back?

"It can be worn as a locket," Harriet's mother said. "There's a chain in the box so you can convert it if you like." She smiled. "I recognize the look on their faces. I've caught you and Will glancing at each other like that a time or two."

Aunt Jinny pressed Harriet into a hug. "Your grandmother would have wanted you to have this brooch for your special day. I think it's a paste piece, but it's still quite pretty and sentimental."

"I love it," Harriet assured her. "Help me pin it on?"

Harriet held still as Aunt Jinny and her mother worked together to pin the brooch into place at the neck of her dress. She reached up to make sure it felt secure before turning this way and that in the mirror to admire the effect.

Harriet's mother and aunt helped her finish getting ready, and she set aside her earlier worries about the reception venue. Nothing could dampen the brightness of her outlook right now.

She was marrying Will.

If Harriet had any doubt of Will's affection for her, it was immediately cast aside when she stood at the entry to the majestic stone church's sanctuary. As Harriet's seven-year-old cousin, Sebastian, carried the couple's rings on a satin pillow and his twin, Sophie, scattered rose petals in the aisle, Harriet caught Will's eye.

The look of love written on his face made her feel as if she floated, rather than walked, on her father's arm to the melodic strains of Clarke's Trumpet Voluntary. Familiar faces in the crowd passed by in a happy blur. Countless parishioners of Will's from White Church. Harriet's kind neighbor, Doreen Danby and her family. Harriet's mother and Will's father. Aunt Jinny, sitting beside her son, Anthony, and his wife, Olivia—parents to Sebastian and Sophie.

MYSTERIES OF COBBLE HILL FARM

Low laughter rippled through the crowd as Sophie blew kisses from the front of the sanctuary. Little matter that her flower girl role was finished. She obviously ate up the attention.

Harriet's focus, however, rested on Will. It was as though the two of them were suspended in time. The only people in the world.

Harriet's father lifted her veil and pressed a kiss to her cheek. Then he left her at the altar before Will and Jared, Will's seminary roommate, who was performing the ceremony.

"You look beautiful," Will whispered, so low that only Harriet could hear.

"You don't look so bad yourself," she whispered back.

Her eyes misted with emotion as she joined hands with him. How special this day was. Her family and friends in attendance and Will's as well. All those they loved best, in one room.

What a winding road that had led her here. Just a short while ago, Harriet had wondered if marriage was part of God's plan for her. A broken engagement had nudged her to relocate from her hometown in Connecticut to England and take over her late grandfather's business and estate. It was a radical move, and one that made her wonder even more at what her future held. Then she met Will, and his tender attention healed her broken heart. Looking back over the pattern of past months, God's plan was clear. In His perfect timing, He brought Will and her together, and today was the fulfillment of that promise.

After Jared gave opening remarks and Will's cousin Emily sang the song she'd written for the occasion, Harriet and Will took turns reading from the Alfred, Lord Tennyson poem, "Marriage Morning."

Light, so low in the vale,
You flash and lighten afar,
For this is the golden morning of love,
And you are his morning star...

Next, they said their vows, joining a long line of couples throughout history who have made the same sacred promises to each other. Harriet smiled as she thought of the brooch pinned to her dress. The commitment of those who had gone before her filled her with gratitude.

The ceremony complete, Jared invited Harriet and Will to face the congregation. "I present to you Fitzwilliam Ringo Knight and Harriet Grace Bailey-Knight."

As the crowd applauded, Will squeezed her hand. "Ready to face the world, Mrs. Bailey-Knight?"

"With you? Always."

After the ceremony, the photographer pulled the members of the wedding party aside to take more pictures. She kept raving about the "golden hour" and how perfect the light was for photography. Hopefully, that meant the pictures would turn out well. Harriet cheesed with Will through what felt like hundreds of photos, and by the time they finished, her cheeks ached from smiling. Finally, it was time to wrap things up at the church and head to the reception.

"Your carriage awaits, my lady."

Past the happy gauntlet of well-wishers throwing confetti, Will led Harriet to the stylish convertible waiting to transport them to the reception venue. Their driver opened the rear passenger door and waited while Will helped tuck Harriet and her dress's voluminous tulle inside. Then Will circled around to take his place opposite his bride.

"What do you think of her?" he asked Harriet as she fastened her seat belt.

Harriet frowned at him. She was just glad he'd left the top up and she didn't have to worry about her hair. "*Her*?"

"Yes, her. The car." Will grinned. "She's something, isn't she?"

All Harriet could offer was a bemused smile. What was with the "she"? Was it like with boats, where men personified them into people?

She shrugged. "I don't know. It's a nice car, I guess." She could tell from the leather interior and sharp details that it was a step above a common vehicle, but her answer must have surprised Will. His eyebrows shot up.

"A *nice* car? You *guess*?"

"I don't know much about vehicles."

"First order of business then." Will winked. "I'm happy to teach you, if you're interested in learning. I've been fascinated by vintage cars since I was a lad."

Will set aside light conversation as the driver eased the vehicle into motion, and both Harriet and he waved through the windows at the group of wedding guests still milling in front of the church. Harriet flinched as a sudden cascade of confetti hit the windshield. Wait a minute. Weren't they done with that?

When the view cleared, however, she could see what had happened.

Apparently, Sophie and Sebastian hadn't gotten the message that the time for throwing confetti was over. Harriet and Will shared a chuckle as Olivia and Anthony lunged to stop the twins from chucking any more at the car. A smile pulled at Harriet's cheeks. The twins were as thick as thieves, and as mischievous too. But what else could you expect from seven-year-olds?

With the twins constrained, the driver honked the horn at the crowd. Then he eased out of the parking lot, leaving Will free to turn back to the matter at hand: sharing his passion for vehicles with Harriet. "For your information, this is more than a 'nice car.' It's a Jaguar E-Type."

He said the last part emphatically, as though it was supposed to mean something. She decided to humor him. "Is that different from a regular Jaguar?"

"Different?" Will nearly came out of his seat. It was really quite amusing. She'd had no idea of his rabid interest in cars before. "I'll say. It's an absolute classic. One of the first cars with disc brakes on all four wheels, as well as monocoque construction."

Amazing. It was like he was spouting Greek. "I'm sorry. What?"

"Monocoque construction. It means that the body and chassis of the car are integrated into a single unit. Plus, it's the same kind of vehicle Joe Root drives. When he's not chauffeured around, that is."

"That's a job I'd jump at." The driver angled an amused look at them in the rearview mirror.

"You and me both," Will replied.

Now, Joe Root, Harriet knew. Will enjoyed watching cricket in his spare time, and Joe Root was his favorite player. "Ah, well. If it has a cricketer's ringing endorsement, it must be quite impressive."

Finally Will seemed satisfied. "That it is. And I rented the car for the entire week. We'll be touring in style for our honeymoon."

She reached across the back seat to lace her fingers with his. Who would have thought? Her new husband had a penchant for vintage cars. Just an hour into marriage, and here she was, learning something about him that she hadn't known before. One of the countless things she would certainly learn about Will over the years.

How she hoped there would be many of them.

CHAPTER TWO

It took less than ten minutes to reach the southern outskirts of White Church Bay, where the reception hall was located. Ravenscroft cast a majestic silhouette against a backdrop of fading light, and the gardens that flanked the castle were in full summer bloom.

How thrilling to be staying here. Will had booked a suite for the night so that they wouldn't have to travel after the reception. Tomorrow they planned to head up the coast for a two-day tour of Wales. Then a couple more days in Ireland followed by France before heading back home to settle into ordinary life. Though it would feel strange to be absent from the clinic for an entire week, she relished the promise of uninterrupted time traveling with her new husband.

But she was getting ahead of herself. First, it was time to enjoy a wedding reception with all their favorite people.

"Look, there's Anthony and Olivia. Anthony must've had a lead foot to beat us here." Harriet pointed out the window at her cousins, who were making their way up the cobblestone pathway that led to the castle's main entrance.

Will exited the car and started to open Harriet's door, but not before a shriek pierced the otherwise tranquil evening. "What?

MYSTERIES OF COBBLE HILL FARM

What happened?" Harriet twisted around in her seat to look out the back window.

"I'm not sure," Will said.

With Will's help, Harriet quickly maneuvered her behemoth of a dress out of the car and hurried toward her family. "Is everyone all right?"

Olivia had a hand pressed to her heart, while the children danced around excitedly. Everything looked okay. No one appeared to be hurt. Nothing too bad could have happened, could it?

Anthony scowled in response to Harriet's question. "One of those birds tried to dive-bomb us. That's gotta be bad luck."

Olivia swatted his arm. "That's just an old superstition. I didn't take you for a believer of old wives' tales, honey."

Apparently, even couples who had been married for years could make new discoveries about each other.

"Everyone all right?" A young man wielding a garden rake gave one final "shoo" at the bird. He looked to be in his early twenties and sported dark, slicked-back hair and a polo shirt and khakis. The hotel insignia on his shirt told Harriet that he must be a Ravenscroft employee.

"We're fine, thank you," Will informed him.

"Pastor Will?" The young man stopped, a surprised expression on his face. "What are you doing here?"

Will squinted without recognition. Then he broke into a wide grin. "I'll be. Benny Carter?"

The young man nodded and extended his hand to shake, which Will did enthusiastically.

"I actually go by Benedict now. Thought it would be a good idea to put my old life behind me, and I started with the name."

Benedict's cryptic allusion to his past piqued Harriet's curiosity, but she wasn't about to poke her nose in where it didn't belong. If there was anything she needed to know, she was certain Will would fill her in.

"Well, Benedict then." Will beamed. "A right good name too. It's been proper donkey's years since I last saw you. How have you been?"

"Grand, just grand. A lot has changed for me." Benedict proudly tapped the stitched insignia on his shirt. "Steady work and honest hands, as you see. I've been working here at the hotel since high school and recently got promoted to manager. I've also been seeing a lovely lass for the last year."

"That's wonderful, Benedict. Congratulations on the promotion and the relationship. What's the lucky lady's name?"

"Lucy Robinson. She works here at the hotel too." Benedict leaned forward as though he was relaying a secret to which only Will and Harriet were privy. "I need to save up a bit more money for a down payment, but I'm planning on proposing as soon as I can buy an engagement ring."

"How lovely," Harriet enthused.

"Sounds like life is treating you well, Benedict." Will placed his hand on Harriet's back. "A lot has changed for me recently too. You asked what I was doing here. May I present my wife, Harriet?"

Hearing Will call her "wife" warmed Harriet even more than the balmy August sun inching toward the horizon. She stuck out her hand to Benedict. "It's wonderful to meet you."

MYSTERIES OF COBBLE HILL FARM

Instead of returning her greeting, a funny look suddenly crossed Benedict's face. His eyes narrowed, his nose wrinkled, and his arm flew up to shield his face.

Achoo! The man sneezed a mighty sneeze into the crook of his elbow.

Harriet slowly withdrew her hand. Oh no. Was he ill with a cold? She wanted to be friendly, but nursing a virus on her honeymoon was not on her checklist.

"I'm so sorry," Benedict apologized. "I've been sneezing a lot. The pollen count is high today. Anyway, I'm happy to meet you, Harriet, and offer my hearty congratulations on your wedding."

Only allergies then. That was one worry checked off her list. She thanked Benedict for his well wishes. Goodness, her cheeks still ached from smiling. She supposed she had better get used to it though. "Can I ask how Will and you know each other? Through the church, I assume?"

Benedict's nose wrinkled again, but the high pollen count didn't seem to be the cause this time. Did Harriet detect a shamefaced expression on his youthful features? "I suppose you could say that."

"Water under the bridge, mate," was all Will said. "What's past is past."

Again with the mysterious allusions. Had Benedict been in trouble before? She darted a glance Will's way for explanation, but he shook his head. Apparently, she wasn't to push it. What had she said that was wrong? Though she'd been careful, it appeared she'd stuck her high-heeled foot in her mouth, and the thought put a small damper on her joy.

The rest of the conversation with Benedict wrapped up quickly. "Gotta get back to work, but I'll catch up with you soon."

"Feel free to stop by the reception if you can," Will offered.

"I might do that," Benedict replied. "If Lucy can step away from watching the front desk for a minute, I'll introduce you to her."

"Please do," Harriet insisted, and she and Will told Benedict goodbye.

As Benedict disappeared around the corner of the castle, Harriet turned another questioning gaze toward Will. "What was that about? Did I say something I shouldn't have?"

"Don't worry about it." Will leaned close and spoke low. His voice tickled her ear. "It's a long story for another time. Let's just say I helped Benedict when he was a young chap. He wasn't on a good path then, but I'm pleased to see he's making good choices now."

Side by side, they walked up the cobblestone pathway that led to the castle's main entrance. Harriet's mother met them at the threshold with a thumbs-up. "Looks like the avian invasion is under control."

"We saw." Harriet explained about seeing Benedict chase one of the birds from the castle with a garden rake. When she relayed Anthony's comment about the dive-bombing being bad luck, Harriet's mother waved her hands as though to shoo away worries. "Hardly. The reception is going to be nothing short of perfect. Come on in."

Harriet reached for Will's hand, and he laced his fingers through hers. Then he gave her hand a tight squeeze. "Shall we make our entrance?"

"We shall, sir." Harriet squeezed his hand in response. Then they walked through the large antique double doors that led to the reception hall.

Evidently, Harriet's mom had alerted everyone to the new couple's arrival, because a cheer rose from the guests as soon as Harriet and Will entered the venue.

"Cheers for the new mister and missus!" Polly cried, and all the guests whooped and clapped. Harriet grinned and shook her bouquet in the air for greeting, and Will made a mock bow to the crowd.

Harriet hadn't seen the hall since the rehearsal dinner the evening before. A few late-night hours of elbow grease from her family and the bridal party had utterly transformed the space. Twinkling lights hung from high beams and cast a warm, soft glow across the room. Lush bouquets of colorful flowers and vases dotted the tables. The normally grand but imposing room was filled to overflowing with lively chatter and shared joy.

"Mom was right. It's perfect," Harriet breathed. Will squeezed her hand again.

Ashley appeared beside them. She still wore her bridesmaid gown, but she had swapped her heeled shoes for more comfortable flats. Harriet wiggled her toes inside her own heels. It would be a relief to sit after several hours of standing.

Ashley led Harriet and Will through the throng to a long table festooned with copious amounts of filmy tulle where the wedding party sat. Will and Harriet took their places, and Harriet happily slipped her feet out of her shoes.

After a quick blessing by Jared, they enjoyed their meal. The guests had their choice of chicken or beef, along with roasted potatoes and green beans almondine. Everything was delicious, and the sustenance was much appreciated after a long afternoon of festivities. Of course, there would be the wedding cupcakes for dessert, but as the food had been served buffet style instead of plated service, they had to wait for everyone to finish eating first.

Harriet laid her fork and knife across her empty plate and removed the napkin from her lap. Before she could do anything else, however, Aunt Jinny appeared at her shoulder. "Can I steal you away for a moment?"

Harriet stood to her feet, reluctantly slipping on her shoes again. "Sure."

"We won't be long," Aunt Jinny assured Will before steering Harriet toward a long table near the entrance that Harriet hadn't noticed before. Framed family photos lined the tabletop, as well as a smattering of sparkling jewelry.

"Yesterday when I was sorting through the family keepsakes," Aunt Jinny said, "I had an idea to set up an heirloom table with the special items I found." She led Harriet up and down the table, detailing the family history of the pieces she knew. "And this necklace belonged to—"

Aunt Jinny was interrupted by Sophie, who tugged on the hem of her blouse. The little girl grinned up at her grandmother, and Harriet noticed the gap in her smile from a recently lost tooth.

"Nan? Do you think I did a good job as flower girl?"

"Yes, of course. The best flower girl I ever saw." Aunt Jinny smiled at Sophie. "You had the crowd eating out of your hand."

Sophie beamed. "Really?"

Harriet nodded. "She's telling the truth. You were great."

The little girl twirled in her dress, appearing to enjoy the attention. However, just past her, standing at the other end of the table, was Sebastian. He certainly didn't look pleased. His arms were crossed over his chest, and his face held a scowl. What was that about?

She didn't have time to ask, as Sophie demanded attention again. She took off the sparkly tiara she had worn as flower girl and handed it to her grandmother. "Is my crown pretty enough to go on the treasure table?"

"The treasure table?" Aunt Jinny looked puzzled for a moment before catching Sophie's meaning. "Oh, you mean this table? With the family jewelry?"

"Uh-huh. It looks like the treasure I have in my treasure box at home. But you have a lot more than I do."

Harriet smiled. Sophie's "treasure box" was filled with all manner of items precious to a young girl: shiny gum wrappers twisted into bracelets, lost beads from broken necklaces, and random hair baubles. A catchall of childish riches.

With Aunt Jinny's approval, Harriet moved some items on the table to clear a space for Sophie's tiara. "Why don't we put your crown in a place of honor?"

Sophie grinned widely, even as Sebastian's scowl deepened. "Okay." She handed Harriet her tiara, and Harriet situated it on the table. Then Sophie skipped off, leaving her brother behind, to go talk to Ashley's son, Trevor, who looked as if he'd grown a foot since Harriet saw him last. Harriet waved at him, and Trevor waved back.

"A little girl who loves jewelry. Tell her I may have a job for her in fifteen years…"

Harriet looked away from Sophie and Trevor when the exuberant voice broke into their conversation. She turned to see who was speaking and came face-to-feathers with a hat that would put any Kentucky Derby attendee to shame. Then the hat tilted, and the person wearing it became visible.

"Talia!" Harriet cried. Worries over the twins flew out of her mind as she threw her arms around the woman. What a surprise! How many years had passed since Harriet had seen her?

Natalia Bishop was an old family friend who spent most of her time running a fine jewelry shop out of town. She had left White Church Bay to open her business about a month before Harriet had relocated to England. Harriet had sent her a wedding invitation weeks ago but hadn't expected her to attend. It was well known that Talia was a workaholic who rarely closed her shop, even for special occasions such as this one. She was a one-woman show and proud of it. "I'm so surprised you're here. I had no idea you were coming."

Talia wrapped Harriet in a tight embrace. "I got here a little late, and I only caught the tail end of the ceremony. I wasn't going to crash the reception, especially after I RSVP'd that I wouldn't be able to attend, but your mother assured me there was more than enough food to go around."

Harriet laughed. "And she was right. How's work?"

Talia shrugged. "Oh, you know how the entrepreneur's life goes. A mountain one day, a valley the next. It's a roller coaster."

Harriet nodded empathetically. Owning a vet clinic was a bit different than running a jewelry shop, but she understood the stresses involved with occupying the helm of a business. She had gotten used to wearing a variety of hats, that was for certain. Before

MYSTERIES OF COBBLE HILL FARM

she could say anything to that effect, however, Talia turned and began studying the jewelry at the heirloom table.

Aunt Jinny stopped her before she got very far. "If you're looking for something like the jewelry you sell in your shop, I'm sorry to say you'll be disappointed. Most of this is paste."

"I don't know about that. I see a few real pieces mixed in. And this one certainly isn't paste." Talia motioned to the brooch pinned to Harriet's dress.

Harriet touched the brooch. "This?"

Talia nodded.

"Aunt Jinny gave it to me to wear today. She doesn't know much about its history, though we do know it was passed down through several generations to her mother and my grandmother, Helen, and then her. You have expertise in this area. Any guesses as to how old it might be?" Harriet carefully removed the brooch and set it on the table next to Sophie's tiara.

"Hmm." Talia studied the brooch. After looking at the outside of the piece, she depressed the clasp that opened the cover. Harriet once again caught a glimpse of the loving couple's image inside. "Well, it's definitely an antique. Likely Victorian."

"How can you tell?" Aunt Jinny asked.

"The intricacy, for one." Talia's finger traced curlicues in the air that mimicked the metalwork on the brooch. "The Victorians thought more was more. Also, the image inside dates to a specific set of years. The first reliably dated daguerreotype was created in the late 1830s by Louis Daguerre, but the process became particularly popular in the 1840s through the 1850s, which is when I would date this piece. Taking everything into consideration—the style of the brooch, the fashion worn by the couple—I'd date the piece to the early 1850s. Daguerreotypes fell out of favor soon after that."

Interesting. Talia's information provided the barest glimpse into the history of the brooch, but it was enough to intrigue Harriet. What story did the piece hold?

Aunt Jinny appeared interested as well. "You say it isn't paste. Does that mean it's valuable then?"

Talia tapped her fingers on her lips. "Oh yes. I think it could be enormously valuable. A lot of people would love to get their hands on something like this. It's a very unique piece. Also, daguerreotypes are delicate. It's lucky that the closed locket has protected the image from light and moisture. It's rare to find a daguerreotype this old in such pristine condition. If I had to venture a guess at the value, I'd say the brooch could bring around eight thousand pounds at auction."

Aunt Jinny's mouth dropped open. "Eight thousand pounds? Are you serious?"

Harriet did a rough calculation in her head. "That's around ten thousand American dollars. Sounds like we'd be wise to pop this in a lockbox."

Aunt Jinny shook her head, clearly still in disbelief at the enormous sum Talia had quoted. "I just might."

The ringing sound of utensil on glass alerted the group to Van Worthington, the local detective constable and Will's best man, standing at the front of the room. "Time for toasts!"

Everyone moved back to their seats, though Harriet noticed Talia continued to hover at the heirloom table even after they left. She also noticed that Benedict had come into the room and stood just inside the entry beside a young blond woman.

Harriet smiled. He must have coaxed Lucy away from the desk for a minute.

She directed her attention back up front when Van began his best man speech. This was followed by a few words from his wife and Harriet's best friend—and matron of honor, Polly. Then Will left Harriet's side to address the crowd.

"A heartfelt thank-you to everyone who could join us today," he began. "I can't tell you what a joy it is to see so many familiar faces." He drew attention to a few people in the crowd before panning a teasing grin across the room. "And believe me, do I have some stories I could tell…"

He paused as light laughter rippled through the group. Harriet waited for him to spill a clever anecdote about a guest. Before he could continue speaking, however, the lights went out and the entire room was plunged into darkness.

CHAPTER THREE

Harriet gasped. What happened? Her other senses kicked into overdrive as darkness robbed her of sight.

There was a brush of feathers by her face.

A shriek of confusion.

A crashing noise.

And repeated sneezing that traveled from the doorway out into the hall. Who was that? What was going on? Was someone leaving? And why had the lights gone out? It couldn't be storms. The evening sky had been clear as a bell when they'd entered the reception hall.

"Will?"

"I'm here." Harriet reached for her husband in the darkness, and he found her. His warm embrace proved a comfort in an uncertain situation.

"Nobody panic." A man's voice cut through the dark. Benedict? Had the sneezing earlier been him? "I think we've had a power surge. It looks like only the lights in here were affected. I'll have things fixed in a moment."

Harriet leaned into Will. Ah, that was a relief. A simple explanation.

Soon, the lights came back on, and Harriet saw the full extent of the damage that had been wrought by the sudden electrical hiccup.

She sighed. "Oh no. The cupcakes."

The poor baker. Imogen Sinclair sprawled on the floor, looking dazed. The yelp Harriet heard must have come from her. Her apron was smeared with icing, and at least a dozen cupcakes lay smashed on the ground beside her.

Will hurried forward to help Imogen to her feet. "I don't know what happened," she kept saying. "I was bringing these to the bridal table. Then the lights went out, and I felt someone rush by me. I lost my balance and bumped into the cart, and now we've lost your bridal cake and some cupcakes."

"It's all right. We have plenty more." Will winked at Harriet to lighten the mood created by the mishap. "And Harriet and I can always eat the smaller cupcakes instead of the bridal cupcake."

How like him, to lift someone else up after a problem. Harriet laughed. "That's exactly right. Don't give it another thought, please."

Imogen seemed slightly mollified. A hotel employee quickly rushed in to clean up the smashed cake from the floor. After cleaning herself up in the kitchen, Imogen wheeled the cart out again and delivered cupcakes to the wedding party.

The rest of the celebration continued, uninterrupted. Harriet and Will ate cake, she threw the bouquet, and then they prepared to exit the hall to the fanfare of their guests. But just as they were heading for the door, Aunt Jinny stopped them.

"Can I have the brooch back, Harriet? I've been thinking about what Talia said. I need to store it somewhere safe while you're away on your honeymoon."

Harriet fingered the neckline of her dress where the brooch had rested. Then she frowned. "I don't have it. I left it on the table. Remember?"

Aunt Jinny shook her head. "No. It's not on the table. Are you sure you didn't pick it up again?"

"I'm certain."

Harriet and Will hurried over to the heirloom table. Sure enough, the space where the brooch had been was now empty.

"The lights going out caused quite a commotion. Maybe someone bumped against the table in the dark, and the brooch fell on the floor?" Will suggested.

He squatted and reached to lift the hem of the tablecloth, only to fall back in shock when someone leaped out at him.

"Gotcha!" Sebastian sounded gleeful that he had surprised Will.

"Sebastian," Harriet chided, "what are you doing under there? Do you know what happened to my brooch?"

Sebastian's eyes grew wide. Then he scowled. "No. I didn't do anything."

"Relax, love." Aunt Jinny coaxed him out from under the table. "No one said you did. We only asked if you saw what happened."

Sebastian's only response was to shake his head.

By that time, Harriet's mother and father and a few other wedding guests had grown aware of the situation and hurried over to help the group search. But after several minutes, the brooch still hadn't turned up.

"It didn't have legs and walk off," Harriet's dad reasonably pointed out. "How can it be missing?"

Sophie appeared at the edge of the group with an uncharacteristically sour look on her face. Gone was the sunshiny smile from earlier. Maybe Sebastian's attitude was catching. "I think somebody took it."

MYSTERIES OF COBBLE HILL FARM

"Took it? Why would you think that?" Harriet asked.

"Because my tiara's gone too." Sophie stuck out her bottom lip and pointed at the table. "See? I think there's a robber here. Someone saw how pretty my tiara was and stole it."

"Wait a minute." Will tried to calm the upset child. "Let's not jump to conclusions. It's probably all a simple mistake."

Harriet wasn't so certain though. She'd been in enough situations in the past eighteen months to warrant a little paranoia. Items had gone missing before, and it was rarely a simple mistake. But why would a thief with opportunity choose a valuable brooch…and a plastic tiara? Why target an expensive piece along with a nearly worthless one? Not to mention that most of the jewelry on the table was small and easy to transport, and the lights had been off long enough to grab more pieces. Why target those two but leave everything else behind? It didn't make sense.

Someone tapped Harriet's shoulder. She turned around to find Polly. "I hate to say it, but Sophie might be right. I saw a woman running from the room just before the lights went out. Knowing that the brooch is missing now—"

"And my tiara," Sophie interrupted.

Harriet smoothed the little girl's hair from her face. "Yes, and your tiara."

"I stand corrected. We mustn't forget Sophie's tiara." Polly tried to get her thought out again. "Anyway, knowing that multiple items are missing makes the person leaving seem suspicious."

"Who was it?" Harriet asked. Time was of the essence, if a crime had been committed.

"I don't know," Polly answered. "I didn't recognize her, and I only saw her from the back. She had on a dark dress, and she had long brown hair."

That could describe any number of women who had attended the wedding. They had to narrow the pool down more. Harriet surveyed the small group gathered around her. "Did anyone else see this woman?"

Everyone shook their heads.

Aunt Jinny chimed in as the voice of reason. "I know it seems suspicious, but let's try not to get ahead of ourselves. Just because a woman was running for the door doesn't mean she stole anything. It might've been bad timing. What if she spilled something on herself? Or felt unwell?"

Polly pressed her lips together then said, "I'm going to find Van and see what he thinks we should do." She left the group to track down her detective constable husband.

"I'll check in the hallway for the woman Polly saw. Maybe she's still here." Will excused himself from the room.

Harriet turned to her mother as an idea came to her. "Did you get any of the reception on your camcorder? That might show what happened."

"Smart thinking, Harriet. Hold on." Harriet's mother hurried back to her table and returned clutching the camcorder on which she had recorded the ceremony. "I did capture footage of the toasts. I was panning the room for guest reactions to Will's speech when the lights went out. All we have to do is check the video, and that should reveal if anything suspicious happened."

Harriet's mom queued up the video at the appropriate spot before angling the tiny screen toward the rest of the group. Before she could press play, however, Sophie and Sebastian came running up to them. Apparently, the twins had decided to take advantage of the sudden distraction from parental oversight to start a riotous game of tag.

"Stop running, please," Olivia called. Sebastian froze in his tracks, but Sophie, who had assumed the role of chaser, wasn't as quick with her reflexes. Her feet tangled together, and she crashed into Harriet's mother.

Harriet watched in horror as the camcorder flew out of her mother's hands and smashed on the hard stone floor. Thankfully, her mom was able to keep herself from falling by grabbing the edge of a nearby table. Her dad and Anthony rushed to check on Mom, while Olivia helped a sprawled Sophie.

"Oh, Sophie," Olivia scolded her daughter, once she had made sure she was okay. "Why were you playing tag? You know better than to do that indoors. Walking feet, remember?"

Sophie's hands clutched into fists, and her eyes filled with tears. "I wasn't playing tag. I was chasing Sebastian because he was being mean to me."

"Sebastian?" Now Olivia turned her attention to her son. "Is that true?"

Sophie stamped her foot and answered Olivia's question before her brother could. "Yes, it's true. He called me names and pushed me. He's been mean to me since the wedding. I don't even know *whhhyyy*." She drew the last word out into a multisyllabic whine as a tear coursed down her cheek.

By now, Harriet's father had left her mother's side to pick up the camcorder. The situation didn't look good. The viewfinder was twisted at an odd angle, and one corner of the body was dented.

"Maybe it's not as serious as it looks?" Harriet tried to offer a glimmer of hope.

Dad rubbed his forehead. "Just great. I knew we should have taken the warranty when we had the chance. Is it working at all, Charlotte?"

Mom pushed a button on the device and waited. The camcorder turned on, but the screen was glitchy and accompanied by an odd humming noise. "There's no menu. I can't even pull up a video."

"Told you dive-bombing birds are bad luck," Anthony muttered to Olivia. "Something about this whole thing stinks. I'll tell you what I think. The thief cut the lights as a clever distraction. Then he—or she—grabbed the brooch. Don't you see? It's clear as day that the two incidents are related."

Will returned from the hall. "The woman Polly saw is nowhere to be found," he said. "But I did find this." He held out a fistful of colorful feathers, which Harriet immediately recognized as a sampling of feathers from Talia's elaborate hat.

She drew in a quick breath. The feel of feathers brushing by her face in the dark came to mind. Could it be true? Had Talia stolen the brooch and run away? The thought wasn't one she wanted to entertain. But why else would she have run from the room?

Concern creased Aunt Jinny's features. "I hate to say it, but Talia was the only guest I saw wearing feathers like that."

Harriet scanned the room, hoping to see Talia. Hoping there was a simple explanation for everything. But there was no sign of her.

"I'm going to run out to the parking lot," Aunt Jinny said. She seemed as reluctant to believe her own eyes as Harriet. "See if her car is still out there. I'll be right back."

By this time, other wedding guests had started to notice something was wrong, and a few people drifted over to Harriet to ask questions for which there were no answers. Aunt Jinny soon returned with the news that Talia's car wasn't in the parking lot. Then Polly came back to the group with Van. A few minutes of explanation caught him up to speed.

"I'm worried we could have a theft on our hands." He addressed Harriet's mother specifically. "I can get your camcorder fixed for you, but I need to take it to the station as evidence. Hopefully, we can recover the footage from it."

Mom agreed, and Van bagged the damaged device. Then he locked down the hall, called in backup, and made preparations to check guests' bags as they left. "If anyone saw anything suspicious, please report it to the station immediately," he instructed the crowd before pulling Harriet and Will aside for a private conversation.

"I hate to ask this, but is there any way you two could stick close until we wrap this up? Just in case we find concrete evidence of theft on the tape and have questions. The process shouldn't take too long. I hope to have you on your way by tomorrow, although you're free to go now, of course."

"Not a problem." Will looped his arm around Harriet's waist, and she leaned into him. "We were planning to stay here at the B&B tonight anyway. I'm sure you'll get things taken care of quickly. The whole situation is probably a misunderstanding."

"Let's hope so," Van replied.

Harriet nodded her agreement, though she couldn't keep her mind from filling with suspicion. Was it a misunderstanding? Or had someone engineered the lights going out, as Anthony had suggested? And who was the woman Polly had seen running from the room moments before? Harriet didn't want to think it had been Talia, but it was too much of a coincidence that Talia had disappeared. Was it possible that one of Harriet's or Will's close friends or family members could be a thief?

It was a difficult concern to voice. Much easier to believe there had been some kind of misunderstanding. The alternative was that her honeymoon—and perhaps someone's future—was in jeopardy.

CHAPTER FOUR

London, England
Spring 1851

What a glorious day.

Catherine Taylor glanced out the window of the carriage that her husband of hardly a month, Alexander, had hired to take them to the festivities in Hyde Park.

The Great Exhibition of 1851—Prince Albert's brainchild come to life despite the crowd of naysayers who had tried to stop him—opened today. It was the first of May, and the grand event was slated to run through the summer into autumn, showcasing over one hundred thousand exhibits from around the world. It was a stunning accomplishment spearheaded and overseen by the British monarchy. The queen and the prince consort had opened the exhibition earlier that morning to much fanfare.

Excitement fluttered in Catherine's middle as she and Alexander drew close to the park. The buzz of the crowd could be heard over the noise of the carriage, and up the path from them stood a glass castle—dubbed the Crystal Palace—that glittered in the sunlight. The palace's gleaming facade was unmarred by dirt or other debris, reinforcing its otherworldliness.

Catherine looked closer. "Alexander, are those trees in the palace?"

Her husband laughed. "I see you're as surprised as I was when I heard the proposal. When the palace was being designed, there were people who wanted to save three full-grown elm trees that were on the site. So, in the end, they constructed the building around and over them."

"How tall is the palace?" asked Catherine.

"The Crystal Palace is one hundred twenty-eight feet tall at its highest point," Alexander informed her. "It's made of 293,000 panes of glass." He raised an eyebrow at her. "Unfortunately, when they enclosed the trees, they didn't realize they would also be enclosing the sparrows that lived in them. You can imagine what sparrows can do to glass."

"Oh no." Catherine laughed. "How did they solve the problem?"

"Sparrow hawks," Alexander said. "I heard that was the Duke of Wellington's idea."

She believed him. Alexander would know the details of the situation better than most. As manager of one of the

MYSTERIES OF COBBLE HILL FARM

largest London banks, he had loaned money to several of the participants, including Edward Sterling, an artisan responsible for one of the main jewelry exhibits. Sterling had peppered Alexander with details of the fair prior to the public knowing, and Alexander had regaled Catherine. What a thrill, to have such inside knowledge.

The world jostling past her window gradually slowed, and the carriage lurched to a halt. She started to stand, but Alexander stopped her.

"Wait, Catherine. Before we go, I want to give you something." He pulled a box from his coat pocket and handed it to her.

She smiled. Her handsome new husband had already spoiled her with gifts. Fancy dresses, hats, jewels. It was the conventional way wealthy husbands of society treated their wives. Catherine once more thought about how Alexander looked all the world like Prince Albert, at least in her estimation. The only difference, of course, was his station, and the contrast of Alexander's dark hair and complexion in comparison to the prince's fair one. Alexander even sported a delicate mustache above his lip similar to the one Prince Albert had. A fine figure he cut.

At Alexander's prompting, she opened the box to find an ornate gold-and-emerald brooch. It was, by far, one of the prettiest gifts he had ever given her. She traced the front of the brooch with a gloved finger.

"Alexander, how perfectly lovely." She looked up with wonder at her husband. Husband. How new the word felt in *reference to him. Yet life with Alexander was already so familiar. They had fallen into a comfortable pattern the past few weeks, as if they'd always been together. Their love was like that expressed in the Alfred, Lord Tennyson poem that she had recently read.*

Light, so low upon earth,
You send a flash to the sun.
Here is the golden close of love,
All my wooing is done…

"Look." Alexander reached across her to push a clasp cleverly hidden on the side of the brooch. The brooch's face swung open to reveal a blank space inside. "We'll have a daguerreotype made."

Alexander helped her fasten the brooch at her throat. Catherine couldn't have been prouder of her husband's sweet offering than if he had planned and executed the entire exhibition himself.

"I'd dare say that bauble can't compete with the splendor the prince has orchestrated for today." Alexander's mouth lifted in a smile as he helped her from the carriage.

Catherine let Alexander guide her through the crowd gathered in the park. She bit back her pride as they wandered through exhibit after exhibit. She marveled at the Koh-i-Noor diamond from India, Cyrus McCormick's mechanical reaper, and Joseph Marie Jaquard's advanced textile loom.

Her love for Alexander cast a golden glow over everything. Nothing could mar her perfect happiness. Of that, she was certain.

Night was falling as they left the promenade and exited Hyde Park to travel home. Suddenly, the carriage Alexander and Catherine rode in jerked to a stop.

Catherine lifted her head from Alexander's shoulder. The day's activities had tired her, and she had almost drifted off. "What happened?"

He inched over to the window. "Looks like a crowd of people blocking the path. Stay here."

He dismounted from the carriage, leaving Catherine behind. She peered out the window to watch her husband's progress toward the group. Their voices sounded angry and riotous.

"Here now," Alexander cried as he approached. Even though he was one man against many, he still seemed like a protective barrier between Catherine and the buzzing crowd. "What's the trouble?"

"Aye, someone's crowing about a theft." A man in a tatty suit piped up. "An item stolen from the exhibition hall early this morning. Guards are checking members of the public as they leave the grounds."

"A theft, eh?" Alexander cast a glance back at Catherine. His profile appeared paler than normal in the failing light, stark against the dark color of his day coat. *The paper had warned of this possibility.* Open the gates to one and all at a mere shilling, *declared an editorial,* and you'll reap a harvest of lawlessness. *Had the words proven true?*

Another man weighed in. "Gossip is, the theft's connected to that fellow who snuck in the royal procession this morning. It's these highbrow folk, causing all the fuss…"

The rest of Alexander's conversation with the crowd was indistinguishable as another coach approached. After a brief word with the driver, Alexander returned to Catherine.

"What's happened?" Catherine asked her husband as the crowd dispersed and their carriage started moving again.

Alexander took a handkerchief from his pocket and wiped sweat from his brow. The day had been unbearably warm. "No more than a case of petty thievery by a fellow down on his luck. Nothing for you to worry over, my dear."

Petty thievery. Nothing to worry over. The words formed a cadence in time with the clatter of their horses' hooves on the road. She tried to lean her head on Alexander's shoulder again, but he inched away.

Her stomach tightened. He had never acted so with her. What could be wrong?

He motioned to the brooch pinned at her neck. "I forgot to mention it, but take care to wear that only around home, my dear."

She reached up and touched the brooch. It was a fine work of art. "Only wear it around home? What would be the point in that?"

MYSTERIES OF COBBLE HILL FARM

"I know you've worn it all day, but I've changed my mind." Alexander's reply was uncharacteristically sharp. *"It's far too valuable to wear in public. Heaven forbid you lose it or a pickpocket pinch it from you. Tensions in town are high lately. The exhibition has unsettled things."*

So he didn't want her to wear the brooch where others could see it? How odd. He had never made such a strange request of her before. It didn't make sense. She had proudly worn the brooch at the exhibition only minutes before. Its rarity had been paraded in front of the whole of London society, it seemed. Why was it deemed such a sensitive matter now? Something must have happened.

Alexander refused to talk about the topic anymore with her. The rest of the way home, Catherine struggled to push down her worries as Alexander mopped sweat from his brow.

CHAPTER FIVE

Harriet and Will gave one more round of goodbyes before gathering their suitcases from the Jaguar and heading up to their room. Harriet couldn't stop thinking about the turn things had taken at the reception. As the day's adrenaline ebbed from her, stress crept in.

Will glanced at her. "Don't worry. We'll figure out what happened to the brooch."

Harriet grimaced. "Today would have been perfect if that hadn't happened. I mean, it still was wonderful, but—"

"It cast a bit of a shadow over the celebration?" Will gently finished her sentence.

"Maybe a little." Harriet sighed. "I promise not to let it get to me too much."

"I hope not." Will playfully bumped her shoulder with his. "We have a honeymoon to enjoy."

If they ever got to go on it. "What do we do if Van is wrong and he doesn't find the thief quickly? I love White Church Bay, but I was excited to travel somewhere more exotic with you. This is the start of our new life together."

"Aye, but it's no use borrowing trouble. Let's take Van's word for it. Things will wrap up soon. Maybe we can scout around and help

MYSTERIES OF COBBLE HILL FARM

the matter along in the meantime. For right now, though, the only thing I want to focus on is you."

Oh, his smile. It absolutely melted her, and her shoulders relaxed at his reassuring words. He was right. Of course he was right. How many worries had kept her up at night but had never materialized in the end?

After a long flight of steps, which they had to bump their suitcases up because the elevator was being repaired, they finally reached their room. Will took a key card from his suit pocket at the door and slipped it in the reader. A tiny light glowed green, and he opened the door into their suite.

Harriet started to go in, but Will stopped her. "I thought you were a traditionalist," he joked. "No carrying you across the threshold, Mrs. Bailey-Knight?"

She hadn't even thought about it. Was he seriously going to pick her up, along with her ungainly wedding dress? Apparently, that was exactly what he was going to do. Will propped the door open with their suitcases and then attempted to sweep her off her feet— literally. The riot of tulle on her dress, however, made it difficult.

Harriet couldn't help but laugh. "I should have warned you. I'm a walking cloud in this thing."

"You're lovely. Don't rain on my parade," Will quipped.

He pressed a gentle kiss to her lips before carrying her inside.

The suite was lovely. It had a small kitchen and even a sitting room, which held a gift basket of various fruits and chocolates. A tiny card with curling script beside the basket read, *Enjoy your stay at Ravenscroft.*

Oh, and the views! Harriet drew her breath in as she peered out the glass doors that led to the balcony. The entirety of the gardens in full summer splendor lay spread before them. This more than made up for a broken elevator. The tension of the day began to melt from her muscles.

"Look how beautiful the sunset is." Harriet turned to catch Will's eye.

"It has competition." Her heart fluttered again as Will pressed another kiss to her lips.

Early Sunday morning, Harriet awoke next to Will. A golden glow at being his wife swept over her. Even if he did snore.

She hummed a happy tune as she slipped away to the bathroom to get ready for the day. The hotel had advertised a lavish breakfast spread, and though she didn't want to dine without Will, she might be able to snag two cups of hot tea to bring back to the room. As cute as the small kitchen in their suite was, she couldn't for the life of her locate a teakettle. So a quick beverage run downstairs, it was. If she planned to surprise Will with caffeine, however, quietness was essential.

Or was it? It only took a few minutes of puttering around the suite to realize that her new husband was apparently also a much heavier sleeper than she was. He didn't even stir when she accidentally dropped her hairdryer on the bathroom counter. She added another observation to her list of things she was learning about Will. Vintage car enthusiast. Now she could add "saws logs and sleeps like the dead" to the list.

At least she knew the way he took his tea. That wasn't a surprise. Brewed strong with a heavy splash of milk.

She slipped on a sundress with a pair of leather sandals and grabbed her key card. She took the stairs to the lobby but couldn't find the breakfast spread promised by the hotel.

She scanned the room once again. She couldn't even smell food cooking. Where were the sausages and potatoes? The toast? The tea? Had she gotten the time wrong? It didn't seem possible. What sort of establishment would stop serving breakfast before eight thirty in the morning?

Harriet made her way to the front desk, where a young woman with a blond ponytail sat behind a computer. Harriet recognized her as the person she had seen standing beside Benedict at the reception. This must be his girlfriend, Lucy.

"Hi, I'm looking for the breakfast buffet? And do you know when the elevator will be fixed?"

"Our maintenance man has been working on the lift for the past couple of days," Lucy replied. "It should be repaired soon. And the breakfast buffet is right over there." She pointed to a small table that held two carafes, an assortment of tea bags, and a napkin-lined basket of pastries.

No wonder Harriet had missed it. She thanked Lucy and crossed the room to check out the display. The coffee was already brewed and kept warm in a carafe, as was hot water for tea. She fixed beverages for Will and herself before assessing the pastries. She used tongs to sort through them and see if there were any interesting flavors, like almond or cheese, only to be met with disappointment. What a letdown. They were all just plain doughnuts with the smallest amount of glaze drizzled on top.

Despite her deflated expectations, her stomach still grumbled. She supposed it was a silly thing to be irritated over. At least she could take some pastries up to Will to go with his tea.

Harriet finished fixing their tea and wrapped up several doughnuts in a napkin. Before she went upstairs, though, an idea came to her.

She approached the front desk again and addressed Lucy. "Excuse me. Were you here in the lobby yesterday when the wedding reception was going on?"

Lucy ceased tapping the keys on the computer. "I was. Though I'm exhausted today. I don't fancy an evening shift and a morning shift back-to-back. Especially on the weekend. Wait a minute. I recognize you. You were the bride, weren't you?"

Harriet nodded. She had hoped Benedict would introduce them to Lucy last night, but then he'd had to deal with the power outage.

Lucy beamed. "I thought you looked familiar. Congratulations on your marriage. Sorry about all that fuss when the lights went out. I heard about what happened with the breaker tripping because of a power surge. I hope it didn't cause any major issues."

The tiniest flicker of suspicion rose in Harriet as she remembered what Anthony had said about someone cutting the lights on purpose to steal the brooch. "Is there someone I can talk to about that?" she asked. "Could I talk to the maintenance man?" Might as well go straight to the source. And it never hurt to investigate. The

MYSTERIES OF COBBLE HILL FARM

sooner law enforcement could wrap things up, the sooner she and Will could leave for their honeymoon.

"Of course." Lucy consulted a paper schedule hanging behind the desk. "His name is Nigel Wharton. He's on the clock, but I'm not sure where he is right now. Maybe check back here at the desk a bit later, and I, or whoever else is working, can help track him down for you."

"Sounds great. Thanks for your help," Harriet said. "Could I bother you with one more question?"

"Sure."

"You didn't see anyone run into the hallway after the lights went out, did you?"

Lucy shook her head. "No, but I wasn't at the front desk when that happened."

That was right. Harriet had forgotten that Lucy was standing by Benedict during the toasts.

A look of concern crossed Lucy's face. "Why? Did something else happen?"

"Hopefully not." Harriet explained the situation with the missing brooch. "I hope it's all a mistake and nobody stole anything."

"I don't know." The young woman sounded skeptical. "I think you're right to question what happened. It doesn't sound like an accident to me. The lights go out and then the brooch disappears? It's too coincidental."

"You think so?"

"I do. I think you need to speak with Nigel and see if you can find out more. If you discover that the situation with the lights was

44

intentional, there's your answer." Lucy drummed her fingers on the desk. "Find the person who cut the lights, and you'll find your thief."

Harriet thought again about what Anthony had said yesterday at the reception. *The thief cut the lights as a clever distraction. Then he—or she—grabbed the brooch. Don't you see? It's clear as day that the two are related.*

Harriet said goodbye to Lucy and navigated through the maze of hallways to find her suite. The tea was still quite hot, and it was a balancing act to keep from spilling any—or dropping the pastries— as she dug her key card out of her pocket. She slipped the card in the reader and waited for the green light.

But the light didn't appear. She hefted a sigh, pulled the card out, then popped it back in again. Still no green light. A few more unsuccessful tries prompted her to knock on the door.

"Will? I don't think my card is working. I'm locked out."

She waited for him to open it. When he didn't, she knocked on the door a little louder. It was a feat to keep tea from splashing onto her dress.

"Will? Are you there? Hello?"

Maybe he was in the shower? She pressed her ear to the door.

Snores. It sounded like Will was taking a chainsaw to a hapless tree in there.

So, he was there at least. "Will?" She finally set the tea and pastries on a nearby table beside a small artificial plant. Then she knocked even more loudly on the door. "Will, it's Harriet! I'm locked out!" she called.

Nothing. She would have to trek down to the front desk and see if she could get a new key card. Then the tea would get cold. She

MYSTERIES OF COBBLE HILL FARM

pressed her ear to the door once more to see if she could hear sounds of Will stirring. Instead, she heard the pealing ring of the landline phone. Thankfully, Will answered it. After a brief and indistinguishable conversation, the door to their room opened.

Will stood in his pajamas with adorably mussed hair. "Harriet? What on earth are you doing out here?"

So he didn't hear her frantic knocking, but the landline…that had awakened him? He was a complex man. She motioned to the tea and pastries in reply, and his eyes brightened. He helped her carry everything inside and then handed her the phone. "Perfect timing. I wondered where you'd gone. The call is for you. Your aunt's on the line."

"Aunt Jinny? Why is she calling?"

Will shook his head. "She didn't say. Just that she needed to talk to you right away."

Was it something related to the missing brooch? Had Van recovered the damaged video from her mom's camcorder? Or maybe a witness had come forward, claiming to have seen something suspicious?

Harriet's heart fluttered as she pressed the receiver to her ear. "Hello?"

"Harriet, thank goodness you're still here." Relief filled her aunt's voice. "Did you realize you left your passport at your house? Your mum and dad saw it on the kitchen table when they got up this morning."

Her parents planned to stay in England to watch over Harriet's home and animals while she and Will were on their honeymoon. Harriet had been so grateful when they'd offered. It was a load off her mind to know her pets would be well taken care of in her absence.

46

And here was another reason to be thankful for her family. She didn't want to think what would have happened if she'd shown up at the border without her passport.

"Why weren't you answering your mobile?" Aunt Jinny asked.

Harriet sank onto the bed with a groan. Then she reached over to fish in her handbag for her phone. Of course. In all the commotion, she'd forgotten to charge it last night, and it was dead as a doornail. Likely filled with voice mails from her parents, worried she would hit the open road without proper documentation.

"It's dead," she explained to her aunt. "Taking care of it now." Will, apparently listening in on Harriet's side of the conversation, handed her a charger, and she plugged in her phone. She blew him a silent kiss in thanks, and he responded by raising his cup in return.

Harriet turned her attention back to her aunt. "I can't believe I left my passport at home. Tell Mom and Dad I'm going to swing by the house and pick it up now."

"I'll let them know," Aunt Jinny replied. "Come to the cottage though. Everyone's over here. Anthony and Olivia brought the kids. Sophie and Sebastian are staying with me for the first part of the week. I wanted some Nana time with them before they went back to school, and I'm planning to throw a little end-of-summer party with the neighborhood children before they leave. How fun will that be?"

Harriet was glad Aunt Jinny was enjoying her grandmotherly role. She only hoped Sebastian and Sophie had ended their spat and were getting along. "Sounds like you have a great time planned. I'll be at the cottage in a bit."

She settled the receiver back in its cradle. The day was already filling up with little tasks when all she really wanted to do was relax and spend time with Will. She needed to remember to find Nigel and talk to him as well. As she and Will ate breakfast, she filled him in on what Lucy had told her about the lights cutting.

"Hmm." Will took a sip of tea. "It could be nothing. But even if it is, maybe Nigel saw or heard something out of the ordinary at the reception that will lead to another clue."

Harriet smiled. "You're certainly getting the hang of this mystery-solving thing pretty quick."

"What can I say? I've watched you do it for the past year-and-a-half. Makes sense that I would've picked up on a few tricks."

He was right. Over the last year, Will had been at her side many times, helping to solve mysteries and even sometimes being an extra pair of hands when she was tending to a sick or injured animal.

She slowly chewed a bite of her doughnut as she realized she wanted to be a part of his work too. But what could she do? What niche would be a good fit?

"You look stressed. Why don't we divide and conquer?" Will's voice broke into her thoughts. Obviously, her demeanor had broadcast a different emotion to him. Anxiety. "You go get your passport, and I'll try to track down Nigel. I need to stay here anyway to rebook some of our travel plans."

"Sounds good to me." Harriet gave him a kiss goodbye.

Hopefully, when she returned, he would have answers and they would be one step closer to leaving on their honeymoon.

CHAPTER SIX

When Harriet arrived at the dower cottage, Sophie and Sebastian were playing in the front garden.

"Wow!" Sebastian gazed admiringly at the Jaguar. "That car is so cool. I didn't know that was what Pastor Will drove!"

"It's only a rental for the honeymoon." Harriet stepped out of the driver's side and pocketed the keys. What was this love for cars that men and boys had? She wasn't sure that she understood it, but Sebastian seemed awfully impressed with the vehicle. Sophie, on the other hand, didn't bat an eye.

"Harriet!" The little girl ran to her and gave her a hug.

"Hi, sweetie." Harriet hugged Sophie back before reaching forward to ruffle Sebastian's hair.

"You looked so pretty in your wedding dress yesterday. Just like a princess," Sophie gushed as she grabbed Harriet by the hand and led her to the front door of the cottage. "So did that lady in the big hat. I saw her at the wedding."

Sophie must be talking about Talia. "Did you know she's a friend of our family? She owns a jewelry shop."

Sophie bounced on her toes. "Really? She owns a jewelry shop? I want to have a job like that someday. Or be a tiger trainer."

Harriet laughed. A jewelry store owner or a tiger trainer? Quite a big difference between the two, but Sophie didn't seem to think so. Meanwhile, Sebastian tried to divert attention back to his own interests. "Why does that lady wear such a big hat? Is she trying to hide something?"

Sophie stopped, and her mouth fell open. "Like my tiara. What if she stuck it under her hat and stole it?"

Harriet still wasn't ready to consider Talia as someone who might have stolen the brooch, but the children had no such qualms.

Aunt Jinny appeared in the doorway with an odd expression that Harriet couldn't quite decipher. "Sebastian? Why don't you and Sophie come inside? I just took some biscuits out of the oven, and you can have some while the grown-ups talk."

"You don't have to ask me twice!" Sebastian crowed. He beat his fists on his chest like a he-man, and Sophie hurried into the house after him, all worry over her stolen tiara dismissed.

As soon as the children were inside, Aunt Jinny stopped Harriet on the threshold. Her face still held the unreadable expression Harriet had noticed earlier. "I need to talk to you about something," she said. "Sophie might be right. I think Talia could have had something to do with the brooch's disappearance."

Harriet stifled a gasp. For her aunt, who was even closer to Talia than Harriet, to suspect something, the situation must be serious indeed. "You're joking. You can't think Talia stole the brooch. You said yourself, running from the room wasn't an indicator of guilt. She could have done that for any number of reasons."

"I know what I said," Aunt Jinny replied. "But I've had time to reconsider. Talia told me something worrying at the reception."

"Go on."

"She confided in me that her business was on the rocks. She's planning to close soon if the bottom line doesn't improve. I think she came to the wedding for help. She asked me if I would consider floating her a loan."

"Oh no." Harriet sighed. "She didn't talk much about the shop with me, but it sounded as though things were going okay. Just busy. I had no idea the jewelry store was failing or that she was cash-strapped. What did you tell her?"

Aunt Jinny brushed a wayward piece of hair from her face. "I told her I didn't feel comfortable lending her money. I've seen situations like that ruin too many good relationships. I offered to give her a smaller amount—as a gift with no strings attached—but she refused. I suppose it was all or nothing, in her opinion."

Poor Talia. Harriet couldn't help but feel for her. She didn't have much family to speak of, outside of the honorary family she considered Harriet's to be. "So you think she was desperate? She knew the brooch's value, grabbed it, and ran?"

Aunt Jinny nodded. "I hope I'm not jumping to conclusions, but I haven't been able to get ahold of her. I tried to call her mobile, but I wonder if I have the number wrong in my contacts. I can't seem to reach her. I tried the shop too, but I got her machine. I'm worried that even if she is innocent of any wrongdoing, she'll avoid my calls because she feels embarrassed about asking for a loan. Could I ask you a small favor?"

"Sure, anything."

"Would you try to contact her? She might be more willing to answer the phone for you."

"Of course."

"You're a lifesaver." Aunt Jinny handed Harriet a slip of paper with a couple of phone numbers scribbled on it. "This first one is her mobile, and the other is the shop." She waved Harriet into the sitting room, where her parents were engaged in lively conversation with Anthony and Olivia.

"You're telling me Americans only get two weeks of vacation leave? Per year?" Anthony appeared aghast.

Dad nodded. "That's the standard after a few years of employment, and then it can increase after that. You get more?"

"I'll say. Two weeks is a drop in the bucket. Anyone in the UK who works five days a week is entitled by law to twenty-eight days of vacation a year."

Harriet thought her dad's eyes were going to pop out of his head. "Twenty-eight days? That's…that's…" She saw him doing the calculation in his head. "That's more than five weeks! How do you get anything done with everyone gone so much?"

"Hi, Dad." Harriet nudged her father before he could start an international incident.

"Hey, sweet pea." Dad jumped to his feet to press her into a hug. Then he reached over to the coffee table for her passport. "Bet you're here for this, aren't you?"

"That would be it. Thanks so much." Harriet tucked the passport into her bag.

"I'm so relieved you were still in town." Harriet's mother hugged her too.

"Actually, Will and I might be staying in White Church Bay for a few extra days." Harriet explained about Van asking them to stay close until the situation with the brooch was resolved.

"I'm sure you're anxious to start your honeymoon," Olivia said, "but it looks like everything worked out. At least as far as your passport."

"I guess so." If that was the silver lining to this whole situation, Harriet would take it. Speaking of the reason she was still in town, though... "I don't suppose Van has called here about the video yet, has he?"

Mom shook her head. "No. But I promise you'll be the first to know when he does."

Aunt Jinny pressed a hand to her heart. "I just hope we can recover the brooch. I had no idea it was so valuable until Talia said something. I could kick myself that I didn't secure it right away."

"Who could've known someone would try to steal it?" Harriet said. She was fairly certain it hadn't been on any of their radars.

Just then, Sebastian charged into the room with a scowl. His mouth was smeared with chocolate from the biscuits Aunt Jinny had made. "Can you tell Sophie I'm done playing tea party with her teddy bears? It's boring. I want to do something else."

Sophie trailed behind her brother, a plush teddy bear squeezed under one arm. "Not just any tea party. A *royal* tea party. This is the queen. Except she doesn't have her crown, because my tiara is still missing."

Tiara or not, Harriet decided to play along. She put on her most serious face and dropped a curtsy before Sophie and the stuffed animal. "Your Highness."

Sophie stuck a hand on one hip and glared at her brother. "You see? Harriet understands. Why don't you?"

"Because it's a silly game. And I don't want to play." Sebastian crossed his arms over his chest. "Why do you always get to pick what we play? What makes you so special?"

"Sebastian…" Olivia's voice held a warning tone.

Anthony backed up his wife. "Be nice to your sister, young man."

What had happened between the two of them? Sebastian and Sophie had had a tiff yesterday. But they were playing so nicely in the yard just minutes ago. Sebastian seemed unusually defiant. Should she chalk it up to a case of sibling rivalry? Or was there something else going on?

While Olivia and Anthony mediated between the twins, Harriet stepped outside with her parents. Together, they walked the short distance to Harriet's house, where they were greeted by her pets, Charlie and Maxwell. Though she had scarcely been away from them for a day, it was still wonderful to see them. By the time she finished giving them both attention, her dress was covered in pet hair.

"What a clever girl," she cooed to Charlie as she scratched the patchy calico behind her ears. Charlie purred contentedly in response.

Then, to Maxwell, "Guard the clinic, okay, boy?" The little dachshund devotedly followed her to the door, dragging his wheeled prosthesis behind him.

"We'll take good care of them," Mom assured Harriet.

"I know you will." Harriet clasped her in a tight embrace. "Thanks, Mom. It's so good to have you and Dad here."

Harriet finished telling her parents goodbye and headed back to the car. She smiled as she made a half-hearted attempt to swipe the hair from her clothes. That was a happy occupational hazard she could live with. Where would she be without the job she loved and the sweet animals she cared for?

Before she could think about it too much, her phone rang from her bag. She took it out to see Will's picture on the screen. She smiled and answered the call.

"Hello?"

"Harriet." Will sounded out of breath. "I wanted to call you right away, so I didn't forget any details."

Harriet pressed the phone closer to her ear. "What happened? Did you find Nigel?"

"I did. Though I almost wish I hadn't."

What exactly did he mean? Why would he regret finding someone who knew the truth about what happened with the lights at the reception? That information could only lead them closer to the truth, couldn't it?

Will didn't explain his statement. "So I went downstairs, and Lucy found Nigel for me."

"And? What did he have to say? Did he know anything about the lights going out?" Harriet couldn't keep the questions from tumbling past her lips.

"Wait a minute. I'm getting there." Will's voice held an edge of determination. "Nigel was reluctant to talk at first. He claimed he didn't know anything. But I could tell that he did."

Tightness gripped Harriet's throat. "Go on."

"I explained to him about the missing brooch and that it was a family heirloom. Very sentimental. He softened at that and seemed a little more open to helping. He confirmed that the cause was a power surge, which tripped the breaker, like Benedict claimed. He said it had something to do with the hotel lift overloading the circuits."

Harriet supposed it made sense. A power surge could easily be the root cause of the issue. Yet something still didn't sit well with her. She couldn't quite put her finger on the reason why though.

Then it dawned on her. "Will! It couldn't have been a power surge from the elevator. It wasn't working last night, and when I checked with Lucy this morning, she said it's been broken for a couple of days. A power surge couldn't have been caused by the elevator if it was broken during the reception. Nigel and Benedict aren't telling the truth. Am I imagining things?"

"You're not imagining things." Will's tone was grim.

"How do you know?"

"Because I haven't finished telling you all I discovered yet. When Nigel left the desk, I followed him. I felt there might be more to the story than he was telling. He called someone on his mobile from the stairwell. He told the person on the other end of the line that he'd lied to the police and also to me about the reason the lights went out."

"So are you beginning to think it wasn't an accident?"

"What else is there to think? Someone flipped the breaker on purpose. And the person Nigel was talking to encouraged him to lie about what happened."

"Why? Who was Nigel talking to? Did he say the person's name?" Why didn't Will just cut to the chase already? The tension was unbearable. He certainly knew how to draw out a story for maximum dramatic effect.

Will leveraged a huge sigh. "He did. That's why I almost wish I hadn't confronted him. Harriet, the person on the other end of the line…was Benedict."

After finishing her chat with Will and climbing into the Jaguar, Harriet tried to call Talia at the numbers Aunt Jinny had given her. The cell phone number yielded a "number unobtainable" message, and the shop number rang through to an answering machine, as Aunt Jinny had said. Harriet left a quick message at the shop before driving back to Ravenscroft. The mystery was getting deeper. They had two suspects now regarding the theft, and neither Benedict nor Talia was particularly appealing. Yet, the truth remained. The brooch was missing, and someone had likely taken it. Harriet had to get to the bottom of the matter, and quickly.

The weather wasn't unreasonably warm, so Harriet and Will decided to take a stroll through the gardens before lunch. The marigolds and roses were in full bloom, and the scent coming off the flowers was heavenly. She also spied a lovely violet-blue flower, which the staked placard informed her was Meadow Cranesbill. She made a mental note to see if she could purchase some from a nursery to add to her garden at home.

They found a cool spot on a bench under a shade tree and sat. Harriet had already shared what she knew of Talia over the phone.

MYSTERIES OF COBBLE HILL FARM

Now it was Will's turn to talk more about the implications of the conversation he had overheard between Nigel and Benedict.

"Remember that long story I promised you yesterday?" Will asked.

"You mean the one about Benedict?"

"His name is Benedict Carter, though I knew him as Benny. We first met when he was a teenager, only thirteen. He was a bit of a troublemaker back then, and his mum, Violet, had gotten worried over his rebelliousness. She wrangled him into attending a service at White Church. I think she hoped the church would provide a calming influence. After the service, however, I caught Benedict pinching money from the offering plate."

Harriet gasped. "Really? He stole from the church?"

"I chalked it up to youthful folly." Will sighed heavily. "He was surrounded by bad influences at school at the time. I let the matter go, but he stole again later that fall, from the benevolence fund. I talked to my superior, and we agreed we had to turn him in. There was no other option."

Harriet shook her head. Such a sad situation. "What happened?"

Will's shoulders slumped. It was clear he would rather forget these memories of Benedict. "What you'd expect. He appeared in youth court and wound up paying penance under a YRO."

"And that is...what exactly?" The term didn't ring a bell with Harriet.

"Sorry." Will chuckled. "You've become so much a part of life in White Church Bay that I forget you haven't always lived here. YRO stands for Youth Rehabilitation Order. It's a program comparable to juvenile community service in the States. Anyway, I negotiated for Benedict's community payback time to be with the church. I made sure he personally met the widows and shut-ins he had stolen from.

It was an experience that seemed to change him in a radical way. At least I thought it had."

"So what do you think this new development means?" Harriet waved away a bee that ventured too close to her face. "He engineered the lights going out so he could steal the brooch? Why would he do that? When we spoke to him, it sounded like his life was going well."

"I don't know what motivation he would have for stealing. Or why he would lie. Unless…" Will sat up straight. "Oh no. Harriet, do you remember what he said? He needed money to buy an engagement ring for Lucy. You don't think he would've taken the brooch so he could sell it and then buy a ring, do you?"

"I don't know." Harriet reached out to him, as he was clearly upset. "I don't know him as well as you do. Do you think he's capable of such a thing?"

"It's anyone's guess. He certainly was at one time, but that was so long ago. He was young. I wouldn't have suspected him at all, if it wasn't for that conversation I overheard between him and Nigel. But he's trying to cover up something. That's obvious, from what Nigel said about Benedict asking him to lie to the authorities. I regret to say it, but I think it would be wise to keep an eye on him."

Will's tone was laced with defeat. How discouraged he must be, to think he had made a positive difference in a young man's life, only to find out that all his work might have been in vain. Harriet placed a hand on his shoulder. "We don't know anything for certain yet. We still need to get ahold of Talia and see what she knows. Besides, there's one thing in Benedict's favor."

"There is?"

Harriet nodded. "I never saw him go near the heirloom table. He was at the entry, which was at least fifteen feet away, and only for a few minutes during toasts. If he had wanted to swipe something, he certainly didn't have convenient access."

Even as she tried to convince Will of Benedict's innocence, an irritating worry surfaced in her mind. What about the sneezing noise she had heard in the dark? Should she tell Will about that? Or avoid troubling him until she had a more concrete reason to suspect Benedict?

After waffling a bit, she chose to keep quiet. Plenty of time to mention that later if it proved more relevant.

Unaware of her internal monologue, Will responded to Harriet's earlier assessment. "I suppose you could be right. Benedict could be innocent. We need to tell the authorities about what I overheard though. I don't want to smear Benedict's good name if he's innocent, but I don't see how I can let what I heard go unreported."

At that moment, Harriet's cell phone rang inside her bag. She dug it out to discover that someone from the police station was calling. How timely.

"It's the station," she said to Will, and his eyebrows lifted. She answered the call. "Hello?"

Van's voice greeted her. "I just contacted your family and communicated the news to them. We were able to recover the footage from your mum's camcorder. Can Will and you come down to the station?"

CHAPTER SEVEN

London, England
Summer 1852

Even though Catherine stood on solid ground in front of the famed Augustin Clavette's photography studio, the earth still swayed beneath her.

She pressed a gloved hand to her mouth as dust from the street kicked up in a noxious cloud. Her throat felt dry, and her stomach roiled. Maybe she shouldn't have insisted on keeping the appointment, but Alexander wasn't the only one who harbored a secret...

The trip to London from home hadn't been lengthy, but the ride had felt more uncomfortable than usual. Street smells blew into the carriage cab—coal smoke, horse sweat, and the occasional whiff of food vendors. The feeling of unease hadn't left her when they arrived at the location of Monsieur Clavette's new studio at 150 Picadilly. Though they'd disembarked from the carriage moments earlier, it didn't feel like it.

"Feeling ill, my love?" Alexander steadied her with his strong grip. "Are you unwell? Do we need to turn back?"

"No, no." She reached into her reticule to ensure the brooch was still secure. She hadn't worn it in public since last spring, though she still didn't understand the reason behind Alexander's command. Why was he so interested in keeping it hidden? What was the purpose of giving it to her if she couldn't show it off? They had waited months to secure an appointment with the city's best daguerreotypist for a likeness to fill the brooch's hollow space. If they canceled, they might not be so fortunate to book another appointment anytime soon. And time was of the essence. They weren't turning back now. "The carriage was a bit oppressive."

"Let's go inside. Perhaps Monsieur Clavette can provide you with a drink of water. Would that make you feel better?"

She nodded gratefully. Yes, that did sound good.

Alexander took her arm, and they headed toward the studio, passing by a dirty-faced newsboy hawking the latest dispatch.

"Read all about it!" the boy shouted. "Jewelry heist at exhibition continues to baffle police! Thief still at large one year on!"

Catherine clutched Alexander's arm tighter. Couldn't they escape the reminder of what happened last year? It was the one thing that blighted her perfect joy. Alexander had acted so odd during the carriage ride home that she had finally confronted him. He brushed off her concern and said he knew nothing of the theft, but some knowledge she wasn't privy to gnawed at him. She could see it etched on his face. His hours at the bank stretched far into the evening. He spent the remaining hours until bed poring over newspapers by lamplight and muttering under his breath. Why was he avoiding her?

If only he would talk to her. Yet he refused to confide, and she didn't know why.

The boy addressed Alexander. "Buy a paper, sir? Only a penny."

At first, she thought Alexander would turn it down. His jaw tensed. But then he fished in his pocket and flicked a penny in the boy's direction.

"Thanks." The boy reached into his bundle to hand over a paper.

Alexander tucked the paper under his arm. Then he led Catherine into the studio, which was an airy space carved out of the larger building. A skylight let in the sun, while flickering gas lamps chased off lingering shadows in the wings. A hulking camera set up on a wooden tripod dominated the space. A man with neatly combed white hair stood over the bellows. He must have heard them enter, because he swiveled to face them.

"Monsieur Clavette," Alexander greeted the man, "it's a pleasure to meet you. My wife feels faint and needs something to drink. Could we trouble you for refreshment?"

"But of course." The artist clapped his hands. "Pierre, you are needed."

A wiry young boy with unruly hair rushed into the room at Monsieur Clavette's command. "Yes, monsieur?"

The proprietor gestured to the youth. "This is Pierre, my apprentice. He'll be assisting me today. Pierre, please fetch the lady some water."

The boy bobbed a nod and rushed from the room, quickly returning with a tumbler of water, which he handed to Catherine. She took a greedy sip. Though the water was lukewarm, it took away the dry feeling in her throat and calmed her stomach as well.

Monsieur Clavette led them to the studio space, where a velvet settee welcomed them. Catherine sank onto the seat gratefully and pinned the brooch to the neck of her dress in preparation for the daguerreotype. Alexander took his place beside her, setting the paper he had purchased off to one side.

"Have you seen the headlines today?" Monsieur Clavette made easy conversation as he fussed with the photography equipment.

"I purchased a paper," Alexander replied. "But I haven't read anything in depth. What news is there?"

"Word is that Edward Sterling has passed away."

"Passed away?"

"Yes," Monsieur Clavette confirmed. "The police found a journal he wrote with speculations about who stole from his display at the prince's exhibition last year. They have some new leads on the thief, and they believe him to be of the gentry."

Alexander's brows rose. "Oh? Why do they think that?"

"Proximity. It had to be someone with access. Someone who knew the inner workings of the exhibition. The brooch is rumored to be quite expensive. Well over sixty pounds, they're saying."

Catherine stifled a gasp. Over sixty pounds! Why, Alexander had scarcely made more than that in a year when he started at the bank. It was an enormous sum and not a trifle that someone had stolen something worth that amount.

Monsieur Clavette left his camera to arrange the couple the way he wanted on the settee. He fussed over the lighting for an eternity. All the while, Catherine's thoughts tormented her. She was certain she had seen a familiar tension on Alexander's face at Monsieur Clavette's speech. Yet there was no time to question her husband again now. She tried to remain focused on the task at hand.

"Remember the day we married?" As if sensing her discomfort, Alexander leaned in close to Catherine while Monsieur Clavette situated his camera. His mustache tickled her ear.

She relaxed as the memory came into clear focus. The wedding had been out of a dream. It had taken place at the revered St. Paul's Cathedral, and she had worn a white silk taffeta gown with a sumptuous train.

Alexander couldn't be guilty of anything wicked or underhanded. Of that she felt certain. Perhaps she was imagining all of it. His avoidance. The tension. It was a figment of her imagination, heightened by the emotions of impending motherhood.

She told herself what she wanted to hear, and the tight smile on her face softened as she remembered Alexander's recent kind gestures. Bringing her toast and tea in bed when she wasn't feeling well. Purchasing tickets to that new swoony play she had wanted to see at the theater. He wasn't hiding anything. He was only being cautious. He was thinking of her. He didn't want her to be a target for pickpockets.

Monsieur Clavette took multiple pictures of the couple, muttering in a creative frenzy after each one. Finally, he proclaimed the session over.

"Wonderful." He clapped his hands in satisfaction before addressing Alexander. "The development of the images should not take long. Your telegram mentioned something about setting the daguerreotype in a piece of jewelry? Is that correct?"

"Yes." Alexander motioned for Catherine to remove her brooch. "My wife would like our image fitted inside this piece, please."

"Ah, a lovely choice."

Catherine started to remove the brooch, but as she did so, her eyes fell on the newspaper Alexander had purchased. A phrase below the headline captured her attention. The stolen item of jewelry is purported to be an emerald brooch, custom made by artisan Edward Sterling.

A sudden flush came over her, accompanied by a wave of nausea. She hadn't heard that detail mentioned before. An emerald brooch? Like the one clasped at her neck? Could it be a coincidence? Was she being naive?

"Alexander?" His name was the only word that would push past her lips.

"A moment, my love." Unaware of her need, he continued giving directions to Monsieur Clavette, who excused himself to contact a jeweler about the timing of the daguerreotype fitting.

"Alexander?" Catherine bid for her husband's attention again. She reached for the brooch. Clawed at it. It was choking her. When she couldn't remove it, she reached for him.

Then the room went dark.

"Catherine, can you hear me?"

She stirred at the sound of her husband's voice. She lay on the floor. A flock of birds flew past the glass panes of the skylight. She turned her gaze so that Alexander's face came into focus beside her. Concern etched lines into his handsome features.

What could she say? That she suspected her dear husband of stealing the brooch from Sterling? Then hiding it within the shelter of their home? What possible reason would he have for doing that? There was no bad blood between the two men as far as she could tell. Alexander wasn't hurting for money. His promotion to management at the bank had brought with it a hefty pay raise. It didn't make sense for him to steal anything and keep it hidden. Yet the facts were still unsettling.

MYSTERIES OF COBBLE HILL FARM

Her hand fluttered to the neckline of her dress. The brooch lay tangled in a web of lace. "Where did you get this?"

"What?" Alexander's face crinkled into confusion. "Why are you asking me that? You are ill."

She wasn't to be dissuaded, however. She repeated her question. "I'm not ill. Where did you get it?"

Alexander blinked stupidly. "I told you before. From Edward Sterling. He gave it to me with his blessing on our marriage."

"He gave it to you? You're certain?"

"Of course I'm certain. I remember the day as clear as a bell. I'm not a complete fool."

His snappish response startled her. What nerve had she touched, to unsettle him so?

"I'm sorry. Forgive me, my dear." Alexander looped his arm behind Catherine's shoulders in support. "You're ill, and I'm berating you."

Catherine struggled to sit up. "I'm not ill."

Pierre, Monsieur Clavette's assistant, came back into the room at that moment. He scurried over with a sachet of salts. Alexander must have asked for them when Catherine fainted.

Catherine managed to shove herself up by her elbows. She repeated her earlier words. "I'm not ill, Alexander. I'm with child."

The shock her husband showed! Then he expressed his delight, but not before she caught the look of fear that momentarily crossed his face. It made no sense. Did she really know him as well as she had thought? Who was this man before her?

"Is something wrong?" This time, she turned a question on him.

He cleared his throat. "No, my love. Only taken aback. What wonderful news."

Pierre discreetly glanced away as Alexander pressed a kiss to her mouth. Her heart thumped painfully in her chest.

She had revealed her secret. They were to have a child soon. They were going to become a family.

But family or not, Alexander was still hiding something from her.

CHAPTER EIGHT

When Van called to tell Harriet and Will about the tape, a few clouds already dotted the sky. It didn't take long to get back into town. Will eased the Jaguar into a parking spot in the lot nearest the station, and then he and Harriet walked the rest of the way.

The exterior of the police station was crafted of local stone with a tiled roof. Salt from seawater blew inland far enough to weather the stone in a way common to buildings in the area. As Harriet followed Will up the steps that led to the entry, she thought of the many people who had sought justice there over the decades that the station had been in service. Would the answer to who stole the brooch come from within these four walls?

Van met them at the door and immediately ushered them down the hall into his office. "Have a seat."

He motioned to two chairs opposite his desk, and Harriet and Will both sat. Van settled into a rolling chair behind the desk and got right to business. "Thanks for coming. Here's where we stand right now. We spent last evening and this morning reaching out to a few people we think might've seen activity surrounding the brooch's theft, but we didn't gain any helpful information."

Harriet exchanged glances with Will. They had to tell Van what they knew about Benedict, even if it was difficult.

"Actually, we wanted to talk to you about something," Will said. He filled the detective constable in on the information they had regarding Benedict, his past, and the way he had involved Nigel in his scheme.

"Hmm." Van scribbled a note on his desk blotter. "That's certainly an avenue to investigate. I did talk to Mr. Carter, but I didn't find any reason to question his story. Perhaps I should have, although the video doesn't show any suspicious behavior on his part."

"What does it show?" Curiosity nagged at Harriet. Whatever evidence the video revealed obviously wasn't cut and dried. Otherwise, Van or some other officer would have made an arrest already. Yet, as far as she could tell from the tension in Van's jaw, that wasn't close to happening.

"I'll let the footage speak for itself." Van swiveled his computer screen so Harriet and Will could see it more clearly. Then he pressed play on the video.

"The time stamp on this footage is approximately one minute before the lights went out, after which we presume the brooch was stolen," Van explained.

Harriet watched the moving images on the screen with rapt attention. Ah, this was where Will had given his wedding toast. The camera zoomed in as he started to speak to the crowd. Then the focus broke away from him as Mom panned the room to capture guest reactions. Most people were smiling, a few covering their mouths in amusement as Will spoke. Someone in the back of the room, however, caught Harriet's attention.

It was Benedict. His reaction stood in stark contrast to the rest of the group. Instead of showing enjoyment, he appeared... stricken.

MYSTERIES OF COBBLE HILL FARM

There was no better way to describe the deer-in-the-headlights expression on his face. But Will's tone was teasing, not serious, and everyone else seemed to be enjoying his speech. Why not Benedict? Why would his reaction be anything but lighthearted?

"Can you please pause the video?" Harriet asked. Van did, and the frame froze on a shot of Benedict as he pulled his cell phone from his pocket. Harriet shared what she had observed. "Benedict looks like he's reacting to the toast. Will, you said, 'Believe me, do I have some stories I could tell...' What story *were* you planning to tell?"

Will scrubbed his hand over his chin. "Nothing to do with Benedict. It was only a lark that happened the first year I was in full-time ministry in the Islands. Believe it or not, the sheep outnumbered parishioners the first time I assumed the pulpit. We had a jolly mishap with some of them getting inside the sanctuary."

"Benedict must've thought you meant something else. Something about him, perhaps?" Harriet touched his arm. "Think. Is there a certain incident your words would remind him of?"

"I can't think of anything. I was quite vague," Will said slowly. "I may have looked at him when I queued up the story about my early days in ministry."

"Let me rewind the video." Van ran the tape back. "Listen carefully. Knowing what you've told me about Benedict, his reaction does seem telling. If we can figure out what's happening with him, that might help us out. I certainly need to speak to Mr. Wharton too, especially since I can't account for his whereabouts at the time of the power outage. In the meantime, here's another person of interest..."

Harriet leaned in to study the tape more closely.

"Can you tell me who this is?" Van pointed at the screen where a woman stood alone at the heirloom table. Harriet knew right away who it was because of the hat the woman wore. The woman suddenly threw up her hands and bolted for the door, passing by Sebastian, who dove under the table. Then all went dark.

Harriet frowned. "That's Talia. Natalia Bishop." She caught Van up to speed with information about Talia and how she was a longtime friend of the family. "I assume Polly told you that she noticed someone running from the room around the time we think the brooch went missing? And that we think the person she saw was Talia?"

Van nodded.

Harriet thought for a moment. She couldn't bring herself to implicate her friend, no matter what the evidence implied. Now it was Will's turn to give her a meaningful glance. "Harriet, you have to tell Van about the conversation you had with your aunt," he gently prodded.

Van looked at Harriet expectantly. She felt as much of a need to protect Talia as Will did Benedict, but he was right. They had to tell Van everything they knew. He needed their absolute trust if they were going to discover what happened to the brooch.

"All right." Harriet bit her lip before saying, "Aunt Jinny told me that Talia confided in her at the reception. Her business is in trouble, and she wanted my aunt to loan her some money. Aunt Jinny told her she couldn't do that."

"Hmm." Van tapped his pen on the desk. "Is it possible that Ms. Bishop was desperate enough for quick money that she would have nabbed the brooch?"

"It's possible," Harriet answered reluctantly. With her connections in the jewelry business, Talia might have opportunity to sell a stolen item. But would she go to such lengths to save her business at the risk of losing relationships? And if so, why would she disclose the brooch's value before stealing it? Unless taking the brooch had been a spontaneous decision...

"Desperate times press people to extreme measures," Van said grimly. "Has anyone been in contact with this woman since last night?"

"No, though we have tried." A fact which now seemed ominous. It had been easy to think of innocent reasons Talia might have left the reception early. At first, Harriet had comforted herself with the thought that Talia was simply being...well, Talia. A workaholic dropping into their lives to say hello and then, just as quickly, winging out again. When Aunt Jinny hadn't been able to reach Talia at the shop, Harriet had imagined she would get back to them when she could, her reply sandwiched in between never-ending appointments and travel. But was that the truth? Or was it what Harriet wanted to be true? "We haven't been able to reach her. My aunt has tried, and I've tried too. I didn't think much of it at first, but now..."

"Do you know what she's reacting to?" Van continued his line of questioning. "Or why she's running for the door?"

"I assume she isn't reacting to my toast." Will was only half joking. Talia had begun running before the lights went out and was gone when they came back on. Was she running from someone? Or running to escape with the brooch?

Will placed a hand on Harriet's shoulder. "Harriet? Any theories?"

Harriet drew in a deep breath. "I'm afraid not. All I can think is that it looks like she's getting out of there fast."

She thought back to the confusing moments after the room had gone dark. She had heard a shriek. Then she had felt Talia's hat brush by her face, followed by a crash. Next, repeated sneezes. Had that been Benedict, or someone else?

No, wait. She had the wrong order. The brush of Talia's hat came first. Then she heard someone yell and the crash. Perhaps on the way out, Talia had knocked into Imogen? That lined up. But now she had a new question. Why had Talia started for the door and then changed direction to come near Harriet at the bridal table before turning back around and leaving?

Harriet's mind swam with confusion. Was it possible that financial desperation could have driven Talia to steal from the same people she called honorary family? Or was it all a huge misunderstanding?

"I can see you're struggling to absorb this." Sympathy softened Van's features. "It can be difficult to process something disturbing like a crime when loved ones are involved."

Will placed an arm over Harriet's shoulders, repeating the reassurance she had offered him earlier regarding Benedict. "I'm sure there's a reasonable explanation."

Van gave them a moment before pushing forward with the tape. "There is one more person we haven't been able to identify who is implicated in the video. We're hoping you can help us?"

Harriet sat up straighter. "We'll try," she said.

She squinted at the screen as Van scrubbed the tape back even more. Before the lights cut and the brooch disappeared. As Talia lingered at the heirloom table, an elderly woman wearing a forest-green skirt suit and carrying a brown handbag came alongside her. She bent over the jewelry, studying each piece carefully. When a hotel employee approached her, she engaged in a brief conversation with him before wandering toward the exit. A few seconds after she left, Talia ran, the lights cut, and the screen went dark.

Van stopped the tape. Then he jabbed a finger at the screen. "Any idea who this is? She isn't top of my suspect list, because she doesn't fit the profile, but I need to include her for the sake of a thorough investigation."

"I don't know her." Will glanced over at Harriet. "Is she someone from your side of the family?"

Harriet's heart sank as she studied the woman's image. Van may not think the neatly dressed woman fit the profile of a criminal, but there was certainly something suspicious about her. Starting with the fact that Harriet had zero idea who she was.

"That's not one of our wedding guests. I've never seen that woman before in my life."

A momentary silence followed Harriet's confession.

"So, what are we dealing with here?" Will asked.

It seemed laughable to describe the unobtrusive woman on the video as a wedding crasher, but wasn't that the truth? If Will didn't know her and Harriet didn't know her, what could she possibly be if not an uninvited trespasser?

Will offered an optimistic solution. "Maybe she's a random guest from the hotel who accidentally wandered in?"

"Perhaps." Van seemed skeptical though. "I'll need to go back to the hotel and speak to some of the employees again. Do more in-depth questioning."

"Could we have some still prints of the mystery woman to take with us?" Harriet asked.

"Certainly." Van recapped his pen before standing. "Sit tight, and I'll get those for you right away." He isolated the video feed, pulled a few screenshots, and retrieved the printouts. Harriet and Will assured him they'd contact him immediately if they found out anything, and he promised to keep them in the loop as well.

Will held the door for Harriet as she stepped out onto the sidewalk. The warm August sun beat down, but she could feel a shift in the air. The atmosphere was electric and charged, and the temperature had noticeably dropped a few degrees. Proof a summer storm was blowing in, bringing with it a drastic change.

Given the circumstances, the weather had never felt more appropriate.

CHAPTER NINE

We'd better hurry to the car. I have a feeling we're going to get a downpour soon," Harriet said.

Will agreed, and the two of them started back to the Jaguar. But the storm descended quicker than even Harriet had anticipated. Fat raindrops began to dot the sidewalk.

"The printouts!" She tried to slip the pages Van had given them into her handbag, but they were too large for her small travel crossbody.

"Here." Will grabbed her hand and tugged her into one of the nearby businesses lining the street. The scent of fresh baked goods and brewing coffee met her nose. She was pleased to see their detour had landed them in a familiar restaurant: the Happy Cup Tearoom and Bakery. The last time she had gotten food from there—sausage rolls and cucumber salad, if memory served her—everything had been delicious. Not a bad place to wait out a little rain.

Or a lot of rain, as it turned out. The heavens outside the tearoom's windows opened, and a verifiable deluge poured down. Yikes. They were definitely staying for a while.

Will adopted the same train of thought as Harriet. "Feel like lunch? Or did you eat at your aunt's?"

"No, I haven't eaten since the pastries this morning." Her stomach growled on cue. "A real meal sounds great."

They chose a booth in a cozy corner with a good view out the windows facing the street. Not that there was much to see. Foot traffic all but halted as rain pelted down. When the server, a woman with a curly mop of brown hair, arrived to take their drink order, Will requested hot tea for the table.

After the young woman served them, Harriet fixed herself a cup of tea and added a hearty splash of milk. She supposed she was properly British now. It felt odd to drink tea any other way. She took a tentative sip of the hot beverage, taking care not to scald her tongue. Then she passed the printouts to Will.

He took a sip of his own tea before setting the cup down to study the photos. "This woman doesn't look familiar at all. Quite odd, considering how small White Church Bay is. Why wouldn't we have run into her around town?"

Harriet didn't have any answers for him. "I'm not sure. Maybe we can show her picture around. If she lives anywhere near here, surely someone will recognize her."

"We can go ahead and send it to Polly and your aunt," Will said. "That's a start."

"That's a smart idea."

Will snapped some closeups of the photos and spent a few minutes composing a message on his phone while Harriet mulled over the current suspects list. None of the options quite made sense. First, there was Benedict. He had an established history of stealing and was obviously covering up something related to the power outage. He apparently had no qualms lying to the police and encouraging others to do so as well.

But what could his motive be? When they'd talked to him, it had seemed as if his life was on an upward trajectory. He'd appeared proud of his position at the hotel, his relationship with Lucy, and the general direction his life was heading. He made no bones about the fact that he had turned over a new leaf. Was that all idle talk? If not, why would he put his future in jeopardy with another criminal charge? He mentioned needing more money to purchase an engagement ring for Lucy, but was that a good enough reason to commit a criminal act? Even if the brooch was worth an enormous sum, Benedict could outstrip that amount by doing honest work at Ravenscroft. Was he really willing to trade six months of aboveboard labor for potentially years in jail if he was caught stealing?

Then there was Talia. Harriet didn't know her as well as some other family members did, but up until recently, the woman had given her no reason to suspect her of anything criminal. But if she wasn't guilty, why did the video show her running from the room just before the lights went out? With her business in financial trouble, she had a motive for stealing. Add the fact that she was all of a sudden out-of-pocket, and no one was able to reach her? The dots connected to form a picture that was too large a coincidence to ignore.

Finally, Harriet mused over the mystery's newest development. Who was the elderly woman at her wedding? And if she wasn't on the guest list, why was she there? White Church Bay was an insular community. Why didn't they recognize her?

Just then the server returned to take their food order. "What can I get for you?"

"Let's see…" Harriet set her questions aside to study the menu in front of her. She needed fuel if she was going to solve this mystery. It was tempting to get the same thing she had ordered before. It was really delicious. But part of the fun of going to restaurants was escaping the tried-and-true and opting for an unfamiliar dish. After all, it could become a new favorite. "I'll take a Welsh dip sandwich, please."

"Right." The server scribbled on her pad of paper. "That comes with crisps and a small salad. That work for you?"

"That'll be great."

Will ordered the sausage rolls and a bowl of gazpacho.

"I'll bring your food right out." The server gathered their menus and hurried off.

Will bent over the printouts again to study them more carefully. "Wait a minute…"

"What?"

"Look at this." Will angled the papers toward Harriet. Then he pointed at a small detail that had escaped Harriet's attention. "See the key fob she's holding?"

"Yes. What's special about that?"

"The logo on that fob is for quite a unique car. The Aston Martin DB5." Will shook his head in disbelief. "I can't believe I didn't notice it before. If we find the car, we find the mystery woman who crashed our wedding reception."

Hmm…maybe Will's knowledge of cars was going to come in handier than Harriet had thought.

"We need to get back to Ravenscroft," she said. "Lucy sees a lot of guests come and go at the hotel. Maybe she can help us."

The server brought their food, and Harriet and Will enjoyed their lunch. The Welsh dip sandwich wasn't as good a choice as the sausage rolls, but thankfully, Will was kind enough to share some of his with her. Yet another perk of married life. The rain slowed as they savored their last sips of tea. People began walking by the window again. First, there were only a few as the skies cleared, but the small trickle soon grew to a steady stream.

Harriet nudged Will. "Should we make a run for it, now that the rain has stopped?"

When the server came over to their table to check on them, Will paid their bill. Then the newlyweds hurried back to the car. The sidewalks were wet from the rain, and they had to skirt a fair number of puddles along the way.

Once they arrived at their car, Harriet pulled her phone from her handbag. Since Will was driving, she might as well use the opportunity to make some calls. The first one was to Aunt Jinny. Studying the printouts had reminded Harriet of Sebastian popping up from under the table just after the brooch's disappearance. The video from the police station had shown him standing beside the table prior to the lights going out. Even though he had denied taking anything, she wanted to question him again. Maybe he hid something under the table, or maybe he had more information about someone else involved. Any scrap of evidence they could gather would be helpful.

Aunt Jinny answered after a few rings. "Harriet! I didn't expect to hear from you again so soon. Is everything all right?"

"Everything's fine," Harriet assured her. She explained everything they'd learned at the police station, ending with the appearance of the mystery woman. "I know Sebastian said he didn't take the brooch, but I'd like to talk to him again. If he was under the table when the theft occurred, maybe he saw something that can help us make headway on the case."

"Of course," Aunt Jinny answered. "Hold on."

Harriet heard a muffled sound, as if her aunt was covering the receiver with one hand. "Sebastian! Come inside, please." Aunt Jinny's voice was followed by the opening and closing of a door and the thump of running feet.

"What is it?" Sebastian sounded out of breath.

"I'm talking to Harriet," Aunt Jinny replied.

"Oh, can we do a video call?" Sebastian pleaded. "Please?"

"Only as long as you don't get distracted with filters. Harriet wants to see you. Not a cartoon cat face. Deal?"

"Okay…" the little boy agreed begrudgingly.

The video feature switched on, showcasing Sebastian's grubby face. Dirt smeared his ripped T-shirt, and there were long, red scratches on his arms.

Harriet gasped. "Sebastian! Did you get hurt?"

"No," Sebastian replied, appearing perplexed at her question. "Why?"

Aunt Jinny grimaced. "He's been climbing trees, apparently. He says he's Jack climbing the beanstalk. I read him that story last night at bedtime. Children and their imaginations."

Aunt Jinny rested a hand on Sebastian's shoulder. "Sweetheart, we know you said you didn't take the brooch, but you were hiding under the table at the reception. Can you answer some questions for us?"

At this, Sebastian's boldness fled. He ducked his head. "I guess."

"It's okay, buddy." Harriet tried her best to soothe his nerves. It wouldn't do to scare him off. She had no idea which way this situation was going to go. It was still possible he'd taken the brooch and wasn't being truthful. If he thought he was in trouble, he might not be as forthcoming with her. "First, can you tell me why you were hiding under the table in the first place?"

Sebastian shrugged. "I was playing a game."

"What kind of game?"

"I pretended I was a brave knight. The bravest of them all."

Harriet hid a smile behind her hand. Her wedding reception had been in a castle. From a child's perspective, it was barely a hop, skip, and a jump to living in medieval times. "Wow, a knight. That's so interesting. Go on."

Sebastian beamed, seeming to enjoy the attention. "I pretended that the table with all your jewelry was a treasure to guard. Anytime somebody came close, I would watch them. First, there was that lady with the big, feathered hat. I pretended she was a lady-in-weighty."

A laugh burst past Harriet's lips. "A what?"

"A lady-in-weighty. You know."

"Do you mean a lady-in-waiting?"

"That's what I said." An edge of impatience snuck into Sebastian's voice at Harriet's correction. "Then there was an older lady. She was the queen. That man in a uniform by the door was a knight."

"And?" Harriet held her breath. It seemed like a childish game of imagination, but what if Sebastian had witnessed something nobody else had? "Did any of those people try to take the treasure? Do you know who the queen was? Did she say anything?"

"I don't think so." Sebastian's brow wrinkled. "But I didn't see everything. I had only guarded the treasure for a little bit when a big, scary dragon swooped down. I made sure to stay hidden in the cave."

A dragon? Harriet's breath whooshed out in an exhale of disappointment. So, no help at all then. Just a little boy's imagination working overtime. "The cave? You mean, you hid under the table?"

"It wasn't a table. It was a cave. Weren't you listening?"

Harriet smoothed things over as best she could. Then Aunt Jinny waved Sebastian outside to go play again.

"I think he just wants attention," Aunt Jinny murmured into the phone. "It's been difficult for him lately. Sophie did well in school last year, but Sebastian fell behind in reading. Olivia has been working with his teacher, who's given him summer reading assignments to help him catch up. I think Sebastian is worried about the start of a new school year and he's harbored resentment toward his sister as a result. I'll keep talking to him about the brooch, but I doubt we'll get much more out of him than we already have."

Another voice, Sophie's, suddenly joined the conversation. "Sebastian's lying, Nana! He stole my tiara, and he broke it too! Look!"

"What happened?" Harriet asked. All the action was taking place off-screen, so to speak, and she couldn't see anything. What was Sophie talking about?

"Oh my." Aunt Jinny held up Sophie's flower girl tiara so Harriet could see. Clearly, it was no longer missing. The sparkly crown was snapped cleanly in half. "Sophie, where did you find this?"

Sophie bobbed into view. Her eyes were red, and tears streaked her cheeks. "Under Sebastian's bed. My ball rolled under there, and

MYSTERIES OF COBBLE HILL FARM

when I went to get it, I saw my tiara. It's absolutely ruined! I'll never forgive him. Never, never, never!"

Aunt Jinny sighed. "This paints a different picture. I'm going to go talk to Sebastian again. I promise I'll call if I find out any more about the brooch's disappearance. Okay if I let you go?"

"Of course."

Harriet thanked her aunt for her help and hung up. So, another wrinkle in an already complex mystery. What if Sebastian did know something about the brooch? And what if the irreplaceable heirloom had been damaged too, like Sophie's tiara? A quick glance out the car window assured Harriet that they were only halfway back to the hotel. Just enough time for one more call.

She punched in the phone number for Talia's shop that Aunt Jinny had given her previously. Things had been so busy that she hadn't tried calling again. The phone rang three times before a young woman answered.

"Hi, who's this?" A fumbling at the other end of the line. A clearing throat. "I'm sorry. I mean, Golden Radiance Fine Jewelry, this is Sandi speaking. How may I help you?"

The second try was clearly a pass at redeeming professionalism. The young woman sounded unsure of herself, as if she wasn't used to answering the shop number. Had Talia hired help?

"Hello," Harriet said. "I'd like to talk to Talia, if she's there?"

A rustling of papers. "Um, Ms. Bishop can't come to the phone right now, but I'd be happy to take a message?" Her voice ticked up at the end, as if her sentence was a question instead of a statement. She sounded as if she was reading from a script.

Borrowed Trouble

That was odd. Shouldn't Talia be back home by now? Her store was only a couple of hours away from White Church Bay. And as far as Harriet knew, if the shop was open, Talia was there.

"Could I ask where she is, please?"

"Um…" More shuffling papers. "Um, I don't know that… I'm not really supposed to…"

"It's okay." As with the earlier call with Sebastian, Harriet tried her best to smooth over the uncomfortable situation her questions had created. "Will she be back today?"

"I can't really say…" Sandi sounded on the verge of tears. Then she dropped all pretense of professionalism. Her words rushed out in a jumble. "I'm so sorry. I've been an employee here for a while, but this is my first day managing things on my own. I'm a bit overwhelmed. Ms. Bishop left me so many pages of notes that I can't keep everything straight. All these people keep calling asking for things, and I don't have answers for anybody. Someone even threatened to leave a bad review online. They can't do that. They just can't!" A long sniffle punctuated the end of her monologue.

"I'm sure things aren't as bad as all that," Harriet said in a soothing tone. How well she remembered her first stumbling steps into a leadership role in her career. Clinical rotations in veterinary school had sent her scrambling to find the real adult on call—only to find to her surprise that it was her! "All I need is a phone number or some other way to reach Talia. She's a friend of my family's, and I have something important I need to talk to her about."

"I think she left a cell phone number somewhere…" Sandi's voice sounded a bit more confident. "Oh, here it is."

MYSTERIES OF COBBLE HILL FARM

Harriet scribbled the number Sandi gave her on the back of a receipt in her handbag. Aha! It looked like Aunt Jinny had written Talia's number down incorrectly. But swap a "7" for a "9," and they were in business! "Thanks so much, Sandi. I'll make sure to tell Talia how helpful you've been."

"Really?" Sandi sounded as if she was forever indebted.

Harriet told Sandi goodbye and ended the call just as Will parked outside Ravenscroft. After she grabbed her handbag and got out of the car, she tried to call Talia with the cell phone number Sandi had just given her. When the call pinged to voice mail, she drew a breath to leave a message but stopped cold as the greeting played.

Hello, you've reached the voice mail of Lindell Gruber. Please leave me a message unless you're a solicitor, in which case, hang up now...

Harriet ended the call without leaving a message.

Lindell Gruber? Who on earth was that? And where was Talia?

CHAPTER TEN

D o you think Sandi gave me the wrong number on purpose? Or was she just confused?"

Harriet hashed out the situation with Will on Sunday evening as they ate what he called a "traveler's dinner" on their hotel balcony. Cubed cheese, prosciutto, crackers, olives, and orange wedges made for a simple but tasty meal. Since the mistaken call to Lindell Gruber, Harriet had tried a couple of times to contact Sandi again at the shop without success.

Will shrugged. "Difficult to say. If you keep calling, surely, she'll pick up. Then you can get things sorted out."

"I hope so, but—"

The muffled ringing of the landline inside the suite interrupted Harriet's reply.

"I'll get it." Will popped a last bite of cracker into his mouth before pushing to his feet. He left the balcony to answer the phone. After a quick conversation, he hung up and returned to Harriet.

"Who was that?" she asked.

"Imogen Sinclair."

"Why is she calling?"

"She wanted to apologize for what happened at the reception. She asked if she could speak to us in person, so I gave her the room number."

MYSTERIES OF COBBLE HILL FARM

In a few minutes, a knock sounded at the door. When Will opened it, Harriet saw Imogen standing in the hallway holding a white cardboard box. "Imogen, how nice to see you. Won't you come in?"

"Yes, thanks." Imogen entered the room before extending the box to Harriet. "I got word you were still in town and wanted to bring you this."

Harriet took the box. "What is it?"

"Just an apology gift." A questioning expression must have crept onto Harriet's face, because Imogen rushed to explain. "I felt horrible that your bridal cupcake got destroyed. I know your husband said it wasn't a problem, but tradition is important. I couldn't stand the thought of ruining your special day."

"That's so thoughtful, Imogen, but you don't need to feel bad. What happened to our wedding cake wasn't your fault."

"I know. But I still wanted to make it up to you by bringing you another cake."

"Come in, please." Harriet waved Imogen into the suite's sitting area. She set the box on a table and flipped open the lid. Inside nestled a two-tiered sponge cake liberally dusted with confectioner's sugar. A lovely, sweet aroma rose from the box to meet Harriet's nose.

"That smells absolutely delicious," she said.

"It's Victoria sponge cake," Imogen replied. "Classic vanilla layered with strawberry jam and homemade whipped cream. I made it fresh this afternoon. Just be sure to eat it soon so the cake doesn't get soggy."

"It looks wonderful." Will gave the cake an appreciative sniff. "Smells wonderful too."

"I agree," Harriet said. "I can't wait to try some." She smiled at Imogen. "Would you like to have a piece with us?"

"No, thank you," Imogen said. "I really need to get going. But I'm so pleased you like it." She turned toward the door. "Let me know when you get settled in at home after the honeymoon, and I'll bring you another bridal cupcake for your freezer. Earl Grey cake with blackberry filling and lemon frosting. Just like yesterday's."

"That's so kind of you. We'll give you a call." Harriet thanked Imogen again before showing her to the hall. Then she returned to the suite to admire Imogen's handiwork. What a treat the cake was. She would definitely make sure to leave a glowing review on the bakery's website.

Once she and Will had stuffed themselves with dessert, Harriet felt fortified enough to press forward on the mystery.

"Should we go check the front desk again?" Lucy hadn't been stationed at her usual post when they arrived, and Harriet was anxious to talk to her. Apparently, she was in more of a rush than Will was, however. He still had half a slice of sponge cake left.

A bit of gentle prodding sped up his efforts, though not without the addition of some good-natured grumbling.

As soon as they'd cleaned up, they headed downstairs to find Lucy. Thankfully, she was at the desk this time.

"Still here?" she asked with a smile as they approached.

"Still here, and pretending to be Poirot," Will joked. "At least until we find out who took Harriet's brooch."

"I wish I could help," Lucy said.

"Maybe you can." Harriet handed the printouts that she and Will had received at the station to Lucy. "Do you recognize this woman?"

Lucy leaned closer to study the papers. Then she shook her head. "No, she hasn't been a guest at the hotel. I'm certain of that. I'm very good at remembering faces, and I don't recognize her."

Harriet released a sigh. They weren't making very quick progress with the mystery. How long were they going to have to postpone their honeymoon? Van had originally acted like all would be cleared up in twenty-four hours. Now they had pushed past that, with little progress to show for their efforts.

"We also noticed that the woman has a special key fob, which indicates she drives an Aston Martin," Will said. "Do you know anyone around here who drives that vehicle?"

Lucy laughed. "Now you're even less likely to get an answer. I know next to nothing about cars. But I do know somewhere you might find the information you need." She pulled a binder off the shelf behind her and flipped through pages until she found what she wanted. She swiveled the book toward Will and Harriet. "I keep up on all the events happening in the area, in case a guest wants suggestions. There happens to be a vintage car show going on at the Station Lot right now."

Harriet read from the page. "The White Church Bay Classic Car Show?"

"Someone there will know who drives an Aston Martin," Lucy said confidently.

Will thanked Lucy and gathered up the printouts. Then he turned to Harriet with an imploring expression. "A car show. Fancy that. Don't suppose I could persuade you to goggle at some cars for a bit, could I?"

"I guess we could do that…" The words came out more hesitantly than she intended. Not that she wanted to begrudge him his interests, but they had been running around all day, and she would prefer to spend what little remained of the day relaxing. She hadn't intended for their sleuthing to take them outside the hotel walls.

"Never mind. We don't have to. It's your honeymoon too." Will must have caught her wavering tone.

Oh goodness. How could she deny him something that would make him so happy? Even if she didn't care about cars as much as he did, she supposed she could always learn. Plus, this might help them track down the mystery woman. "No, I'd love to go. You can tell me about all the different vehicles. And a lot of people will be there. It'll be an opportunity to show the photos around. Even if no one knows about the car, someone might recognize the woman."

Will's eyes lit up. "Great. I promise you'll enjoy it. Car shows are fascinating."

Harriet warmed to the idea as they left the hotel to travel to the show. Maybe this would be interesting. But she could feel herself zoning out as soon as they arrived and Will started in with talk of chassis and carburetors again. He oohed and aahed over the vehicles on display, asking the owners question after question. She was an intelligent person, but it was safe to say she understood roughly five percent of the lingo Will threw around.

But that was okay. Cars weren't in her wheelhouse like they were his. It was unlikely Will would know what she was talking about if she referenced information from the BSAVA, the manual that British veterinarians in small animal practices commonly used. Maybe she could still prove the trip to the event worthwhile though. She scanned the area, and her gaze fell on a small information booth set up in the corner of the lot.

"I'll be right back." Harriet touched Will's arm to let him know she was leaving.

"Sure, of course." Will waved at her. "See you in a bit."

With the printouts from the police station clutched securely in hand, Harriet approached a man and woman who appeared to be running the information booth. More than likely, they'd had eyes on an enormous number of participants already. It was a shot in the dark, but it was all Harriet could think to do right now. Until she could come up with something better, this was the plan.

"Hello. I'm Graham Fletcher," the man said when Harriet approached the booth. "And this is my wife, Rosalind. Is this your first time at the show?"

"Yes, it is."

"Wonderful. Let me grab a brochure for you." Rosalind gave Harriet a wide smile before digging in a cardboard box behind her and handing over a colorful brochure with information about the cars in the show.

"Thank you," Harriet said. Graham elaborated for a few minutes on some of the highlights visitors could expect to see at the show. "Are you a car enthusiast?" he asked.

"I don't know much about vintage cars, to tell the truth," Harriet admitted. "But my husband enjoys them. He rented a Jaguar E-Type for us to drive on our honeymoon."

Graham whistled through his teeth. "Nice set of wheels. Did you know Enzo Ferrari said the Jaguar E-Type was the most beautiful car ever made?"

"No, I didn't," Harriet answered.

Rosalind broke into the conversation. "You sound like me when we were first married. I wasn't very knowledgeable about vintage cars. Or very interested, to tell the truth."

Yikes. Was Harriet's tepid response that obvious? She hoped Will hadn't noticed her lack of enthusiasm.

Rosalind continued. "Over the years, I took more of an interest. It was a huge part of Graham's life, so it was natural that it became part of mine too. Turnabout's fair play though." She winked. "He took up birdwatching with me."

"Who would've thought those little fellows were so fascinating?" Graham grinned. "That's the secret to being married forty-five years. Build a life together and try not to fuss more than necessary along the way."

Forty-five years. What an achievement. They seemed delighted to be in each other's company too. Graham and Rosalind must be doing something right, to keep the spark alive for that long. Harriet thought of the times Will had changed his plans to help her investigate clues or track down suspects. It was only fair that she make the effort to show interest in his hobbies. If that meant learning about carburetors and pistons, then so be it. If she wanted their life as a couple to be as seamlessly entwined as the Fletchers' seemed to be, she would need to exert some effort.

"Anything else we can help you with?" Graham asked.

"Yes, actually." Lost in life lessons, Harriet had nearly forgotten why she had wanted to talk to the couple in the first place. "My husband and I are trying to locate someone in the area. It's about something related to our wedding." No need to give all the details of the theft. No one wanted to give information that might implicate an acquaintance.

She handed the photos to Rosalind. Disappointingly, Rosalind said she didn't know who the woman was. She handed the papers to her husband. "Recognize her? You seem to know almost everybody."

"Huh. Let me get my specs." Graham took a pair of readers from his shirt pocket and put them on. Then he scrutinized the image with a scholarly intensity. "No, I don't think I know her."

"How about someone who drives an Aston Martin DB5?" Harriet asked. She pointed out the key fob that Will had noticed during lunch.

Graham froze. "Wait a minute. Now *that* I can help you with."

CHAPTER ELEVEN

Wonderful! A breakthrough. Harriet stifled a sigh of relief.

"An Aston Martin DB5?" Rosalind repeated Harriet's words. She glanced at her husband. "Weren't there only a little over a thousand of those in production in the entire country?"

"Spot on." Graham appeared impressed at his wife's knowledge of his hobby. "Only one owner of that vehicle in this area that I can recall. Used to come to the car club meetups all the time. He rarely missed a get-together."

"What was the man's name? Do you remember?" Harriet tried not to stake her hopes on his reply, but this was important. Maybe the man was the woman's husband? Or a brother? This could be the clue that they needed. It was possible that the elderly woman who had appeared at their wedding contained all the answers to the mystery's questions. If they had a name, they could track her down.

"Hmm, what was it? Pendleton... Pennington..." Graham stared into the distance as if he were trying to pluck the correct name from the air.

"Pembroke!" Rosalind suddenly blurted out.

Graham snapped his fingers. "That's it. Rosie beat me to it. Robert Pembroke. That was his name. And his wife's name was Florence."

MYSTERIES OF COBBLE HILL FARM

Harriet borrowed a pen from the table and scrawled the name on the edge of the brochure that Rosalind had given her. Then she tucked the brochure into her bag. "Thanks so much. Really. You don't know what a huge help that is."

Warm hands squeezed her shoulders from behind. Will. "I see you're making friends."

"She couldn't help but make friends with Graham." Rosalind laughed. "He's never met a stranger."

"It's true." Graham nodded. "From what your wife says about you, it sounds like we need to chat cars, young man."

Oh no. As encouraging as Rosalind's example had been, Harriet didn't want to get sidelined at the car show for another hour. They had a name for the woman who had shown up unannounced at their wedding. This could be the piece of information they needed, and it was important to act fast.

Thankfully, Will picked up on the fact that Harriet was anxious to get going. "I'd love to visit with you sometime soon. Is the show hosted by a local car club or something?"

"It sure is. And you're looking at the chairman." Graham proudly puffed out his chest. "We meet on Tuesday evenings at six. Details are in the brochure Rosalind gave to your wife."

Will and Harriet thanked the Fletchers before heading toward the parking area where they had left the Jaguar. They hadn't covered much distance before Harriet took the brochure from her bag and shoved it at Will. "Look at this. Isn't it exciting?"

Will frowned at the brochure. "You mean about the car club? Goodness, you're being supportive. I thought you were bored to tears."

98

"No... I mean, I was, but I'm not... Oh, never mind." Harriet stopped walking and flipped the brochure over to show him the name she had scribbled down.

"Florence Pembroke?" Will appeared perplexed. "Who's that? Does she have something to do with the car club?"

"No, forget the car club. I asked the Fletchers if they recognized the woman in the police printouts. They didn't, but they perked up when I mentioned your car tie-in. They know a man who used to be in the car club who owned that vehicle."

Once Will understood Florence Pembroke was connected to the owner of an Aston Martin, he seemed as impatient as Harriet to get to the car. He slipped into the driver's seat while she used her phone to do a quick online search for *Florence Pembroke*. When that didn't return any viable results, she tried typing in the husband's name, in case the phone listing was under him instead. "Robert... Pembroke..." she said out loud as she tapped in the letters.

A bit of scrolling yielded a phone number, which she promptly called after checking the time to make sure it wasn't too late. Mrs. Pembroke picked up right away. After a short conversation, Harriet scribbled down an address under her previous note on the car club pamphlet. After she ended the call, she said to Will, "She gave me her address, and she's expecting us."

Will drove to a small cottage just on the outskirts of town.

It took Harriet a moment to gather her bearings. "I don't think we're far from the Danbys' farm. Or the clinic." How odd, to know they were sitting so close to her property, yet she had never ventured along this stretch of road. It was no wonder she hadn't been aware of its presence before though. The Pembrokes' home was located on a remote cul-de-sac tucked neatly behind a copse of trees. A newcomer would need a map to wind up here.

They parked in an open grassy area in front of the house. The Pembrokes' cottage was modest, with a thatched roof, stone walls, and painted front door. It contrasted sharply with the gleaming silver sports car in the driveway. Harriet and Will exited the Jaguar, and Harriet waited while Will got his fill of gawking at what she assumed must be an Aston Martin DB5.

After a few minutes, they walked up the path that led to the house. The front porch was swept clean, and the railings looked newly painted. Someone was taking care of the place, at least on the outside.

Harriet knocked on the door. No one answered, so she rapped again, a little harder. "Hello? Anyone home?"

"I'm coming." After the click of a lock and the rattle of a knob turning, the door opened a crack, and an elderly woman peered through the opening. She didn't seem to recognize them, though Harriet immediately identified her as the woman on the videotape.

The woman squinted at them. Then she reached for a pair of glasses hanging from her neck on a gold chain. As soon as she put them on, her eyes widened. "Ah, the couple from the hotel! The one with the lovely wedding reception. I didn't put two and two together when you called."

So that explained why she hadn't immediately recognized them. Mrs. Pembroke opened the door even more to reveal a rather intimidating English Mastiff standing guard. Harriet's years as a veterinarian had given her a comfort level with animals, so she went down on one knee and extended a flat palm for the dog to sniff. Will, however, stayed back.

Mrs. Pembroke must have detected Will's concern. "Hercules is a big sweetie," she said. "Aren't you, fellow? He wouldn't hurt a fly, but strangers poking around my place don't need to know that. Good thing you two come with a stamp of approval from Graham. He and my husband went back a long way."

Went back? *Why not* go *back?* The wording, in firm past tense, caught Harriet off guard. She tested the conversational waters. "Does your husband still participate in the car club?"

Mrs. Pembroke shook her head sadly. "No, my Robert passed last year. Gets lonely in this old house without him. Care to come in for a cuppa while we talk?"

Harriet and Will agreed, and Mrs. Pembroke led them inside. To say Harriet was shocked when she entered the widow's sitting room was an understatement. Far from the cozy, neat environment she had envisioned, especially given the well-cared-for exterior, the home more closely resembled a bachelor's pad. Every surface was piled high with items, and books and bric-a-brac had taken over. It was an absolute mess.

Mrs. Pembroke appeared nonplussed. She waved her hand at the clutter as if it was nothing. "Sit wherever you'd like."

The ring of a phone pealed from another room, but the noise sounded muffled. Hidden under a mountain of items, more than likely.

"That must be the bank. Excuse me, I must take this." Mrs. Pembroke appeared eager to not miss the call. "I'll fetch us some tea as soon as I'm done. The kettle's already on." She excused herself from the room, leaving Harriet and Will standing in the middle of the disarray. They locked eyes for a moment.

Will's forehead wrinkled in concern. "I didn't expect Mrs. Pembroke's home to look like this. The fact that her husband passed away and now she lives alone… It's worrisome. It would be so easy for her to trip over something and break a hip. I wonder if I should try to contact someone at the church. See if I can get her some help with all of this."

The widow hadn't appeared to lack physical strength on the videotape they had viewed at the police station, but Harriet had to agree that maybe Mrs. Pembroke needed assistance. She took a few tentative steps toward the sofa and accidentally nudged a tower of shoeboxes with her foot. Thankfully, the tower didn't fall over, though it did wobble a little.

Hercules, who had been cautiously sniffing Will's shoes, left to go bark at animals through the windows. Smudges from his nose were all over the bottom half of the glass. Yet another thing to clean.

At least the home smelled fresh. No sensory evidence of dirty dishes or pet messes anywhere. Mrs. Pembroke seemed spry and able to get around. Capable of taking care of herself.

So, the place was clean, if a bit dusty. Incredibly cluttered, however. What reason could there be for holding on to so many items? But then again, the Pembrokes probably had a lifetime of accumulated items and mementos in this home.

While Mrs. Pembroke took her phone call, Harriet made her way to the sofa before clearing a few books from the coffee table so they'd have room for tea. A cardboard box beside her seat held a small stack of titles. There was quite an impressive collection of vintage books inside.

"Oh, look." Harriet reached across the table to pick up a cloth-bound volume. "The collected poems of Alfred, Lord Tennyson."

Will smiled. "That makes me think of the reading at our wedding."

Had their wedding only been yesterday? It felt as though a lot of time had passed since then.

Harriet smiled back. "Me too." She gently flipped through the book to find "Marriage Morning."

Once she located the poem, Will leaned over her shoulder to read the words he had quoted during the ceremony. "'Heart, are you great enough for a love that never tires?'"

"'O heart, are you great enough for love? I have heard of thorns and briers…'" Harriet leaned into the crook of Will's arm, relishing the wave of affection that washed over her in his presence. What an interesting thought. Those words, penned so many years before, had been read by countless couples. Now she and Will were reading them, and they'd be read years after them as well. She wasn't naive enough to imagine that she and Will would never have trials in their marriage, but their love was rooted in God and would only grow stronger with time. Of that, she felt certain.

The sound of Mrs. Pembroke's raised voice on the phone brought an abrupt end to Harriet's thoughts. "The end of the week? How am I supposed to have that done by the end of the week? You're being completely unreasonable."

Before she had answered the call, Mrs. Pembroke had mentioned she thought it was someone contacting her from the bank.

MYSTERIES OF COBBLE HILL FARM

Harriet glanced at the piles of paperwork and mail on the coffee table. Peering closer at a stack of unopened envelopes, she saw the sender was Bayview Trust Bank. Harriet could put two and two together. "Do you think Mrs. Pembroke might be in financial trouble?" she whispered to Will.

"I don't know."

The widow's voice rose even higher. "I won't leave my home. Do you hear me? I don't care what you try to do." She ended the call with, "I don't want to talk about this anymore."

They didn't have time to discuss the matter further because the clatter of teacups alerted them to Mrs. Pembroke's presence. She stood in the doorway, holding a tray laden with cups, saucers, and a teapot.

Will stood to his feet. "Let me help you with that, Mrs. Pembroke."

"I don't need your help," she snapped. "I'm not an invalid, you know."

Her sudden change in demeanor was like a slap in the face. "I didn't mean to offend you," Will said with more kindness than Harriet might have shown.

Mrs. Pembroke shuffled across the room to set the tray on the empty space Harriet had cleared on the coffee table. Her cheeks flushed pink. "Looks like my mouth has run away with me. I got some information just now that has me a bit agitated. No excuse for poor manners though. I hope you'll accept my apology, and I hope you'll call me Florence."

"Of course." Will's response was quick and gracious, and Florence calmed at his soothing tone. "We were just looking at your impressive vintage book collection. Are you a collector?"

A new emotion washed over Florence's features. She pointed at the book still splayed open on the table. "I'm not a collector, but my husband was. Robert was a particular fan of poetry. He was a gentler soul than I am, but I've become more nostalgic since his passing. I need to let go of some things, but I don't want to lose the reminders I have of Robert."

Harriet cast another glance around the room with a new perspective. The random hodgepodge of items suddenly made sense. The books. The bric-a-brac. The piles of clothing—all suits and ties, she now realized. All items presumably belonging to Mr. Pembroke. Was it any wonder his widow was reluctant to clear the clutter?

"All of this belonged to your husband?" Harriet asked.

Florence nodded. "Yes. I'm afraid I'm having trouble sorting through all of it. I'm too sentimental, but I need to let go. His loss still feels so fresh. I confess I'm frozen without him."

"That must be terribly difficult," Will empathized. "Is there any way we can help you?"

By all appearances, Florence seemed to be in a bad state. Grieving, unable to manage cleaning and decluttering, and possibly in financial straits after her husband's death. Her house could be close to foreclosure. Harriet felt nothing but sympathy for the woman.

Florence shook her head in response to Will's offer of help but then paused. She glanced around the room with a defeated expression. "Actually, there is something you can help me with. Could I trouble you to take a few boxes to the charity shop for me?"

"We would be happy to help with that," Will said.

"People can be kind. You don't know me at all, yet you're willing to help me." She smiled. "So, what did you want to talk to me about?"

Harriet took a deep breath. It wasn't easy to broach the subject, but it had to be done. She got straight to the point. "We're here to talk to you about why you attended our wedding reception. Forgive me for being blunt, but you weren't an invited guest. Why were you there?"

"Oh, that." Florence waved off Harriet's questions. "I was at the hotel for a birdwatching seminar. I took a wrong turn and stumbled into your reception. I know I should've left right away, but I suppose I got a little wistful. Robert and I married in the summer of '62. I was looking at that lovely table of photos and jewelry when a hotel employee approached to see if I needed help finding a seat at a table. When I told him I was there for the seminar, he said he could show me where I needed to be."

Her story squared with the footage Harriet's mom had recorded. Florence had left before the lights cut out. Did that also mean she left prior to the brooch's disappearance? The view on the videotape had been taken from Mom's seated position. The angle didn't show when the brooch was taken. It could have been swiped before the lights went out.

Harriet decided to test the waters and see what Florence knew. "What about the brooch? Do you know what happened to it?"

"What are you talking about? What brooch?" The woman certainly seemed to know nothing about it. If she was pretending, she was quite an accomplished actress.

"There was a brooch on the table you were looking at," Harriet explained. "It was there before the lights went out. When they came back on, it was gone."

"Oh, I don't know anything about that. I'm sorry to hear it. I didn't even know the lights went out."

They talked for a while more, but the conversation didn't yield any new information. Will finally tapped his watch. "Would you look at the time? The evening's gotten away from us. Harriet and I need to get back to the hotel. Thanks so much for your hospitality."

"Of course." Florence stood to her feet and showed them to the door. Hercules remained glued to her side. "I think I'm going to turn in early."

"Good night." Harriet and Will loaded a few charity boxes into the car's trunk and back seat and then told the widow goodbye.

Harriet assumed the driver's seat so Will could call his dad on the way to Ravenscroft. She had to admit, the Jaguar did handle nicely. Maybe there was something to Will's car obsession after all.

After he ended the call with his dad, all Will could talk about was his concern for Florence's situation. Harriet, on the other hand, couldn't suppress a flicker of suspicion. The most unlikely people could commit crimes, and something about the way the elderly woman had spoken to the person on the other end of the phone made Harriet distrustful. The bank might be threatening foreclosure, but it sounded as though Florence wasn't planning to leave her home without a fight. That established motive, and the woman's presence at the wedding had given her clear opportunity to take the brooch.

As they turned in to the hotel parking lot, Harriet's phone rang from the cupholder.

"Could you see who that is, please?" Harriet asked.

Will picked up the phone and glanced at the screen. "It's Polly. Want me to answer?"

"Sure."

Will accepted the phone call and spoke briefly with Polly before switching to speakerphone. "Polly, repeat what you just said for Harriet. She needs to hear this."

"Hi, Harriet." Polly's voice came in loud and clear. "I was checking my email, and I saw Will's message. Did you find what you were looking for?"

Ah, yes. The email he had sent out while they were having lunch. The one asking if Polly or Aunt Jinny knew Florence.

Harriet pulled into a spot and turned off the car. "Yes, we did discover the identity of the woman. Her name is Florence Pembroke."

"I was just calling to tell you that," Polly confirmed. "Do you know about her interesting past?"

"No. We didn't find out much about her. Only that she's recently widowed and likes birdwatching."

"The only thing I know about her isn't very good." Polly's tone grew grave. "A few years back she used to work with Cressida Barnett at the Gullywash Restaurant as a hostess, but she was let go because the till always came up short at the end of her shift. Word around town was that she pocketed the extra cash. It didn't help matters much when soon after she quit the Gullywash her husband bought some fancy car."

Harriet drew in a sharp breath. The Aston Martin.

Polly wasn't given to gossip. If she reported something, it likely stemmed from a reputable source. And it was true that greed could lead even the mildest of personalities to embrace desperate measures. Florence had nearly convinced her that her presence at Ravenscroft was mere happenstance. Polly's information painted a different picture.

What if Florence's appearance at the wedding reception wasn't as innocent as she claimed? Had the hotel even hosted a birdwatching seminar? Harriet made a mental note to verify Florence's alibi with someone at the hotel. Maybe she was telling the truth, and maybe she wasn't. It was possible that she had resorted to dishonest means to suit her purposes before. Who was to say she hadn't done it again?

CHAPTER TWELVE

London, England
Fall 1854

"Mummy!" *Eager to go to her mother, one-year-old Mary wiggled until Nanny Dotson set her on the floor and let go.*

Catherine held out her hands to encourage her little daughter to walk toward her. When Mary began crawling, Catherine gently ticked her finger in admonition. "No, sweet one. Walk to me. Show me what a big girl Daddy will see when he arrives home."

"Daddy...home!" *Mary parroted. But she didn't look around for her father. Why would she, when she had scarcely known him before he'd left for Crimea?*

Nanny took hold of Mary's pudgy hands and pulled her to standing. "Take a step, there. That's a girl." *She helped the child take a few assisted steps before she let go. Mary fixed her eyes on her mother as she wavered on her feet. Then she shuffled a small step forward, her dimpled arms held out for balance and her pink tongue sticking out in abject concentration.*

"Good girl! Come to Mummy." Catherine's heart swelled with pride. If only she could bottle this moment for her husband. How his heart must ache, being away from his only child when she was tender in years. She would write to him later. All the details of their domestic life contained within the flourish of ink on paper. Small consolation, but it was her connection to him now.

After three momentous solo steps, Mary plopped onto her ruffled seat, her fall cushioned by an ornate Persian rug displayed underfoot. Catherine leaned down to press a kiss to her daughter's dark, wispy curls before straightening to address Nanny Dotson. "I must oversee luncheon for the ladies' society meeting. It will be starting soon."

"Very well, ma'am." Nanny gathered Mary and bustled to the nursery for milk and shortbread.

Catherine set her hand to preparations for the luncheon. She clarified menu details with Mrs. Hosten and instructed Robert Bend, the gardener on retainer, to cut some of the fragrant English roses for nosegays for the guests' places.

With the mouth-watering scent of Cornish hens wafting from the kitchen, Catherine allowed herself to sit and reflect for a moment. Alexander's last letter burned like a coal where she had tucked it in her sleeve. She removed it to read for the hundredth time.

The date at the top of the letter was October 20, 1854. The last time she had heard from her husband. Yet now it was well into December. It wasn't altogether unusual for communication to be sparse. Perhaps the regiment was on the move and Alexander had little time for scribbling a note back home. But something told her that wasn't the case. Something was amiss.

The war had stifled her concerns about the brooch, however the matter still weighed on her. Was her husband the man she thought he was? Marriage, done properly, was a melding of two persons into one. But how could she experience unity with her spouse when she didn't know who he was? Was Alexander a selfless hero? Or a selfish swindler?

She shoved the letter into her apron pocket before reaching up for the brooch she wore daily. It was as much a reminder of her marriage as her filigreed wedding ring. Just as quickly, however, she jerked her hand back as though the brooch were on fire. The metal, white hot. A single thought seared her brain.

Thief or not, will my husband come home to me?

His photo was buried in the hollow compartment. Buried as the man himself might soon be. This new worry clawed at her. Oh, why hadn't she heard from him? She'd sent three letters to his one. Word of dying men reached the city every day. Did she really think her family was immune from tragedy?

The front doorbell rang, and the butler answered it. Mr. Redburn would turn fifty years old this May, and she might have to let him go. She'd been monitoring the finances in Alexander's absence, and funds had grown tight. But little matter, if Alexander was safe. Little matter, if he was alive.

She recognized the greeting of her dear friend, Elizabeth, and Elizabeth's husband, Colonel Frederick Powell, as they entered the foyer.

A twinge of envy pierced Catherine's heart. Elizabeth hadn't lost her husband. The colonel hadn't been fit for war. He had fought previous battles and gained a title and a limp. He walked with the assistance of a gold-tipped cane. Why couldn't the same be true for Alexander? Much better to have him here, unsteady but in one piece, than still in the uncertainty of the fray.

She was getting off course though. The real question was, why was the colonel here, at her home? Elizabeth visited regularly, but Colonel Powell had no business attending a ladies' luncheon. Normally he would be occupied elsewhere during the day.

She started into the foyer to greet her friends. She desperately needed the clarity and reassurance that Elizabeth could provide. She halted just outside the door as her friends' conversation filtered in.

"How are we going to tell her?" Elizabeth's voice was low and measured. "It will devastate her. A woman looks up to her husband. He is her confidant. She thinks him invincible…"

Colonel Powell answered his wife. "It can't be avoided. Perhaps all will end well. None of us know the future, my dear."

It was clear they were having a private conversation. Something Catherine had no part in. Yet it affected her. They had to be talking about Alexander. Did they know something she didn't? Were her suspicions valid?

She clutched at the brooch as she had that day at Monsieur Claudet's studio a couple of summers past. The fiery furor over the brooch stolen at the exhibition had cooled to glowing embers with time. Now she rarely heard of the matter. Even if it was still on her mind occasionally, she found she resented anyone else fanning the flame.

She didn't want to hear it. She set her mind. It was time to put this behind her. She had tried to talk to Alexander about the brooch before, only to be met with the same story he had told her that day at Monsieur Clavette's studio. Edward Sterling gave it to me with his blessing on our marriage…

She made a show of calling into the kitchen for Mrs. Hosten to check on the progress of the Cornish hens. That way, the Powells would be aware of her presence. How awkward it would be to walk in on them discussing her family's affairs. Decorum offered her a shred of dignity. Convinced that they had heard her approach, she entered the foyer to greet her guests.

"It's wonderful to see you both. Please, come in." She smiled at the colonel and pressed Elizabeth's hands between her own.

To her surprise, Elizabeth's eyes immediately filled with tears. "Oh, Catherine."

This was it, then. They had both come to tell her the truth. Her husband was no more than a common criminal. She braced herself for the blow.

Colonel Powell cleared his throat. "I'm afraid we bear some bad news. I have a nephew in the same regiment as Alexander. Knowing that you haven't heard from your husband recently, I contacted Rupert. He wrote back with some news. Your husband is..."

"Yes?" Her heart hammered in her ears. The pulse of blood felt almost painful.

"Your husband is..."

Before he could say another word, Elizabeth threw her arms around Catherine in a frenzied display of emotion. "Oh, Catherine! Alexander isn't with the regiment. He's missing in action."

CHAPTER THIRTEEN

That night, sleep eluded Harriet. Her mind was occupied with going over the new piece of information Polly had given her. Could Florence Pembroke be a habitual thief?

Will was already sound asleep and snoring. Rather than toss and turn, Harriet decided some light bedtime reading was just the cure for her busy brain. She had asked Will to carry one of the widow's donation boxes up to the room, and she riffled through it now.

The box was mostly full of books. Harriet picked one up that sounded particularly intriguing.

"*The Jewel of Deception* by Kate Tyler." She traced the gold-embossed letters on the cover with one finger. Then she flipped to the copyright page. 1872. Wow, this book was old. Why would Florence donate such a valuable item? It might have monetary if not sentimental value. Harriet made a mental note to hold on to the donations until she could talk to the elderly woman again. She had seemed emotional yesterday. Perhaps she'd made a mistake and given them the wrong box.

In the meantime, it wouldn't hurt Harriet to distract herself a little. She took the book back to bed and snuggled under the covers. Then, by the light of the bedside lamp, she began to read. The story was entertaining. It was a Gothic-style mystery of a woman who suspected her doting husband of secretly stealing the crown jewels from the Tower of London. Harriet was several chapters in when she fell sound asleep.

She woke to the sound of a ringing telephone. The book had fallen to the floor. Still half asleep, she picked it up before reaching across Will to answer the phone. "Hello?"

"Harriet?" It was her mother.

Harriet rolled back over to glance at the clock. Six thirty. She was pretty sure her mother wasn't calling with good news at such an early hour. She had fetched her passport yesterday. Surely she hadn't forgotten anything else at the house. Had she?

"I'm here, Mom. Is something wrong?"

"Nobody's hurt, don't worry." Her mother was quick to reassure her. "But that sudden rainstorm we had yesterday must've damaged the art gallery's roof. Ida stopped by yesterday to pick up something and said she noticed a small leak. When your dad and I checked it this morning, we realized the leak was a little more extensive than any of us realized. It seems that the thatching was damaged."

"Oh no." Harriet's late grandfather had been a veterinarian but was also well known for the oil paintings of flora and fauna that he created in his spare time. The gallery on the estate held a trove of her grandfather's artwork, and Ida Winslow managed the place for tourists. "Are Grandad's paintings okay?"

"I think so. But there were a few boxes in the attic that may have gotten wet."

Well. That was news to Harriet. She hadn't realized there were any items in the gallery's attic. Most of Grandad's belongings were stored in the house.

MYSTERIES OF COBBLE HILL FARM

Harriet's mother continued. "Dad and I moved everything to the house and put buckets under the drips, but we still wanted to let you and Will know in case you want to check the situation out for yourself."

Harriet pressed her fingers to her temple. A nasty tension headache was already brewing. Great. She loved living on Cobble Hill Farm, but repairs were a constant concern. While the thatched gallery roof was undeniably charming, it didn't last as long as a tiled roof. She had known it was a matter of time until the thatching would need to be redone. It was pure providence that nothing worse had happened.

"We'll be right there, Mom."

Harriet ended the call and then contacted Ida and informed her that the gallery would be closed for the day. Then she woke up Will to tell him the bad news. Thankfully, he rolled with the punches a little better than she had. He didn't seem too put out as he shrugged on a clean T-shirt and shorts. She should probably take notes on his easygoing attitude. She got ready as well. Instead of a floaty sundress and sandals, she also put on a T-shirt and shorts. Who knew what mess they might encounter at her—now their—home?

They fueled up with sugar and caffeine at the meager breakfast buffet just in time to witness a hotel employee removing signage related to the past weekend's birdwatching seminar.

"I guess Florence's alibi checks out," Will murmured. "The hotel did host a seminar, like she said."

"Looks that way."

As they stood to leave, Harriet remembered the dead key card in her handbag. She asked Will to wait a moment while she went to get a replacement at the front desk. "I definitely don't want to get locked out again."

"Meet me at the car when you're done?" Will asked. "I'll get the AC going."

"Okay." Harriet sat in an armchair to fish her key card from her bag. From across the room, she could see Lucy's ponytailed form at the front desk. She must have gotten stuck with morning shift again.

Before Harriet could find her card and approach the young woman, however, Benedict swooped in. "Hello, babe. Working hard?"

Lucy smiled at him. "Fairly slow this morning. Do you have something you need me to do?"

Benedict shifted his weight from foot to foot. "No. But I do have a personal matter to discuss. Would you like to have supper with me this evening?"

"I think I can arrange that." Lucy grinned, and her voice held a teasing tone. "Where are you taking me? Better be somewhere special."

"How about the Mariner's Table?" The Mariner's Table was an upscale dining establishment located on the water near the Victoria Hotel. Servers in tuxes, white tablecloths, candles, the whole nine yards. The place cost an arm and a leg. "I snagged us a spot with the best view of the water. Is that special enough?"

Lucy's grin widened. "I'll say! That place is brilliant. Isn't it a bit spendy, though?"

Benedict shrugged. "It's fine. I found a way to make some money on the side."

"Doing what?"

His reply was another shrug.

"You're keeping secrets from me, Benedict." She playfully shook a finger at him, but he didn't give her any more information.

Harriet narrowed her eyes. Why wouldn't he tell Lucy about his side hustle? Unless he was doing something underhanded to make money...

Lucy continued. "Are you sure you aren't overextending yourself, Benedict? Managing a hotel takes up a lot of time already. Things haven't been running very smoothly around here lately." Lucy caught sight of Harriet in the background, and her face flushed pink. She immediately lowered her voice. "I've been fielding complaints left and right. Guests have been really upset about the lift being out..."

"Nigel just got that fixed," Benedict interrupted. "I promise, this is a short-term situation. I just need to make a little extra money. Trust me?"

"I do trust you." Lucy leaned closer to him across the desk. "You know I don't expect to be showered with diamonds and rubies, right?"

Benedict took her hand. "Nothing's too good for you, Lucy," he said. "Pick you up around seven?"

Lucy and Benedict finished their conversation and Benedict left, leaving Harriet free to approach the desk. She handed Lucy her key card. "Good morning. My key card isn't working. I need to replace it, please."

"I'm sorry, what?" Lucy appeared dazed. The young woman was starry-eyed over Benedict, that was certain.

Harriet understood the feeling. She had been quite smitten with Will when he'd finally asked her out. That first rush of infatuation was delightful and distracting. Her only worry in Lucy's case was Benedict's trustworthiness. Was Lucy's love so blind that she would overlook obvious red flags in the relationship?

Harriet repeated her request regarding the key card.

"Ah, yes, I can do that. Give me a moment." Lucy turned to her computer.

While Harriet waited for her to reprogram the card, she took the opportunity to dig a little. "Things seem to be going well between you and Benedict."

Lucy's cheeks tinged pink again. "Oh yes. Very well."

"How long have you known each other?"

"Almost a year. We started dating last summer. Of course, a lot of the relationship has been long-distance. I only work here at the hotel during the warm months. The rest of the time, I attend Teesside University."

Teesside was located in Middlesbrough, approximately two hours away. A year was a significant amount of time to date, but it sounded as though only a few months of that had been spent in the same town. How hard would it be to hide your real self from someone who only saw you intermittently?

"This is an awkward question to ask…" Harriet lowered her voice in case Benedict was still within earshot. "But it's important. Has Benedict ever done anything to make you think he isn't who he says he is?"

Lucy stared at her, eyes wide. "Why would you ask that? Benedict's a nice guy. It's one of the things that drew me to him in the first place. He's really, really honest."

MYSTERIES OF COBBLE HILL FARM

Even though Lucy's defense of Benedict was vehement, her demeanor didn't exactly reassure Harriet. She fumbled through the rest of the process with the key card. It took her three tries to activate it, but she finally declared it fixed.

"Here you go. You might test it in your door right away to make sure there aren't any issues." Lucy gave her an apologetic smile as she handed over Harriet's card. "Good news, though. The lift's fixed."

This place certainly had its quirks. Broken lift, dead key card, lackluster amenities. But Harriet supposed she couldn't expect everything to work perfectly in an antiquated building like Ravenscroft any more than she could expect things to always go smoothly with her grandfather's estate.

She thanked Lucy and rounded the corner that led to the elevator. She pressed the button to go up and waited...and waited...and waited some more.

She tapped her foot impatiently. It might have been quicker to take the stairs. She reconsidered as strains of conversation echoed from the nearby stairwell though. Maybe she had been delayed for a reason. The door to the stairs was propped open, and she stepped closer to hear. One of the voices was Benedict's. "I'm absolutely chuffed, Nigel. I'm taking Lucy out tonight, and after this afternoon, I should have enough for the down payment on the ring. I just hope I don't catch her off guard with a proposal. Do you think I'm rushing things?"

Nigel. Harriet's ears perked up. Maybe the men would say something about the lights cutting out. Anything that would divulge more information related to the theft of her brooch.

"I don't think so," Harriet heard another man—Nigel—say. "Lucy is smitten with you. She talks nonstop about you when you're not around. I hear her gabbing with Julia when they're cleaning the lobby."

Benedict laughed. "Listening in on private conversations, are you?"

Nigel laughed with him. "It's the drama of the week. Where are you taking her to pop the question?"

"The Mariner's Table."

Nigel whistled. "That's a pretty penny now, innit? How're you swinging that?"

"Plan on promising them my firstborn son," Benedict joked.

"Right." Nigel chortled. "More like you robbed the till."

At Nigel's light jab, all lighthearted tones dropped from Benedict's voice. "Nigel, be quiet. What if Lucy heard you? You think I want her getting the idea I'm a crook?"

"All right, all right. Sorry. Touched a nerve, eh? I only wondered how you got the money."

"It just so happens I found a side hustle that pays off, and quick. Is that a crime?"

"I suppose not." But Nigel's tone was flat.

"I should be flush with cash in plenty of time for tonight. If I'm not, I'll have a phone call to make…"

By now, the men had ascended far enough up the stairwell that Harriet could no longer hear them. The elevator bell dinged, and she got on with only her whirling thoughts for company.

Thanks to Will, Harriet knew of Benedict's past mistakes. But why did the young man have such a strong emotional response to his friend's comments? And why hadn't he denied "robbing the till," as Nigel had put it? Instead, his focus had been on what Lucy would think. Did that mean he hadn't strayed so far from his criminal roots as he would like people to believe? What was his lucrative side hustle, and why was he keeping it secret? Was it possible he was reaping a profit from stolen goods?

Harriet exited the elevator at the third floor and quickly checked her key card in the door to their room. Thankfully, it worked this time. She tucked the card in her handbag and hurried down to the parking lot where Will waited.

"Took you a while. The car's as cool as Antarctica now," Will teased as she slipped into the passenger's seat.

She caught him up to speed with what she had overheard. She shared with him her worry that someone who knew Benedict as well as Nigel did seemed so suspicious of him. "Nigel questioned the source of Benedict's money, and Benedict immediately went on the defensive," she explained. "He told Nigel he didn't want Lucy to suspect he was doing anything wrong. That doesn't sound like the way an innocent person would react. Does it?"

Will's brow wrinkled. "No, it doesn't. I would feel better if he had just outright denied it."

"That's what I thought. Do you think we should try to get a reservation at the Mariner's Table on short notice? For tonight?" The closer an eye they could keep on Benedict, the better.

"Good idea. If Benedict did something wrong, though I'm still praying he didn't, he'll slip up at some point. He'll do or say something that reveals the truth."

Will took out his phone and located the number for the restaurant. After a brief conversation, he ended the call with a dejected expression.

"They're booked two months out." He slipped his phone back into his pocket. "I gave them my number. They said they'd contact me if they had a last-minute cancellation."

Harriet sank into the passenger's seat as Will navigated out of the parking lot. Oh well. It had been worth a shot.

One problem at a time…

Harriet sucked in a deep breath as they pulled up in front of the clinic. How strange it felt to be arriving here on a Monday morning when normally she would be seeing clients around this time. Instead, she was on her way to assess a leaking roof. At least she'd enjoyed the ride. Will had put the car's top down, and they had a good laugh when she imagined how her clients would react if she showed up at their farms driving a Jaguar instead of the old Land Rover she'd inherited from her grandfather.

Please, don't let anything be ruined. She sent up a silent prayer as she and Will exited the Jaguar and headed across the garden. Her mother met them at the French doors that led into the kitchen.

"Sorry to bother you both, but this is your property. I figured you would want to deal with it."

"I'm glad you called." Harriet rubbed the back of her neck. Her headache was spreading. "Did much get wet?"

"Not a lot that we've found so far. One box took most of the brunt."

They exited the house, walked across the yard to the gallery, and entered the building. "There's the damage, as you can see," Harriet's mom said, pointing.

Harriet looked up to see a hole the size of a dinner plate in the thatched roof. Buckets caught the few drips that still trickled from above.

"The forecast doesn't call for more rain, which is good," her mother continued. "But we'll leave the buckets there just in case."

Harriet's father paced the floor with a cell phone pressed to his ear. From what Harriet could pick up of the one-sided conversation, it sounded like he was arguing with someone about repairs. He heaved a sigh once he ended the call.

"Bad news?" Mom asked.

"Frustrating news, more like," he answered. "I can't get a contractor to come today. The earliest booking is Wednesday."

"Oh, Dad." Harriet's headache ramped up another notch. "I'm sorry, I should have told you. I have a guy who can fix the roof. I'll call him and see if he's available." Mike Dane was a handyman who had done some work on the roof the year before.

"That's okay." Dad sighed. "I just hope he can come soon. Otherwise, if we have more rain, we could be in trouble."

"Should we fix a tarp up there in the meantime?" Mom suggested.

Dad stared at the hole in the roof. "All right. Though I don't relish climbing up there again." He crossed the room to shake Will's hand. "Sorry, Will, I haven't even said hello. You're looking well. Married life agrees with you."

"Being with Harriet agrees with me," was Will's sweet response. She leaned into him with a grin, and her headache went away. Just like that.

Her mother smiled. "I hope your honeymoon hasn't been ruined because you've had to stick around town?"

Harriet shook her head. "No. It hasn't."

Though she was surprised to say it, it was the truth. She and Will might not have driven off into the sunset like she had anticipated, but they'd spent nearly every waking moment working together toward a common goal and learning about each other in the process.

"Good." Mom appeared satisfied. "How about a look at some of the items that got damaged? We carried them to the house."

"Just a minute. Let me call Mike about the roof first. Before I forget." Harriet left a voice mail for the handyman, letting him know the situation was urgent. Then she followed her mother back to the house while her father exited into the garden, muttering something about needing to find a tarp.

"I'll help," Will offered, and the men went off together to divide and conquer.

"And then there were two," Mom said as she and Harriet entered the house, this time through the side door. Charlie and Maxwell greeted them, and humans and pets made their way to the kitchen. "Here's what we took from the gallery." Mom showed Harriet the contents of the affected boxes, with damp items spread out to dry.

Harriet walked the length of the counter. The damage wasn't severe, but any family history lost saddened her. She saw a few vintage greeting cards, some yellowing playbills, a leather journal with the initials *EP* stamped on the cover, and a letter that looked very old indeed.

"What's this?" She pointed at the letter. It had started to dry, and its edges were crispy and curled.

Harriet's mother inspected the pages. "Looks like a wartime letter from a husband to his wife?"

"I wonder which war." Harriet strained to read the writing. "World War II? Or something else?"

"It's further back than that," Mom said. She pointed at the date written at the top of the letter. "Looks like it's dated 1855."

Oh my. Harriet leaned over the letter to read it. Water damage had erased some of the writing, but she could make out the date—August 1—and half of the first page.

"Listen to this." She cleared her throat. "'I only wish I had a token of remembrance with me on the field, as you do. I think often of that day in the studio where we had the image taken for your emerald brooch. It was the same day you told me we were expecting with our dear Mary. So destroyed by nerves was I over the bank's failing that I could not take hold of the joy your announcement brought me. If I survive this illness, precious Catherine, I vow to never lose a moment of our lives to ghostly worry again. Your affectionate husband, Alexander.'"

Harriet stopped as realization took hold.

"Wait a minute. He has to be talking about our family brooch. The one I wore at my wedding." She glanced up at her mother. Excitement fluttered in her chest. "The couple in this letter must be the man and woman in the daguerreotype."

Her heart in her throat, Harriet hurried from the kitchen to find the family Bible. It provided an extensive record of her grandfather's family lineage. If the letter had been deemed important enough to keep, it must have a connection to a relative. She scanned the names written in the front of the Bible but didn't see an Alexander or Catherine Taylor listed.

Maybe they were relatives on her grandmother's side? Or close friends of the family? That was possible, though it would be significantly more difficult to track down.

"Any luck?" Mom asked.

"No." Harriet double-checked the Bible in case she had missed something. But the names weren't there. Who were Alexander and Catherine Taylor? And why had a letter from Alexander been found on her grandfather's estate a hundred and seventy years after it had been written?

CHAPTER FOURTEEN

Harriet and her mother puzzled over the contents of the letter until Will appeared, looking sweaty and disheveled. He addressed Harriet. "Your dad and I can't find a tarp. Do you think your aunt would have one at the cottage?"

Harriet set the letter aside and stood. "I'll go see."

Will slipped off his wedding band and dropped it into an empty dish on Harriet's counter. "Don't want to damage this while we're working. Remind me to get it before we leave?"

Harriet smiled at him. "I'll help you remember."

At her mother's request, she propped open one of the French doors to let in a light breeze. Then she crossed the estate grounds to her aunt's house. The entry was unlocked, so she let herself in. "Hello? Aunt Jinny?"

"In the kitchen."

Her aunt was washing dishes when Harriet entered the room. She glanced up from the soapy water. "Hello, Harriet. What are you doing here?"

Harriet explained what had happened at the gallery.

"Oh my. Was anything damaged?"

"Not much," Harriet replied. "Only a few items, including a letter that Mom and I think mentions my missing brooch. It's from an

Alexander Taylor to his wife, Catherine. Do you recognize their names? We thought they might be relatives, but I can't find any reference to them in the family Bible."

Aunt Jinny shook her head. "The names don't ring a bell with me."

Hmm, that was curious. Her aunt was even better versed in family history than Harriet. Who were these people, if Aunt Jinny hadn't ever heard of them? Harriet made a mental note to conduct a thorough search online for the Taylors when she got back to the hotel.

In the meantime, her father and Will were waiting on the tarp. She explained what they needed.

"Your dad was over here earlier to borrow my ladder," Aunt Jinny said. "I know I have a tarp, but it might take me a few minutes to find it. The twins are out in the garden. Can you keep an eye on them, please?"

Harriet followed her aunt outside. Sophie sat on a picnic blanket with her treasure box at one end of the yard while Sebastian slouched on the front steps.

"I take it they haven't made up yet?" Harriet asked in a low voice.

Aunt Jinny sighed. "No. They're still bickering. Sophie's upset over her tiara getting broken, and Sebastian's angry because he has some summer reading assignments to finish up. Maybe you can talk him into getting them done?"

"I can try."

Aunt Jinny went in the direction of her shed, and Harriet approached Sebastian. "Can I sit with you?"

Sebastian lifted his head. "I guess."

She settled on the step and decided to lead with a positive topic of conversation. "So, your nana told me that she's throwing an end-of-summer party for you and the neighborhood kids. Are you excited about it? What a fun thing to do before school starts again."

Sebastian's response was less than enthusiastic, however. The only answer he provided to Harriet's question was a disheartened grunt.

"Come on," Harriet prodded. "You'll have a wonderful time at the party."

"Not with Sophie still mad at me."

Harriet looked across the garden to see the little girl carefully laying her treasures out on the blanket in neat rows.

"Sophie!" Sebastian called.

The little girl didn't even lift her head. A bird swooped past her before disappearing into the tree in whose shade she sat.

"Sophie!" her brother called again. "I'll even play tea party with you if you want. I'm sorry I said it was boring. I'll pretend your bear is the queen."

Sophie addressed Harriet. "Please tell Sebastian that I'm not talking to him. He broke my tiara. It was my most special treasure."

Sebastian pleaded his case with Harriet. "I did take her tiara off the table because I was mad at her. But I promise I didn't break it on purpose. It was an accident. I dropped it when I ducked down to avoid the dragon."

Harriet smiled. Again with the dragon. What an imagination he had. If he got more confident at reading, there was no telling the fun he would have, escaping into worlds of adventure and intrigue.

"Anyway," Sebastian continued, "I brought it home and hid it because I was scared to say anything. I didn't think anyone would believe me. And I was right. Sophie sure doesn't."

"She'll forgive you. She's just upset right now. Give her time."

Sebastian didn't seem content to wait, however. Patience wasn't a seven-year-old's strong suit. "I'm going to make it up to you, Sophie," he shouted across the garden to his sister again. "I'm going to get you the best gift ever. Then you'll see how sorry I am, and you'll have to forgive me."

Sophie wasn't ready for peace yet. "Unless you can get me a new tiara, I'm not interested, Sebastian."

He looked dejectedly up at Harriet. "See? She'll never forgive me. She thinks I broke the tiara on purpose because I'm jealous of her."

"Are you jealous?" Harriet asked gently.

"I don't know. Maybe a little. I wish I was better at reading."

"We might be able to change that with a little practice."

Sebastian's Spiderman backpack rested between them. Harriet unzipped it and pulled out a thin book. "I heard you've been working on some summer reading assignments. Want to make some progress now?"

"Not really."

"Why?"

Sebastian scowled. "Because I'm rubbish at reading."

"Don't say that. You're a smart kid. Reading is tough, and people learn at different speeds. I'm sure you'll get it in time." Sebastian didn't respond, so Harriet opened the book to the first page. "*Jack and the Beanstalk*. I heard you were reading this with Nana. Sounds pretty exciting."

"Maybe a little." Sebastian scuffed the toe of one sneaker against the step.

MYSTERIES OF COBBLE HILL FARM

"Why don't we read it together?" She patted the empty space between them, and Sebastian cozied up next to her. Harriet read the first few pages to the little boy, who seemed more than content to listen. She stopped when she got to a particularly interesting part of the story and prodded him to pick up where she had left off.

"Jack… cl…clim…" He huffed out a frustrated breath. "That word is too hard. I don't know what it is."

"Climbed," Harriet told him gently. "Jack climbed."

"Climbed… up… the…bee…an…" He stumbled through the sentence, mispronouncing vowels and pausing after every word. "I can't do this!"

"You can. You're close. 'Jack climbed up the beanstalk.'" Harriet tried her best to cheerlead Sebastian's efforts, but it was clear he still struggled. She was concerned, because she was afraid Sebastian might fall behind in other school subjects if he couldn't read on grade level.

She tried to get him to read some more, but instead, he frowned in Sophie's direction. "Why doesn't she have trouble with reading? She doesn't have to practice anything this summer. She gets to play. It's not fair. She's so much smarter than I am."

"Sebastian, you're smart too."

"No I'm not." The little boy looked miserable. "Did you know I'm in the Robins reading group at school?"

Harriet didn't know what that meant, but she tried to keep her tone cheerful. "The Robins group? That sounds nice."

Sebastian's frown drooped even more. Obviously, that wasn't the answer he wanted. "The Robins group is for the dumb kids. The ones who are the slowest. Sophie's in the Sparrows. The

Sparrows are the smart kids. I want to be in that group. But I can't."

Oh my. Harriet's heart ached as she silently berated a system that so transparently grouped children according to their ability and caused Sebastian to feel "dumb." She wrapped her arms tightly around the little boy. "Sebastian, you're not dumb, and neither are any of the other children in your group. You're one of the brightest boys I know, and like I said, everyone learns different subjects at different speeds. Don't give up on reading. You can do it. It just might take some time."

She encouraged him to try again, but after a few attempts, he threw the book on the ground. They were interrupted by Aunt Jinny, returning with a folded gray tarp clutched in her arms.

She handed the tarp to Harriet. "This should do. And for goodness' sake, tell my brother to be careful if he's climbing up on that roof."

"Don't worry. Will's with him, and I've put a call in to Mike Dane as well," Harriet assured her. "Trust me, I have no intention of anyone getting a broken leg." That was the last thing any of them needed right now.

She told her aunt and the twins goodbye and carried the tarp back to her house, where Polly stood in the garden. "What are you doing here?" Harriet asked her friend.

"I heard the commotion from the clinic."

Ah, that was right. It was Monday and a workday for Polly. Harriet had wanted to keep the clinic open in her absence so Polly could retain her normal schedule. Her tasks for the week were to care for the boarded animals and catch up on administrative chores while the

MYSTERIES OF COBBLE HILL FARM

clinic's summer intern, Brody, fielded any emergency calls. Harriet had made arrangements with one of her colleagues, who agreed to be available if a situation turned up that was beyond Brody's capabilities.

"Thought I'd pop over and see what all the fuss is about." Polly shielded her eyes from the sun to look at the gallery. "What happened?"

Harriet filled her in on the details of the damage before ending with the discovery of Alexander's letter to his wife.

"Wow," Polly said. "And you think the letter refers to your brooch? The one that went missing?"

"I think it might. The description fits, the timeline fits," Harriet said. "I just don't know why the letter was in Grandad's belongings. What connection could he or my grandmother have had to the Taylors?"

"Maybe it's some family history that's gotten lost over the years. It happens." Polly shrugged. "Mind if I pop in as a Girl Friday?"

"Oh, Polly. You don't need to help."

"It's okay. I want to. Things are slow at the clinic this week since you aren't here. I have time. If you're okay with it, I'll look at the letter and try to find out more about it or the man who wrote it." Polly stared in the direction of the gallery again. "Is that Mike Dane?"

Harriet turned to see Mike and Will perched on the gallery roof. Mike certainly hadn't wasted any time. He must have received her message and hurried over.

Mike yelled down to Harriet. "There are better ways to get a skylight in the gallery, you know."

Harriet laughed. "Very funny," she called back.

"Are you certain the roof was damaged by the storm? Because it looks quite intentional. Like someone's been plucking at the thatching with a tool."

Harriet stared at him. Was Mike suggesting that someone had purposefully damaged the roof? She hadn't even considered that possibility. Now, knowing that the gallery had held the letter made the thought seem kind of credible. What if her parents had unknowingly scared off an intruder this morning? It wouldn't be the first time someone was on her property without permission. "I—I don't know."

With that unsettling thought on her mind, how could Harriet say no to Polly's offer to research the letter? It would be helpful to have another person on the case. She and Will still needed to find out what was going on with the other suspects anyway. Not a small feat, considering how complicated the situation had grown.

Polly headed back to the clinic as Harriet watched Will and Mike work on the gallery roof. A few minutes of elbow grease and erstwhile effort yielded a temporarily patched roof.

Dad held the ladder steady as the two men climbed down. Mike wiped a forearm across his brow. "That should hold until we can get proper repairs made."

"Let's hope so," Dad replied. "I don't want to haul more wet boxes out of there." He poked around in the open toolbox that rested on the ground. "Where did my watch go?"

"Can't find it?" Will asked.

"No. I know I put it in here earlier, when Charlotte and I first looked at the roof. Didn't want to scratch it while I was up there."

"I'm sure it's around here somewhere," Harriet said. "Maybe you put it in your pocket?"

Dad patted his blue jeans before shaking his head. "No, not there either."

"That reminds me. I need to get my ring." Will jogged across the lawn and entered the house through the open French door. He soon returned empty-handed with a deep frown on his face. "My wedding band's gone too."

That made Harriet sit up and take notice. One missing item could be a mistake. Two missing items… Well, that was harder to explain away. Especially since they already suspected a thief was in their midst.

Will took Harriet's hands in his own. "Harriet, I feel awful. That ring is the symbol of our marriage. It represents my love for you. I never should've taken it off."

Harriet tried her best to comfort him, though she knew she would feel the same way if she lost her wedding ring. "Try not to worry. We'll find it, I promise."

All possibility of coincidence was erased when Aunt Jinny hurried across the grass toward Harriet. She opened her clutched fist to show a single pearl earring. "Harriet, you didn't see an earring in the grass anywhere when you watched the twins, did you? I took one off when I was on the phone and set it on the table by my chair outside. Now it's missing, and all I have is this one."

"No, I didn't see anything."

"That's odd." Aunt Jinny's face crinkled with concern.

Was it odd? Or were someone's intentional actions behind the missing items? Harriet didn't have to explain what she was thinking to Will. He was immediately on the same page. A brief explanation caught Aunt Jinny and the rest of the group up to speed.

"This is too much of a coincidence to ignore," Harriet said. "Did anyone hear a car come up the drive? Or see anyone on foot?" Scattered denials peppered the group.

Harriet turned to her mother. "You were in the house. Did you see anything unusual?"

"No, nothing." Mom was resolute. "I was in the kitchen the entire time. No one could have taken Will's ring without me knowing...except..." Her eyes widened.

"Except what?" said Harriet impatiently.

"Except I did run upstairs to fetch my glasses. But I was only gone for a few minutes."

That would have been enough time for someone to sneak across the garden, through the open door, and leave again with ring and earring in tow. And the men were away from the gallery looking for supplies. But surely someone would have seen something? How likely was it that a thief could sneak past all of them in broad daylight and then disappear into thin air?

Yet it was clear something had happened. Something calculated and coordinated.

Aunt Jinny brought the twins before the group, even though Harriet knew it was unlikely that either of them had taken anything. After all, she had been sitting in the garden with them for quite a while. Still, they hadn't been supervised the entire time.

Aunt Jinny put a hand on each twin's shoulder. "Sophie, Sebastian, would you help me search your rooms? We need to look everywhere. Harriet and Will can search the gallery, and your aunt and uncle can comb the house."

Harriet had to give her aunt a lot of credit. It was clever of her to include the children in the hunt for the missing items so that they wouldn't feel accused. Harriet hoped that neither one of them had taken anything or lied to the adults. Sebastian had admitted to taking Sophie's tiara, and the brooch had been on the heirloom table next to it. What if he had brushed it off the table by accident when he grabbed the tiara? The brooch was delicate and easily damaged. Didn't it stand to reason that he might try to hide it as well?

An hour later, a thorough search of the children's rooms, the cottage, Harriet's house and the clinic, as well as the grounds, turned up zero evidence of the missing items. It seemed that Sebastian had taken only Sophie's tiara and was in the clear regarding the other items, brooch included.

But if Sebastian hadn't taken the items, Harriet was at a loss for what to do next. Could Florence Pembroke be behind the thefts? It was an odd coincidence that her home was so near the clinic. Yet Harriet couldn't see the elderly woman traipsing through the trees to filch items from the kitchen or the garden. To be honest, she was having trouble imagining how anyone would have been able to approach the house and the gallery, take the items, and disappear without detection.

Another dead end. Why did none of the facts add up? They'd been trying to solve this mystery for two days, and they were no better off than when they started. At this rate, they'd never take their honeymoon trip.

CHAPTER FIFTEEN

London, England
Winter 1855

Two more long months of waiting until, finally, word came of Alexander.

He wasn't missing at all. It had been a misunderstanding, common in chaotic times like these. He had fallen ill at the Battle of Balaclava and contracted typhoid fever. So incapacitated had he been that writing was impossible. When his regiment moved to a new location, he wasn't fit to follow them. His superior telegraphed the news when Alexander's condition worsened, but the message was misrouted and had only now found its way to Catherine.

She read it over once more.

To: Mrs. Alexander Taylor
45 Grosvenor Square
Mayfair
London, England

MYSTERIES OF COBBLE HILL FARM

From: Capt. James Whitaker
Balaclava, Crimea

October 28, 1854

REGRET TO INFORM Stop *ALEXANDER TAYLOR TAKEN ILL AT BATTLE OF BALACLAVA* Stop *DIAGNOSED WITH TYPHOID FEVER* Stop

AUTHORIZE RELEASE TO BRITAIN FOR TREATMENT Stop

Captain James Whitaker

"This is quite a common occurrence," Colonel Powell *tried to reassure Catherine. "All may not be lost. He could rally and make a recovery yet, my dear."*

He had graciously agreed to accompany her to St. Thomas' Hospital, where he had arranged for her husband to occupy a bed. Nerves danced within her at the thought of seeing Alexander again. She wished she could have brought Mary, but the hospital wasn't a place for children. Mary would be happier at home in Nanny's capable care. Catherine had managed to keep Mr. Rayburn on the payroll, but Robert Bend, the gardener, had been let go. She prayed he would find work elsewhere, though she had heard times were tough across London.

The trip to St. Thomas was over in a blink. Her heart in her throat, Catherine entered the hospital with Colonel Powell at her side. The place had come highly recommended by him. One of the best spots for the old fellow *had been his exact words.*

Catherine wrinkled her nose at the unpleasant smells wafting down the main corridor. As she drew closer to the room Alexander occupied, the smells grew even more odious. She pressed her handkerchief to her nose, but it helped little. Masculine cries could be heard from inside some of the rooms. Stone-faced medical personnel rushed past, paying neither the colonel nor her much mind.

What sort of place was this, to differ so from what she had expected? If this was a top establishment by the colonel's admission, how horrid were the other hospitals?

They rounded a corner to enter a large room which held multiple beds. Colonel Powell spoke quietly with the nurse, who pointed down a row of men to a pale stranger engulfed in blankets.

"I'm sorry," Catherine blurted out, "but you must be mistaken. That's not my husband."

The nurse glanced at her ledger. "Alexander Phineas Taylor, typhoid fever?"

Catherine swallowed. The nurse's rattled-off words were akin to a hammer driving in nails. Chances were slim that her assessment was wrong.

Colonel Powell nodded. "Yes, that's correct. Mrs. Taylor hasn't seen her husband for some time."

The nurse nodded briskly before hurrying away to some other urgent task.

Catherine's expectations met harsh reality as she approached the bed at the end of the row. Gone was the handsome man she had strolled with at Hyde Park. In his place rested a skeleton of a human being. Yellow skin stretched over hollow cheeks. Bony arms like sticks lay on the muslin coverlet hiding the rest of his emaciated frame.

"Alexander?" She scarcely dared breathe his name. Who was this figure in front of her?

Dread filled her as he turned. Then she saw his eyes. Yes, it was him. The same eyes she had exchanged glances with so many times in their marriage.

His mouth moved, but no sound came out. Was he trying to say her name? Was he asking after Mary?

"Darling, I'm here." She sank onto a wooden chair beside his bed and did her best to encourage him to speak.

He tried again. "Water."

Not her name, then, or Mary's. Something more pressing instead.

"Only a drop or two." Another nurse stopped her bustling to give a sharp command. "No more."

Catherine clutched the pitcher of water beside his bed to her chest. "He's thirsty, poor man. He shall have what he needs." Heightened emotion made her feel bold and reckless. Who were they to say what Alexander needed? Did they know him as well as she did? Their help had turned him into a ghost.

"What he needs?" The nurse angled a practiced gaze through her spectacles. "If what he needs is a more painful death than the one he is already suffering..."

Her voice trailed off. The nurse didn't wait for an answer, only continued her march down the rows of moaning men.

A more painful death than the one he is already suffering...

Catherine refused to take hold of the implication. Surely Alexander wasn't dying. Not her beloved husband. It couldn't be true.

Once she had given Alexander only enough water to wet his parched lips, the colonel helped him sit up in bed. Then he stepped out into the hallway to give the couple privacy.

"It's good to see you." Alexander finally managed to eke out the words. His voice sounded rusty, and he gazed mournfully at Catherine. It was nearly more than she could bear. "How are things at home? How is Mary?"

A lie seemed kinder than the truth. "We're all fine, just fine."

A glint of hope appeared in his eyes. "You're managing the bills? They're not too overwhelming?"

"I've had to trim a few expenses, but we're managing."

"Good." Alexander had been straining forward as if to see her better. Now he fell back against the pillows. His dark hair contrasted sharply with the white fabric. "I gave a letter to one of the nurses. I'd like you to read it when you leave. I have something to confess. I love you always, Catherine."

Catherine finished talking with Alexander and gently told him goodbye. Her emotions found vent in confrontation once she and the colonel were safely outside the hospital's walls.

"I thought he was to have a private room?" she angrily berated him. "Not be shoved in a warehouse like an animal."

MYSTERIES OF COBBLE HILL FARM

To his credit, the colonel appeared apologetic. "I did my best. The funds you afforded me were only sufficient for what you saw. I'm afraid privacy and better accommodations require more money."

She blinked. She had given him an enormous sum. At least it was in her estimation. Her stockpile of available resources had dwindled since Alexander left for war. He had sent home his pay from his time serving in the regiment, but it was still less than he had made as the manager of the bank. Now, with him ill, the payments had stopped altogether.

What more could she do? She had already trimmed expenses at home. Lesser cuts of meat. Ice block deliveries monthly instead of weekly. No bonbons at Mary's second birthday, which at the time had seemed like a travesty and now felt indulgent. Trivialities like dessert were laughable outside the walls of the hospital.

She supposed her next step would be to sell off the contents of the house and let more of the staff go. But whose position to cut next? Mrs. Hosten, the cook? Or Nanny Dotson? Catherine would be left utterly by herself in the house, and her employees would be alone as well. Mrs. Hosten had no family in England, and Nanny had been orphaned from a tender age. Poor Mr. Rayburn wasn't a spry young man anymore and might struggle to find a solid position.

Catherine set her jaw. She had no choice. She must find other ways to cut expenses. To get better care for Alexander. What would he think if he recovered—when he recovered, she corrected herself—and the life they had built together was gone?

Her thoughts swam. Perhaps they could move to a less affluent neighborhood? But a change of address meant more than a simple geographic difference. Location was tied to so much more. Social status, business prospects, reputation, appearance... If their family lived elsewhere, would that hamper future opportunity?

Every decision without Alexander by her side felt monumental.

As Colonel Powell escorted her home in his carriage, she clenched her fists in her lap and gazed out the window at the passing blur of shops.

Was her life little more than a journey from one worry to another?

CHAPTER SIXTEEN

When Will and Harriet arrived back at the hotel on Monday evening, Harriet called Van to inform him that more items had gone missing. Will worriedly glanced down at the blank space on his ring finger as Harriet relayed the information to the detective constable. Then she asked to speak to Polly.

Moments later, Polly's laugh came through the connection. "I know I volunteered to be your Girl Friday," she said, "but I haven't had time to do much digging yet."

"No, that's not what I was calling about. This is about a different matter," Harriet explained. "I was interested in something you mentioned yesterday. I need to find out more information about Florence Pembroke. You said that she used to work with Cressida Barnett at the Gullywash Restaurant?"

"Yes, that's right."

"Are you certain that Cressida is a reliable source?"

"Oh, definitely," Polly insisted. "My parents have known her for ages, and I'd vouch for her character in an instant."

"Do you have any contact information for her? Or know where she's working these days?"

"Sure, hold on. Let me look up her info." The other end of the line was silent for a moment. Then Polly returned. "So, it looks like

Cressida is working at another restaurant now. Really upscale. It's a fairly new place on the coast by the Victoria Hotel—"

"It wouldn't be the Mariner's Table, would it?" Harriet cut in.

"Yes, that's it. Have you heard of it? I bet you and Will would love it."

Harriet decided not to tell her everything that had happened with Benedict. It was just too long a story. "We tried to get a table there, but the hostess said they were booked two months out."

"That's too bad," Polly said. "Maybe it'll be easier to get in once the new wears off."

"Maybe."

"Are you ready for Cressida's contact information?"

"Sure." Harriet scribbled down the phone number Polly gave her and thanked her for her help. Then she dialed Cressida Barnett.

The woman picked up on the second ring. "Hello?"

Harriet greeted her and explained that Polly had provided her contact information. Then she filled Cressida in on the details of the missing brooch and mentioned that Florence Pembroke was a suspect. "I heard that you used to work with Florence years ago at the Gullywash? Is there anything else you could tell me about that?"

"What's there to say? Money started going missing from the till during Florence's shifts. Once she and her husband bought that fancy schmancy car... Well, we all just assumed that stealing from the Gullywash wasn't the only crime she'd committed to be able to afford it."

It didn't sound positive for Florence, but the woman didn't know for sure if Florence had stolen. It was all just hearsay. "Did anyone ever press charges?"

"Not that I'm aware of."

"Why not?" Harriet asked.

"I don't know that they had enough solid evidence. Some people were saying that another server was the one taking money and that Florence didn't have anything to do with it."

"Hmm. So what happened?"

"It was all let go. Honestly, it's water under the bridge now, but at the time, it really upset me. It's one of the reasons I left the Gullywash and found a new place to work. I guess it's for the best though. My path eventually led me to where I am now, and I really like it."

So there was a chance Florence Pembroke didn't have anything to do with the situation at the Gullywash. It might have been someone else stealing from the restaurant all the time. With that piece of information up in the air, Harriet felt conflicted about keeping the widow on the suspects list. What if Will was right and she was just an innocent woman trying to get over the loss of her husband? Still, after the thefts this morning and the fact that Florence's house was so close to Harriet's meant she couldn't dismiss her as a suspect yet. She tried not to let on that she was rattled and, instead, responded to Cressida's previous statement.

"Oh yes. Polly mentioned you're at the Mariner's Table. I imagine that's a lovely place to work."

"It's a top-notch restaurant," Cressida agreed. She sounded really happy. "Have you eaten there?"

"No, my husband and I would like to, but when we tried to get a table, they told us they were booked two months ahead."

"That sounds about right. It's been crazy since we opened. I'm good friends with the hostess, though. Sometimes we keep an extra table open for emergencies. Are you and your husband free tonight?"

Harriet conferred with Will before replying, "We're free."

"Wonderful. Let me check with Candice, and I'll let you know."

She called back with the good news that there was an open table, meaning they now had a way to keep tabs on Benedict. What a way to kill two birds with one stone. The conversation Harriet had overheard between him and Nigel indicated that Benedict would be flush with cash by the evening. If he had anything to do with the morning's thefts, perhaps he would drop some detail at dinner.

The restaurant's reputation sold it short. The Mariner's Table proved even more opulent and impressive than Harriet had imagined. Dimmed lights made the glowing candlelight gracing each table stand out, and though the place was busy, conversations remained at a low buzz and were pleasantly overlaid with the strains of live violin music.

Delicious scents drifting their way from the kitchen added to the good impression as well. Harriet's mouth watered as she and Will followed the hostess to their table situated in a cozy, private corner of the room. Will pulled her chair out for her, and she let out a happy sigh as she settled into it. After all the hustle and bustle of wedding planning and sleuthing, it was a treat to relax. Not to mention that her dinner partner was quite attractive, and she could think of nothing better than to spend the evening with him. Even if they were technically trying to get information to solve the case.

"Where's Benedict?" Will cast a glance around the room. "I don't see him or Lucy."

Harriet checked her watch. "They won't be here for another hour. He said he was going to pick her up around seven." Until then, she and Will could enjoy their time together.

A server soon arrived at their table to fill their water glasses and take their order. Harriet opted for the stuffed chicken breast with goat cheese and sundried tomatoes. Will chose pan-seared scallops with truffle oil.

When their food arrived, Will said grace, and they began eating. They made pleasant conversation, finally winding up at the grand topic of the future. "I feel a bit silly asking this," Will said. His mouth tipped up at one corner. "What are your hopes and dreams, Harriet? Anything I don't already know about?"

"Oh, I don't know." Harriet looked down at the cloth napkin in her lap. Such things had been on her mind, but she wasn't at all sure she had a definitive answer. "A family would be nice. Children."

"Yes, but we've discussed that before." Will smiled. "Anything else?"

Harriet exhaled a thoughtful breath. "I suppose I'd like to help people somehow."

Amusement made Will's eyes twinkle. "Don't you already do that? Running a successful vet practice? Not to mention scurrying around town like Miss Marple."

Harriet twisted her napkin. "I suppose, but I mean something more altruistic. I'm happy to help people through the vet clinic, but it's my job. As far as solving mysteries… Let's just say they have a way of finding me. I'm not always seeking them out."

"So, what then?"

"I don't know. You've helped a lot of people in your time in ministry. Now that we're married, I think I'd like to get more involved with the church as well. Any ideas what a good fit for me might be?"

Now it was Will's turn to look thoughtful. "Let's see. There's the residential care home ministry…"

"Maybe." She'd joined a Christmas caroling expedition to one of the nursing facilities last year. Sebastian and Sophie had made construction paper greeting cards for the residents. It was certainly a worthy cause but didn't quite feel right for her.

"Is there an age bracket you'd like to help? Most people have a certain group they feel led to work with."

"Maybe children?"

Will's eyes lit up. "That would be great. We're always in need of reliable nursery workers."

Images of crying infants and potty-training toddlers made Harriet shudder. Not that she minded any of the stages of a child's development, but she had so little experience with that age range. She'd grown up as an only child, so she hadn't taken care of younger brothers or sisters. Weren't there all sorts of rules one needed to follow, like no honey until after a certain age or popcorn until another? The thought of running a classroom full of unpredictable children with rules she didn't know spurred butterflies in her stomach. She didn't have experience teaching and felt ill-qualified to run a classroom.

"I'm not sure. That may not be the best fit for me."

"You're wonderful with children. I've seen the way you interact with Sophie and Sebastian." Will took a long sip from his water glass then said, "Just pray about it and see if God nudges you in a particular direction. There's no rush."

Maybe he didn't think there was a rush, but she did feel some pressure. She longed to start off life as a pastor's wife on the right foot.

She didn't say any of that to Will, however. She wanted to give him a chance to share his heart. "Your turn now. Anything else you'd like to do, aside from the ministry?"

To her surprise, Will appeared sheepish. "Oh, nothing important."

Harriet wasn't going to let him off that easily. "Come on. I shared with you. What are you thinking about?"

Will sighed. "All right. But bear in mind it sounds a bit silly when placed next to your altruistic aims. I'd like to join the car club. Is that a horribly disappointing thing for a pastor to say?"

Disappointing? More like a relief. Her saintly husband was human after all. She couldn't help but laugh.

Will scrubbed a hand over his chin. "I think an outlet outside of the church would be good for me. Some place I can go where I'm just Will."

"One of the group instead of shepherd of the flock?"

Will sighed, sounding relieved that she understood. "Yes, exactly."

She started to lean in to press a kiss on his lips but then remembered the meal she had just eaten. The last thing she wanted to do was flirt with her husband with food in her teeth. "Excuse me just a minute. I need to run to the powder room. Be right back."

She left the table and located the ladies' room, which was no less glamorous than the restaurant itself. Vintage gilt mirrors graced the walls, and the floor appeared to be made of expensive marble. An attendant stationed at the sinks waited to disperse after-dinner mints on request.

Harriet washed her hands before accepting a mint. They were likely better than the cheap pharmacy brand she carried in her handbag. She tipped the attendant a pound and popped the mint into her mouth. Its buttery sweetness melted on her tongue as she exited the restroom.

A few steps out the door, she realized she'd forgotten to check her teeth. Thankfully, she had a tiny hand mirror tucked in her bag. She located the mirror and flipped it open. She was right to have trusted her instincts. A piece of tomato skin was wedged between her front teeth. She tried to discreetly remove it with a fingernail but paused as a familiar voice caught her ear.

Benedict.

She checked her watch again. Ten minutes after seven. He was right on time, and his Birmingham accent was unmistakable. He spoke, and then she waited for another voice to chime in.

But the conversation was one-sided. She only heard Benedict's voice, not Lucy's. Taking a deep breath, she moved closer to the voice. It was coming from the direction of the coat check, which was only a short distance from the restrooms. She took the scenic route back to her table, stopping before she reached the coat check.

There it was. Benedict's voice again. She huddled behind the leaves of a large potted plant and peered down the corridor. It wasn't an elegant solution, but she didn't want Benedict to see her. Save rows of hangers dangling from bars, the space was nearly empty. No one checked coats in summer. That meant she had a more

MYSTERIES OF COBBLE HILL FARM

unobstructed view of Benedict, but he could also see her more easily. If he turned around, that was.

She shrank farther behind the plant and peeped out. Ah, now the one-sided conversation she had heard made sense. Benedict had a cell phone pressed to one ear.

"Come on, Nigel." Benedict's voice held a note of pleading. "Be a chum? I just need you to transfer some money into my account. I'll pay you back as soon as my job delivers."

Whatever Nigel said to this, Benedict's response was a frustrated one. "This *is* important. I know I said I had it under control, but the payment didn't come through from the job like I expected. I just made the down payment on Lucy's ring this morning, and now she wants to order appetizers, entrees, and dessert. I'm almost flat broke, mate. I don't know how I'm going to get out of here without scrubbing dishes in the back."

Another pause. "What do you mean, you don't want to get mixed up in something criminal? Some friend you are."

Harriet held her breath, expecting to hear more heated conversation, but Benedict shoved his phone into his jacket pocket and pulled out his wallet instead. He leafed through a few bills before giving a disgusted sigh.

When his phone rang, he looked surprised. Then pleased. He answered the call with a smile. "Hello? I didn't think I'd hear back from you today." A beat, then he said, "No, that's perfect. I'll be right there."

Who was he talking to? Likely not Nigel. Benedict's tone was much more polite and formal than when he had been cajoling his friend. Harriet listened intently to Benedict's side of the brief conversation but couldn't figure out who might be on the other end of the line.

"Can I help you, ma'am?" A voice at Harriet's elbow startled her.

Harriet spun around to face a young server, who stared at her with a puzzled expression. She wanted to hear the rest of Benedict's conversation, but she needed to save face. "No, thank you. I'm fine. I must've gotten turned around on my way back to my table."

She made a show of scanning the room for her table and finding it. "Silly me. There it is."

She rushed off before the server could ask any more questions or draw Benedict's attention to her eavesdropping. Benedict returned to his table as well, but he didn't sit down. He was close enough to where Harriet and Will sat that she could hear what was being said.

Lucy looked up at her date. "What took you so long? I was beginning to think you'd ditched me."

"Aye, I'd be a fool to do that." Benedict's voice wavered. "Though I do have to nip out for a minute. I promise I'll be right back."

Lucy appeared appropriately wary. "More secrets, eh?"

Benedict shook his head. "No, no. I feel a fool, but I left my wallet at home. Horrible timing, I know. Can you stay here at the table while I go fetch it?"

Harriet narrowed her eyes. He was lying. She had seen him take out his wallet and count his cash in the hallway. He must be going somewhere or doing something to retrieve the money he hadn't received during the day. This could be it. If they followed Benedict, they might find out the source of his side hustle.

There wasn't time to catch Will up on everything, so she explained the situation to him in a nutshell.

"So, he's just leaving her here?" Will asked. "Where's he going? It's obviously not home to get his wallet."

"At least Lucy is safe here. The important thing is to follow Benedict and see where he's going. If he's aboveboard, fine. If not, we'll call the police."

Harriet assumed Will would protest, but he didn't. He set his jaw. "You're right. I can't excuse Benedict's behavior anymore. His actions are odd, and I don't know how to explain them. Let's follow him and, like you said, we can call the police if we suspect he's up to something illegal."

He stood to his feet to flag down their server for the check. Benedict had a head start to the parking lot, but Will managed to settle their bill with lightning speed.

Then Harriet and he rushed out into the night.

CHAPTER SEVENTEEN

Even though it was after seven o'clock, the sun still hadn't set. Will and Harriet raced to the Jaguar as Benedict peeled out of the parking lot. Will drove a respectable distance behind him while also keeping his vehicle in sight. Harriet tried to get Benedict's plate number to no avail. The failing light, combined with the motion of the cars on the twisty road, obscured her clear view. Before long, Benedict turned onto a familiar lane.

"Is he going to—" Harriet began.

Will finished her question, his mouth set in a grim line. "Florence's house? Looks that way."

Benedict parked in front of Florence Pembroke's home. The Aston Martin wasn't parked outside, and Harriet assumed that meant she wasn't home. It also meant that Benedict didn't have permission to be there.

Harriet's breath caught as Benedict got out of the car. After patting his pockets, he walked around the side of the house.

Will squinted through the windshield. "What on earth is he doing?"

What *was* he doing? That was a question for which Harriet didn't have an answer. "Is he—is he trying to break in?"

"I'm not sure," Will answered.

159

MYSTERIES OF COBBLE HILL FARM

So Will had been right. Florence hadn't stolen anything. She had been a victim of circumstance all along. Was someone working with Benedict to case hapless targets? Had the second phone call he received in the hall been from a person keeping tabs on the elderly woman's whereabouts?

Harriet watched, horrified, as Benedict jimmied open a window and climbed through it. Now there was no question about it. He had to be an intruder. This was how he was making money. Stealing from citizens in White Church Bay. How horrible, to prey on a vulnerable, elderly woman like Florence. Harriet had to do something.

"He's going to rob her blind. We need to stop him." Judging from the expression on Will's face, he was ready to climb out of the vehicle and run after the man himself. But they didn't know if Benedict was carrying a weapon. A knife? A gun? Who could say?

Benedict was still inside the house. He wouldn't be for long though. If he was robbing the place, he would likely try to get in and out as quickly as possible to avoid detection.

They needed to do the same.

"Let's get out of here," Harriet whispered frantically to Will. "Before he comes out and sees us. We need to get back to the main road." They had to find a less conspicuous spot to park and call the police. Benedict hadn't seen them yet, but he would cross their path if he came down the drive in the next few minutes.

Will hesitated. Surely he wasn't thinking confrontation was the better choice?

She blew out a sigh of relief when he threw the car into reverse and said, "Dial the police. Quick."

He expertly navigated them to a tree-lined outlook set below the main road. They still had a view of the house from their new location, though it was nearly impossible to distinguish any useful details. Harriet punched in the number for the police station and waited breathlessly.

"Oh no. Call failed. I'm not getting any signal." There was only one bar on her phone. She lowered her window and held the phone out to see if a different angle would boost the connection. "Should we drive back toward town?"

"No." Will's tone was resolute, and he still gripped the steering wheel, even though they were parked. "Let's wait here. That way, we might be able to catch his number plate as he leaves. It should be easier to see it since we're parked. The police will be able to track him down quicker if we can give a more detailed description. I promise, we're out of sight here."

She was safe with him. He wasn't a man given to violence or carelessness. If he had a plan, she could trust it.

They didn't have to wait long. Less than five minutes later, Benedict exited the front door of the house. What was he doing? Why wasn't he climbing through the window to exit? It didn't make sense. She watched as Benedict went in and out of the house, loading several boxes into the trunk of his car. Then he climbed into the driver's seat and rolled back down the driveway toward the main road where Harriet and Will waited, hidden. The remoteness of the location made it even more pressing to not draw attention to themselves.

"All right." Will gripped the wheel until his knuckles turned white. "You try again to catch the plate. I'll follow him for as long as I can keep him in sight."

Harriet aimed her phone camera toward the windshield as Will had instructed and waited until the car drew close. "Got it!" she cried triumphantly as the car whooshed by. "Now we just need to get somewhere with a signal."

Will waited until Benedict's car was far ahead but still in sight. Then he pulled onto the road and began to follow behind.

Benedict was looking guiltier by the minute. By all appearances, he had engineered a distraction at their wedding to steal the brooch and now was targeting others around town as well. Dad's watch, Will's wedding band, Aunt Jinny's earring... Perhaps he had taken them all. Exactly how, she had no idea. A thief would have had to be nearly invisible to have crept past all the people at her house. Yet it was possible. And if Harriet hadn't overheard his phone conversation, Benedict would have broken into Florence's house with no one seeing him. Maybe besides the boxes he had taken cash from her house and was headed back to Lucy at the restaurant right now to pay for her dinner with stolen funds.

After a few tense minutes of trailing Benedict on the twisty road into town, Will pounded his fist on the steering wheel. "How foolish of me. I truly thought Benedict was on the straight and narrow. I thought I'd made a difference in his life. Now I see I haven't had as much positive influence as I'd hoped."

"Don't say that." Harriet squeezed his shoulder. "You've impacted so many people over the years, Will. Don't get discouraged."

"It's hard not to feel I've failed him." He rubbed the back of his neck. "We have to report his behavior to the police. Do you have enough of a signal yet to call them?"

She found that she did, so she dialed the station's number. Sergeant Adam Oduba picked up, and Harriet told him what she and Will had witnessed. "The driver of the car is Benedict Carter. I can give you the information from his number plate too."

Sergeant Oduba confirmed the name and plate information. "Do you know Mr. Carter's location now?"

"Yes." By that time, Will had followed Benedict in a loop. He and Harriet wound up exactly where they'd started the night: the restaurant's parking lot. "He's going into the Mariner's Table."

"Perfect," Sergeant Oduba said. "We'll get the details out to the proper channels, and officers should be there soon. Please stay in your car, and don't approach Mr. Carter unless absolutely necessary. Thanks for calling in."

"Of course." Harriet told the officer goodbye and ended the call. Then she watched as Benedict got out of his car and jogged into the restaurant, presumably to meet up with Lucy again.

Harriet's earlier thought about Benedict concealing a weapon in his backpack sprang to mind. What if he saw the police enter and tried something foolish? She was having second thoughts about leaving Lucy behind and worries over the safety of the other restaurant patrons. She turned to Will. "What do we do now?"

Will looked similarly jumpy as he tapped his fingers on the steering wheel. "The police should be here any moment. We need to stay put, like the sergeant said."

"So we wait?"

"We wait."

MYSTERIES OF COBBLE HILL FARM

It felt like an eternity passed until a police car turned in to the Mariner's lot. Sergeant Oduba and his partner got out and disappeared inside the restaurant. They soon reappeared with Benedict between them.

The young man appeared agitated. "Is this some kind of joke? Did Nigel put you up to this? I was just about to propose marriage to my girlfriend."

Sergeant Oduba took Benedict's emotion in stride. "We had a call come in from some witnesses who say they saw you break into Florence Pembroke's house. They suspect you have stolen items. We need to check your vehicle, please."

"I don't have anything I shouldn't in my vehicle. And what's this about me breaking into Mrs. Pembroke's house?"

"We have a report that you climbed through a window and removed items from the residence. Do you deny it?"

Benedict's voice rose an octave. "What? Is that what you're talking about? Are you mad?"

"Excuse me, Mr. Carter." Sergeant Oduba's tone, which had been cordial to this point, grew steely. "I'll ask you once again. Are you denying it?"

"N—no, sir." Benedict backpedaled. "I only meant it was mad to think I'd do anything to harm Mrs. Pembroke. I had permission to go into her house. She gave me a key."

"Then why did you enter through a window?"

"Because I accidentally left my key at home."

Sergeant Oduba raised an eyebrow.

Benedict held up his hands. "I promise. I'm telling the truth. Call Mrs. Pembroke. Search my vehicle."

"All right. Where are you parked?"

Benedict started walking across the parking lot toward his car then stopped. "Wait a minute. You said there were witnesses? Who saw me going to Mrs. Pembroke's house? Her place is out in the middle of nowhere. They'd have to be trailing me to wind up out there."

"I'm sorry," Sergeant Oduba said, "but I can't divulge the identities of the people who contacted us." Did he glance, however briefly, in Harriet and Will's direction?

Harriet slouched in her seat. A futile attempt, she soon she realized. Benedict had seen the car she and Will had taken to the reception, and the rented Jaguar stood out like a sore thumb.

As she had feared, Benedict swung his gaze toward them. The look of betrayal on his face was clear, even across the dusky parking lot.

"Ouch," Will murmured.

"I know." Harriet tried to comfort him as the officers searched Benedict's car. "But it can't be helped. I feel bad for him, but he's the one who got himself into this mess. You're just trying to do the right thing."

A few minutes later Sergeant Oduba loaded Benedict into the police car before approaching Will's window. "Mr. Carter claims he didn't do anything wrong. We found boxes of Mrs. Pembroke's items in his trunk, though, as well as a stack of pound notes. He said he had Mrs. Pembroke's permission to take the items and the money, though we're obviously going to need to verify that. Do you have any contact information for her?"

Harriet looked up the number on her phone and recited it to the officer.

"Thanks. I'll contact her right away to inform her of the situation. Would you be able to meet us at the station to answer any more questions that might crop up?"

Will nodded, and the sergeant headed back to the squad car and drove out of the parking lot. Will turned to Harriet. "I guess that's our cue to leave too."

"Wait, what about Lucy?" The young woman had stayed inside the restaurant as Benedict was ushered out by a police escort. Now she stood on the front steps with her arms wrapped around herself. "I have to go talk to her."

Harriet jumped out of the vehicle and hurried across the parking lot. "Lucy? Are you okay?"

Lucy looked dazed. "I don't know. I'm trying to process what just happened. One minute, Benedict said he had an important question to ask me, and the next, the police are taking him away."

"I imagine that was quite a shock."

"Do you know what happened?" Lucy frowned at her. "What are you doing here anyway? Are you and your husband having dinner?"

Well, this was awkward. *Yes, we're having dinner but also spying on your boyfriend, who may be a criminal…*

Harriet struggled to find the right words. "Yes, we did have dinner here, but… This is tough to say, Lucy, but do you remember yesterday, when I asked you how well you knew Benedict?"

"Yes. What does that have to do with anything?"

Harriet sighed. "Will and I have been watching Benedict since the reception. He's exhibited some suspicious behavior, and we've been worried that he stole my brooch. Tonight we came to the restaurant to keep an eye on him. When he left, we followed him to Florence Pembroke's house, where we saw him break in. Then he drove back here, to meet up with you."

Lucy frowned. "That can't be true. He told me he forgot his wallet."

"He lied to you, Lucy. I saw him take out his wallet in the restaurant. Then Will and I both watched him climb through a window at Florence Pembroke's house and exit with boxes of her things. The police just confirmed that they also found a stack of money in his car. What else could he have been doing but stealing from her?"

"I don't know." Lucy's face crumpled. Harriet couldn't blame her for her reaction. How distressing, to realize that the man she was interested in marrying was harboring such secrets.

She placed a hand on Lucy's shoulder. "Do you want to go to the station?"

Lucy nodded.

"You can ride with Will and me." Harriet wanted to reassure the poor girl. "Don't worry. Everything will work out."

As they drove away, the restaurant became a distant dot in the rearview mirror. Only time would tell if Harriet's words would ring true.

CHAPTER EIGHTEEN

It was getting late by the time Harriet, Will, and Lucy arrived at the police station. Lucy decided she wanted to remain in the car, claiming she wasn't ready to face Benedict yet. Will and Harriet left her and went inside, where Van met them at the reception area.

"We're still in the process of booking Mr. Carter," he told them. Harriet looked past the detective constable to see Benedict standing at a nearby desk, supervised by Sergeant Oduba and his partner. "Mr. Carter claims his actions are aboveboard and that he's done nothing wrong, but of course, we need to verify his story with Mrs. Pembroke when she arrives. Ah, here she is…"

Harriet followed Van's gaze. Florence Pembroke shuffled up the hallway, her handbag slung over one arm. A stern-looking man with a mustache accompanied her. Who was that? Harriet hadn't seen him before.

Van seemed familiar with the man, however. He left Harriet and Will's side to approach the new arrivals. "I think we spoke on the phone. Are you Preston Pembroke?"

The man nodded. "Yes, I am. This is my mother, Florence. Did you find the intruder? I certainly hope he's in custody now."

"We're in the process of booking someone, but we don't know if he's guilty of a crime yet. We need to answer more questions before we can say he's done anything wrong."

"I don't understand." Preston frowned. "You told me over the phone that you had eyewitness accounts of someone breaking into my mother's house. What question is there over guilt? Throw the book at him, that's what I say."

"We have a process we're required to follow, Mr. Pembroke."

Preston sighed impatiently. Then he turned to his mother. "See? I told you something like this would happen. It's not safe for you to live in the middle of nowhere. You're a target for delinquents."

"You're blowing this out of proportion, Preston. I've lived in my home for years, and nothing like this has ever happened before." She shook her head. "I knew I shouldn't have had dinner with you in town tonight. Trouble. That's the only thing I get from leaving the house."

"You need to get out and be with people. You're too isolated where you live." Preston fixed a heavy glare at Van. "If this guy gets a slap on the wrist for what he did, I'm going to have issues. And I'm not going to be quiet about it. I won't stand for crooked police, and I'll shout it from the rooftops if this fellow walks free tonight."

How Van kept his composure was beyond Harriet, but he did. "Sir, we'll do our best to take care of the situation." He turned to Florence. "Could we ask you a few questions in private, ma'am?"

"Mum?" Preston asked. "Are you sure you feel up to that?"

"Of course I feel up to it." Florence's reply was snappish.

"Great. If you'll follow me." Van started to lead her back to an interview room, just as Benedict was being prodded toward another. When Florence saw Benedict, however, she stopped in her tracks.

A look of confusion crossed her face. "Benedict? What are you doing here? Did you help Pastor Will and Harriet catch the robber?"

Benedict shook his head. "Hardly, Mrs. Pembroke. They think *I'm* the robber."

It took Harriet a moment to catch on. This was unexpected. Florence addressed Benedict as if he was an old friend. "Wait a minute," Harriet said. "You two know each other?"

Florence nodded. "Yes, I met Benedict at the hotel during the birdwatching seminar."

Will stepped forward. "I'm sorry to be the bearer of bad news, Florence, but Harriet and I saw Benedict rob you this evening."

"Rob me?" Florence laughed. "He wouldn't rob me. Quite the contrary. Benedict has been an enormous help to me over the past couple of days."

Preston folded his arms across his chest. "How has this fellow been helping you?"

"Delivering my groceries, painting my porch, helping with house repairs..." Florence rattled off a list.

"I could've helped you with that, Mum. Why didn't you ask me?"

"Oh, I couldn't ask you, Preston." Florence shifted her weight from foot to foot. "It was easier to ask someone else for help."

"Easier? It was easier to ask a stranger for help than your own son?" Preston fixed a glare on Benedict. "And if he was helping you, why did he enter your house through a window?"

Florence gasped. Finally! A normal reaction. "Benedict, you climbed through a window?"

"So, he did enter your residence without your permission?" Van asked.

"I'm not sure how to answer that." Florence shook her head. "I didn't tell him to climb in through a window, if that's what you're asking..."

Benedict threw his hands up in the air. "I forgot my key! That's why I had to go through the window. It's all a big misunderstanding. That's what I was trying to tell the officers. I would never rob Mrs. Pembroke. I know it looks bad. But I can explain."

"Please, Mr. Carter," Van said. "This would be a good time to tell us everything."

"Okay, here's what happened." Benedict took a deep breath. "Mrs. Pembroke was supposed to pay me today for my work, but when I stopped by her house before my date, she was gone. So I left her a message saying I had stopped by to pick up my pay and that we'd catch up later. She didn't call me back until I was at the restaurant. That's when she said that her son had come into town earlier than expected and the two of them were having dinner out. She told me to drop by the house and use my key to get in to get my money. But I didn't have my key, so I went through the window instead. I'd worked on it earlier, and it was unlocked. Then I collected my money from the biscuit jar beside the oven and left."

Van broke into the conversation. "Mrs. Pembroke, is that true? He did have a stack of money on him when we searched his vehicle."

MYSTERIES OF COBBLE HILL FARM

"Yes, that's right." Florence smiled. "I felt bad that I hadn't been able to pay him when I promised."

"I'm sorry." Will shook his head. "All of that is understandable, I suppose. But how do you explain the boxes you carted out to your car, Benedict?"

"I was trying to go the extra mile," Benedict shot back. "Mrs. Pembroke helped me out, so I wanted to return the favor. She's been so worried about her son visiting her house. She wanted everything in tip-top shape before he got there. She had the boxes marked as donations, so I figured I could take care of them. Get them out of her way. If things were cluttered, she worried he would take it as proof."

"Proof of what?" Will asked.

Florence assumed control of the conversation again. "Proof that I'm a doddering old lady. Proof I can't keep up with my own house. Preston wants to force me into a care home. He gave me less than a week to get things straightened out. Can you believe it? I told him the same thing I tell everybody. I'm not leaving my home. That's all I have left of my Robert."

"Wait, what? I'm not trying to force you to move to a care home," Preston insisted. "I only want you to be safe. Taken care of."

"I'm fine where I am. I was fine before I cleaned everything up too. I was only taking some time with memories. Your father isn't someone you get over in a few months. Don't you see that?"

"Oh, Mum." Preston's severe expression softened for the first time since Harriet had laid eyes on him. "I'm sorry I've rushed you. I should've listened better and given you the time you need instead of slapping you with an ultimatum. I can still help you clean up the place. We can go through the rest of Dad's stuff together. When you're ready. Do you forgive me?"

"I forgive you, Son. And I'd love to have your help."

There was nary a dry eye in the station as Florence embraced her son and the two mended ways.

"I suppose we're free to go now, Officer Oduba?" Preston dabbed his eyes. At the sergeant's confirmation, he began to usher Florence out of the station.

"Actually, could I speak to your mother for a minute?" Harriet stopped Preston. "Privately?"

"Certainly," he said. Then he turned to his mom. "I'll be out in the car when you're ready."

He made his way toward the exit while Harriet and Florence moved to an empty hallway.

Florence's expression was quizzical. "What do you want to talk to me about?"

"Only a small matter," Harriet answered. "I found an old and possibly valuable book in one of the donation boxes you asked Will and me to drop off. I wanted to make sure you're not giving it away by mistake."

"An old book?" The widow's expression grew pinched. "I gave you many old books, and other items too. I'm ready to let them go."

"Are you certain? Maybe you should look at it before we drop the items off. I'd hate to give away something important."

To Harriet's surprise, Florence waved her off. "There's no need for that. Please, just take them to the charity shop."

Florence appeared adamant. It seemed an odd response, but what more could Harriet do? She had run the matter by Florence as she had intended. Harriet told her goodbye and reentered the lobby to find the officers wrapping things up with Benedict.

Sergeant Oduba dismissed his partner before addressing the young man. "That takes care of everything. You're free to go, Mr. Carter. We apologize for the misunderstanding."

"It's okay. I get it." Benedict sighed. "I'm not happy about it, but I get it."

Van led him to an officer sitting behind a window. "You can pick up your belongings here. You may have a record for the shortest booking time ever, young man."

As Benedict waited for the release paperwork to be signed, Will said, "I'm sorry I doubted you, Benedict. I shouldn't have assumed you were falling back into your old ways."

Benedict shrugged, looking utterly defeated. "I suppose I don't blame you. And now that I'm cleared of suspicion, I need to confess something to you. I lied about the power surge. I came clean to the officers about that on the way to the station."

"Yes, what was that about?" Harriet asked. She had nearly forgotten about the conversation Will had overheard between Benedict and Nigel several days before. "Why did you cut the power if it wasn't for an opportunity to steal the brooch? You didn't take the brooch, did you?"

Benedict looked offended. "Of course not. I'm not mad enough to do something that foolish again."

"Then why did you cut the lights?"

"It was Pastor Will's speech."

"His toast?" Ah, so they had been right. Benedict had reacted to what Will was saying to the crowd.

"I panicked. After our talk in front of the hotel, I started thinking about my past. How Pastor Will knew me. What horrible things I had done as a lad. Stealing from the church. Robbing from those who needed help most. I'm ashamed of my behavior. It's part of the reason I look for opportunities to make amends now. Help people like Mrs. Pembroke. That day at your reception, I assumed that Pastor Will was going to mention something about how he met me."

"I wasn't going to mention anything about that," Will said.

"I didn't know that though," Benedict replied. "You looked right at me. And Lucy was beside me. I couldn't run the risk of her knowing. I switched off the power as a distraction. I know it was wrong, but it was the only thing I could think of on short notice. I figured that it would distract you enough that you wouldn't tell my story. What I didn't count on, though, was something being stolen at the same time. I was going to tell the truth, but then I heard about the brooch, and I knew that whoever cut the lights would be the prime suspect."

"Wait a minute," Will said. "How did you do it? The footage showed you in the room when the lights went out."

"I can control the breakers from an app on my phone." Benedict smiled wryly. "Conveniences of the modern age, eh? Anyway, of course Nigel knew my story about a power surge was bogus, so I asked him to back up my version of the story. If the truth got out that I was the one who killed the lights, I assumed that, with my past record, everyone would think I was guilty."

"Ah, I see now," said Will. "Benedict, I'm so sorry. I feel responsible for this in a way."

"No, no." Benedict shook his head. "You're not to blame at all. It started with me. I should've been honest from the beginning."

One final thought bothered Harriet. "Can I ask one more question, Benedict?"

"Of course. It's all out in the open now."

"Why did you cross the room and come near the table where Will and I were sitting? I heard you sneezing. Then it sounded like you went out into the hallway."

Apparently, it didn't make sense to Benedict either. He looked puzzled. "I was standing in the doorway when I tripped the breaker, and then I left to get the lights back on. Maybe you heard someone else?"

Maybe. But some detail still gnawed at Harriet. Sneezes and laughs were a bit like fingerprints. Everybody's was unique. She was certain she had heard Benedict pass by the bridal table. Oh, well. A minor detail easily explained away, providing it was the only loose end keeping Benedict on the suspect list.

Her thoughts were interrupted by a sound at the window.

"Sign here, please." The booking officer slid a piece of paper and a pen through the opening to Benedict. He scribbled his signature on the paper before taking the plastic bag she offered him containing his personal effects. He opened it and took the items out one by one.

A brown leather wallet. A watch. A tie clip. And a red velvet box.

Will exchanged a glance with Benedict. "Is that what I think it is?"

Benedict shoved the box into his coat pocket. "Aye. Not that it matters now. My proposal got botched by the arrival of some very insistent men in uniform."

"You can still ask her," Harriet said.

Benedict shook his head. "No, I can't. Not after she saw me carted away by the authorities."

Harriet felt for the young man. She could empathize with Benedict's situation. Hadn't she felt ridiculous after her broken engagement? Dustin's ending of their relationship hadn't been without personal fallout. She had considered not confessing that particular vulnerability to Will when they started dating, but then she had realized it wouldn't do to not be fully open with him. A relationship built on anything less than complete honesty was doomed to fail. "Don't you think Lucy should be the one to decide that? You owe her the truth. The choice after that is hers."

Benedict's shoulders sagged. Almost as if his suit coat held him up instead of the other way around. "I know. I've known all along. It's tough when you want something so badly, though. I love her. My biggest regret now is that I wasn't honest from the start. She's squeaky clean. Even if she understands, she won't forgive me."

"Try me." Harriet glanced up to spy Lucy standing in the doorway. "I got tired of waiting in the car. If you have something to tell me, Benny, I'd be happy to listen."

"Really?" A glimmer of hope shone in Benedict's eyes.

Lucy nodded.

"Could I have a moment to talk to Lucy? Privately?" Benedict asked.

"Of course," Will answered with a genuine smile. Benedict shoved the rest of his belongings in his pockets and crossed the room to take Lucy's hands in his own as Harriet and Will exited the station. He would have a lot to explain to her about his checkered past, but the expression on her face showed nothing but empathy for him.

Harriet's muscles relaxed as she climbed into the passenger seat of the Jaguar. What a relief it was to have Benedict's name cleared and to learn that Florence hadn't been in danger after all.

Will slid into the driver's seat, a contented expression on his face. He had made a difference in Benedict's life. His life's vocation had created a positive impact. She was pleased for him. But with Benedict off the table as a suspect, who did that leave? Florence had acted dismissive when Harriet had talked to her about the box of vintage books, but what did that mean? It wasn't a clear indicator of guilt, by any means. No, the next most likely suspect was someone else.

Talia. The person who had never been anything but kind to Harriet. A friend as close as family. Could she really have stolen from Harriet on her wedding day?

The question proved too heavy to tackle. Weariness weighed Harriet down as she and Will waited for Benedict and Lucy to finish their conversation. A familiar Bible verse she learned as a child crept into her mind: *Therefore do not worry about tomorrow, for tomorrow will worry about itself. Each day has enough trouble of its own.* The verse stirred her spirit and lent a measure of comfort in the otherwise dark and confusing time.

She closed her eyes. Tomorrow was a new day. Today had held enough worries, and she was ready for rest.

CHAPTER NINETEEN

London, England
Spring 1855

"Catherine, you're so pale." Elizabeth appeared at Catherine's elbow. *The two women wore the customary black garb, and a fashionable string of jet-black mourning beads hung around Elizabeth's neck.*

Catherine's hand flew to her own neck. It felt bare without the weight of the brooch Alexander had given her. She had worn it nearly every day until his untimely passing. Now it would be many long months before she could cast off her mourning clothes and wear the brooch again.

Even so, it wouldn't be the same. The person who had made the piece of jewelry so dear was no longer with her or with little Mary, who had grown into a quiet and wide-eyed young lass in her father's absence. Small comfort to think that Mary wouldn't miss what she hadn't known. Most of her life had been spent without paternal influence. Colonel Powell stood in as a doting honorary uncle, and Elizabeth as aunt.

"Have you eaten anything today?" Elizabeth continued her parade of concern.

Catherine cast her memory back to the morning. Had she eaten? She couldn't recall. The days since the funeral blended into one continuous block of loss. She stared blankly at her friend. "I—I don't know."

"Right. We must fix that." Elizabeth's tone was brisk and businesslike. She took Catherine by the elbow and steered her into the kitchen.

Mrs. Hosten stood at the sink, peeling a batch of carrots for stew. She was the remaining household employee, as Nanny had been let go. Catherine had sold a dearth of items to reconcile expenses, retaining only enough to save face. It wouldn't do to have the main living areas so sparse as to rouse speculations amongst her neighbors and the few friends who did still call.

"Mrs. Hosten?" Elizabeth addressed the woman who had been Catherine's faithful kitchen employee for years.

Mrs. Hosten turned and wiped her hands on her apron. "Yes, ma'am?"

"I believe Mrs. Taylor needs sustenance."

Catherine gave a feeble protest. Mary played quietly on her own in the nearby sitting room, and she needed her mother near. "I don't have time. Mary's alone."

"I'll watch her. You stay and eat something. You won't be any good to Mary if you don't tend to yourself." Elizabeth

disappeared from the room to care for Mary while Catherine addressed Mrs. Hosten.

"Do you have any dish already made up? I'm afraid I can't wait until luncheon."

"Certainly, ma'am." The cook dipped her head in a quick curtsy. A trip to the larder provided a small mince pie. Mrs. Hosten arranged it on a plate and handed it to Catherine. Then she paused, perhaps waiting for Catherine to take her meal to the adjoining dining room. But Catherine didn't move.

Lately, the dining room had felt cavernous and too formal. Alexander's empty seat at the head of the table mocked her. She avoided the room whenever possible.

"May I eat in here, please?"

Proper society would laugh at her. Asking her employee's permission to be in a room of her own house! But her situation had served to humble her and make her realize she wasn't so lofty as she had once thought. Very little stood between her and Mrs. Hosten's stations in life.

The kitchen was warm, comforting, and full of delicious scents. Catherine could almost trick herself into thinking it was like old times in there. The hustle and bustle of preparation and the nourishment to come. If she discounted the black garb and the oddly disquieting silence of the house, she could almost fool herself.

"Whatever you'd like, ma'am," was Mrs. Hosten's bewildered reply.

Catherine scraped a seat to the round table in the corner and set her plate down to bless her meal. Eventually, Elizabeth came looking for her, with little Mary on her hip. She settled Mary on the floor to play with some wooden spoons. Then she sat and removed an envelope from the reticule dangling from her wrist. She slid the envelope across the table toward Catherine. "I'm sorry to push, but we've been dancing around this since the funeral."

Catherine's eyes blurred as she spied the writing on the outside of the envelope. For my dear Catherine. *Inside lay a letter dictated by Alexander to his nurse while he was on his deathbed in the hospital.*

An acidic taste rose in her throat, and she shook her head. She had avoided the letter since the colonel first tried to give it to her. "Take that away, please."

Elizabeth turned toward the cook. "May we have a moment?" Mrs. Hosten bobbed a curtsy and left the room.

Catherine distracted herself with another bite of the savory pie, but it stuck in her throat. Her mouth was so dry. Nothing worked the way it used to. She coughed to dislodge the bite. Ever a thoughtful friend, Elizabeth fetched a tumbler of water.

Her eyes were pools of sympathy. "I know you're frightened of what Alexander might confess. But how are you to know what he has to say if you don't open the letter?"

Elizabeth was wrong. Catherine knew the contents of Alexander's letter. Though she hadn't read a word, all the evidence she had gathered pointed to him being nothing more than a common thief. The newspaper headlines. His evasiveness. His caution with the brooch. The conversation she had overheard between the colonel and Elizabeth. They knew. They knew, and they weren't telling her. Was it any wonder she didn't want to read the truth in black and white? She didn't want what little was left of his memory spoiled.

Elizabeth patted Catherine's arm. "It might do you good. Give you some closure."

She was trying to be supportive. But Catherine had other things to deal with. How to make ends meet. How to raise Mary on her own. Alexander was gone, and with him, the hopes of the life she had once thought she would have. She needed to move forward, and she couldn't stay mired in the past.

She reached again for the space the brooch had occupied. It was a reminder of sunshine...but also shadow. A plan began to form in her mind.

She pushed the letter back across the table toward Elizabeth. She knew what she needed to do. The question was, was she brave enough to do it?

CHAPTER TWENTY

Early on Tuesday morning, Harriet's cell phone rang as she was finishing her Bible reading. She had spent the last half hour digging into the book of Matthew and doing some heavy contemplation on worry. Talk about timing. As she picked up the phone from the end table, her breath caught in her chest. The number for Talia's shop scrolled across the screen.

Finally! Sandi had decided to call her back. Or Talia. Perhaps Talia had returned and the answers Harriet had prayed for would come quicker than she had thought.

Harriet went to their balcony to take the call. She knew she'd have to play it cool. She had no idea whether or not Talia was guilty of anything. Leaving the reception early wasn't a crime, and neither was being difficult to contact. Yet taken together, Talia's actions added up to something suspicious.

But it wasn't Talia.

"Hi, Harriet." Sandi sounded a bit more confident than the last time Harriet had spoken with her. "I saw you tried to call the shop a couple of times. I'm sorry it's taken me so long to get back to you. What's going on?"

What a delicate situation. Harriet didn't want to misstep. With the suspect list narrowed down one more person, it was even more likely now that Talia had taken the brooch. The last thing Harriet wanted to do was spew out a misplaced accusation that might offend a longtime friend. It wasn't just her relationship with Talia that might be affected. What Harriet said now could also impact the members of her family who were close to Talia.

Harriet took a deep breath and decided to be forthright. "I'm glad I got ahold of you, Sandi. I need to confide in you about a sensitive matter that involves Talia."

A hint of nervousness crept back into Sandi's voice. "Okay…"

"I didn't tell you why I needed to talk to Talia the other day. It involves a rather valuable heirloom brooch that was stolen at my wedding reception. Talia seemed quite interested in it, and then she ran off from the reception in a hurry."

"Wow, that sounds intense."

"A little. It worries me that no one has been able to get in touch with her since the reception. When I tried the cell phone number you gave me, I got somebody else's voice mail. You can see how this looks suspicious."

"Listen, I don't know where the brooch went or why Ms. Bishop left the reception so early, but I can explain about the wrong number," Sandi said. "That's completely my fault. I shouldn't have given you that number for Ms. Bishop in the first place. I didn't realize that she canceled her phone plan recently. Her number must've been given to another customer."

"Okay…" Harriet was willing to accept that Sandi may have been in the dark regarding how to best reach her boss, but that still didn't shed any more light on what had happened with Talia at the reception. "Does she have a new contact number?"

MYSTERIES OF COBBLE HILL FARM

Harriet heard a rustling of papers on the other end of the line. "No, I'm sorry. She doesn't."

Well, that was that then. Who else did Harriet know who might have contact information for Talia? No one. What had the world done before the invention of cell phones? Was she going to have to chase Talia across Yorkshire to find her?

"Sandi, is there any more information you can give me? Where Talia went or how long it might be until she's back?"

"I think she was headed to some jewelry event? She called late last night and gave me an address for this B&B in Kirkbymoorside where she's staying."

"Perfect. That'll work." Harriet would take any scrap of information she could get regarding Talia's whereabouts. She hastily scribbled down the address Sandi gave her. Then she ended the call and stepped back inside the room.

By this time, Will had woken up. Harriet quickly caught him up to speed.

He scrubbed a hand over his face. "Oh boy. You don't think Sandi's in on the theft, do you?"

His reaction surprised Harriet. "The thought hadn't even crossed my mind. Why, do you think she is?"

Will shrugged. "I don't know. Maybe. It does seem odd that Talia would leave someone so inexperienced in charge of her shop. It's not how I would run a business."

Harriet raised her eyebrows. He was better at this sleuthing gig than she'd imagined. She might have to relinquish the proverbial magnifying glass to him.

"I'm not trying to implicate an innocent party," Will continued. "She could be telling the truth." Skepticism laced his voice though. And he was right. With Benedict out of the mix, Talia was their new prime suspect, and if she was going to smuggle a rare piece of jewelry out of local police jurisdiction, one resource she would need was time. What if Sandi was under strict orders to buy her some?

Kirkbymoorside was approximately forty-five minutes southwest of White Church Bay. What if Talia had stolen the brooch and was fleeing to escape prosecution? As far as Harriet knew, Kirkbymoorside was under the greater umbrella jurisdiction of the North Yorkshire police and was a different local policing district. Enough of a geographic difference for bureaucratic red tape to block the way. All it would take was a minor delay, and Talia could sell the brooch to an underground source, pocket the money, and get away scot-free.

Harriet voiced her concerns to her husband. "Oh, Will. What if Talia is planning to hawk the brooch at the jewelry event that Sandi mentioned?" If Talia sold the brooch, it would be that much tougher to track once it left her hands and entered the population at large.

Will shot a startled glance at Harriet. Even if he had suspected Talia's guilt, it appeared he hadn't considered her selling the valuable heirloom through black market channels. Without a word, he shoved back the covers, snagged some clothes from his suitcase, and disappeared into the bathroom. Soon he emerged, fully dressed and with combed hair.

He began to shove his feet into his shoes, but Harriet stopped him. She had a feeling he wasn't this excited about getting breakfast. "Will, what are you doing? You look like you're headed somewhere urgent."

"I am." Will grabbed his wallet and keys from the nightstand. "How do you feel about a quick trip to Kirkbymoorside?"

It was surprising how good it felt to hit the open road. Several days bouncing around Ravenscroft and White Church Bay had Harriet feeling a bit stir crazy. The mercurial weather hadn't helped alleviate her cabin fever either. Thankfully, it was nothing but sunshine as Will drove out of town.

They had called Van prior to leaving and gotten the green light from him to leave White Church Bay for a few hours. All Harriet could hope was that they weren't being led on some wild-goose chase. As Will drove, Harriet passed the time mentally sorting through the information they had gathered on suspects so far. With Benedict off the list, who was left?

Was Sebastian still a suspect? Aunt Jinny had questioned him several times and searched his belongings without finding any evidence of wrongdoing. The little boy had taken his sister's tiara but nothing else. Or so it seemed.

Will remained convinced that Florence Pembroke had nothing to do with the brooch's disappearance. Harriet still had her doubts though. That mysterious phone call Florence had received might have been explained away at the station. She'd been arguing with her son about leaving her residence for a care home. Her house wasn't in danger of foreclosure as Harriet had first thought. But that didn't mean she was innocent. She could still be in financial distress of another sort, and that, paired with the chatter Polly had overheard about Florence's less-than-pristine past… Well, wasn't Harriet right to wonder a little? The woman still stood to gain something by taking the brooch. Harriet had been fooled by suspects who flew under the radar before. Perhaps there was more to Florence Pembroke than met the eye.

Which brought her to the end of the list. As reluctant as Harriet was to point a finger of blame at a family friend, the most likely culprit was Talia. Who else could it be? The woman knew the value of the brooch and had channels in which to sell it. Her business was in financial straits prior to the theft, and she had been caught on videotape and by an eyewitness running from the reception hall. Now, she was suddenly unreachable. Why? There had to be a reason.

Harriet sighed. Will lowered his sunglasses to cast a glance in her direction. Even amid confusion over the brooch, a thrill shot through her. Would she ever get tired of sitting beside him? Holding his hand? They hadn't been married for long, but she wanted this closeness she felt with him now to last forever.

"Everything okay?" he asked. He glanced at her with a light in his eyes that warmed her heart. He was a good man. He came alongside her and shared the challenges of life. If only she could focus completely on him and not this mystery. She longed to have things wrapped up and out of the way.

She forced a smile to her lips. "It's fine. I'm just frustrated. I'd much rather be driving to our next honeymoon destination instead of Kirkbymoorside. I'm eager to start our life together. It feels as though things have been put on hold."

"Hmm." Will looked thoughtful. "I feel that way too. Believe me, I'd much rather be focusing on you than tracking down a thief. But you're wrong about one thing."

MYSTERIES OF COBBLE HILL FARM

"What's that?"

"We have started our life together. We're living it right now. There will always be things to deal with. Illness. Pressure at work. Perhaps even children, one of these days." He smiled.

That made her smile too.

Will continued. "But life is what happens during those things. It's all about how we respond to situations that matters. Are we going to live our lives continually distracted by the challenges? The worry? Or are we going to live life to the fullest in spite of them?"

Words to consider, indeed. Harriet laced her fingers through his in reply. He was right, of course. This moment, rushing to Kirkbymoorside, was part of their marriage and part of overcoming obstacles together.

It didn't take long to reach the address that Sandi had given Harriet. A rustic wooden sign told them they were at the Robin's Nest Retreat. Harriet climbed out of the car and waited for Will to join her, and they entered the small lobby. Chintz wallpaper lent the space a charming feel, and floral ruffled curtains framed the windows. Through the windows, she could spy a glimpse of a lovely traditional English cottage garden overflowing with lavender and hollyhocks.

Too bad they were in such a hurry. The place was adorable and a location to mentally bookmark for later. She would love to stay there with Will sometime. A silver bell rested on the counter with a laminated sign behind it: KINDLY RING FOR SERVICE.

Harriet rang the bell. A few moments later, a flash of movement at a side door caught her eye. A woman in a flowing maxidress and floppy straw hat entered the room, her arms full of cut flowers and greenery. "Can I help you?"

"I certainly hope so." Harriet greeted the woman, who introduced herself as Rebecca, and explained their situation.

"So you're looking for someone named Natalia Bishop?" Rebecca asked.

Harriet nodded.

"Hmm. I don't recognize the name, but if she came in yesterday, my husband likely checked her in. We alternate shifts. Let me see if we're renting a room to her." She shook her mouse to wake up the ancient computer sitting on the desk and tapped a few keys. Then she tapped the keyboard again, a little more aggressively this time. "This hunk of metal couldn't be slower if it were a stone. Looks like I'm going to need to restart it. That'll give me a second to pop these beauties into a vase. Be right back." With the computer in the process of rebooting, she disappeared into another room with her flowers.

Harriet impatiently drummed her fingers on the wooden surface of the desk while she waited for Rebecca. Finally, the computer came on again and Rebecca returned to check the schedule. She clicked the mouse several times and then said to Harriet with an apologetic expression, "I'm sorry. You just missed the person you're looking for. Natalia Bishop checked out this morning."

"Do you have any idea where she went?"

"No, I'm sorry. Now, if you'll excuse me, I need to get back to my work."

Harriet's hopes sank as Rebecca went back out to the garden. She turned from the counter to face Will. "Now what do we do?"

Will shrugged. "Sandi mentioned that she thought Talia was headed to a jewelry event. Maybe we should do a search for local fairs? See if anything comes up?"

Harriet shook her head. "We don't know if the event is even in this town. Talia could be headed anywhere." August was a packed month for events. What were they going to do? Drop in on every jewelry-related affair on the calendar?

Harriet turned to head out the door. Then she stopped. There was a row of wooden pegs on the wall opposite the desk. And a familiar, feathered hat rested on one of them. Beneath the hat sat a linen-bound guest book.

Harriet rushed over to the guest book and read the most recent entry.

> *Thoroughly enjoyed my stay at your lovely accommodations. Thank Gil for the encouraging talk about my business. If I sell a boatload with Wensleydale Auction House, I owe my success to you!*

"Wensleydale Auction House." Harriet did a quick online search. Bingo! The auction house had an event going on at that moment not far from the Robin's Nest. She grabbed the hat from its peg and locked eyes with Will. "Looks like we've found our next stop."

CHAPTER TWENTY-ONE

Harriet and Will drove straight to the event. An open, grassy field served as a parking lot. Will pulled into an empty spot beside a navy blue Vauxhall Corsa.

He turned off the engine. "Ready?"

Harriet slung her handbag over one shoulder. "Ready. Let's go track down Talia."

The task was more complicated than she had imagined. They purchased tickets at the entrance before plunging though the gate and into the fray. The event bustled with vendors, and there were crowded rows of booths as far as she could see. She didn't want to leave Will's side. If she did, how would she ever find him again? Either one of them could easily be swallowed up in the crush of people milling around.

She held tightly to his hand as she twisted in the direction of the parking lot they'd just come from. At least she thought it was the direction of the parking lot. "I've completely lost my bearings. Is the car back that way?"

"I have no idea," Will answered. "This is madness. How on earth are we going to find Talia?"

"Can I help you?" A voice snagged Harriet's attention. Almost hidden behind a colorful display of bracelets, necklaces, and rings stood a bohemian-looking woman with long, auburn hair and an ankle-grazing dress. She extended her hand over the displays. "Ivy Bell," she said.

Harriet shook Ivy's hand. "Harriet Bailey. I mean, Harriet Bailey-Knight."

Will looped an arm around Harriet's waist. "We've recently wed."

The woman raised an eyebrow and angled a glance at Will. "No ring?"

Will glanced down at the spot where his missing wedding ring used to be. "It's missing," he said.

Harriet sighed. "Long story, believe me."

"Hmm. I could help you find a temporary replacement." The woman showed them an assortment of men's jewelry on the counter before her. "It's only nickel-plated, but I promise it won't turn your finger green."

Will exchanged a glance with Harriet. "I suppose it wouldn't hurt to browse."

Will perused the racks while Ivy turned her attention to Harriet. "Anything I can help you find?"

Harriet feigned interest in some glass bead necklaces before pressing forward with the real reason they were at the event. "Actually, we think a friend of ours—Natalia Bishop—might have a booth here. We need to talk to her. Would you happen to know how to locate her?"

Ivy narrowed her eyes. Harriet thought it might help to actually be a customer, so she purchased a few strands of the necklaces. Ivy took her money and said, "The name is familiar. Does she own a shop called Golden Brilliance? Something like that?"

"Golden Radiance. Yes, that's her shop," Harriet eagerly replied. She felt a flicker of excitement. Perhaps they were close to having their questions answered. Maybe they'd find the thief and be free to leave on their honeymoon tonight.

"Let me check my records. I helped organize the vendor hall this year, so I have a list of the participants and their booth assignments." Ivy reached under the table to pull out a binder stuffed with papers. She flipped through the printouts, running a finger down the pages as she searched for Talia's name. "Let's see… Baker, Barnes, Bennett… Well, that's odd."

Will frowned. "What's odd?"

"Your friend isn't on the list as a vendor." Ivy frowned. "I know she attended last year though. My booth was beside hers."

"You mean she doesn't have a booth here?" Harriet hoped they hadn't traveled all that way for nothing. Why would Talia have mentioned she was participating in an event if she wasn't? Was she even in Kirkbymoorside? Or had they ended up with nothing to show for their efforts but a nickel-plated wedding band and a couple of bead necklaces?

Ivy shook her head. "No, she's not listed. Perhaps there's another way you can contact her?"

Harriet had no idea how, given their lack of success connecting with Talia so far. Still, she thanked Ivy for her help. Will purchased a replacement wedding band and slipped it on.

Harriet's stomach sank as they turned away from the booth. "How are we going to find Talia now? And where's the auction? Talia's message in the guest book mentioned the Wensleydale Auction House. All we've seen so far are vendor booths."

MYSTERIES OF COBBLE HILL FARM

"I don't know. All this walking has made me thirsty though," Will said. "Why don't we head toward the entrance? I think I saw a sign for refreshments."

They retraced their steps to find a concession booth selling water and lemonade. A burly man holding a sleeve of paper cups greeted them. "Can I get you something to drink? Refreshments are free for ticket holders." He jabbed a finger behind him at a large, translucent carafe of lemonade with ice cubes and lemon slices floating on the surface.

Harriet's mouth watered. Not that they needed a distraction from finding Talia, but it was boiling hot. A cup of ice-cold lemonade sounded like a welcome pick-me-up while they pondered their next steps. "I'll have a cup, please."

"Me too," Will chimed in. Sweat glistened on his brow. He took their ticket stubs from his pocket to show the man, who fetched them two glasses of lemonade.

Will thanked him before downing his in one gulp. Harriet was a bit more restrained in drinking hers but only a bit.

She addressed the man again. "I don't suppose the name Natalia Bishop rings a bell with you. Does it?"

"No, it doesn't. Have you checked the big building for her? Lots of people over there."

"The big building?" Harriet asked. "You mean there's another space associated with the event?" Maybe they hadn't missed Talia after all. They still had a chance of finding her.

"Sure. The auction building is on the southeast corner of the grounds. That's where you'll find the real excitement." He leaned forward confidentially. "Word is, they're auctioning off some real gems there today. A seventeenth-century clock, a French tapestry, a rare brooch…"

"A rare brooch?" Harriet barely eked the words out. Her heart leaped with hope.

"That's what I heard," the man replied. "If you're interested, you'd better hurry though. If it's anything like the last auction, items are selling fast."

Realization hit hard. All this back and forth, trying to track down Talia, and they still might be too late. Harriet shot a glance of concern at Will.

"Boy, you two are looking peaky." The man slapped his hands on the folding table. "What's wrong? Lemonade not sitting well?"

"No, no. The lemonade was fine," Harriet rushed to reassure him. "We just need to get to the auction house quickly. Can you please show us which direction to go?"

"Sure." The man pointed a burly finger. "Just keep heading straight until you see a large white building. You can't miss it."

"Thanks for your help." Harriet dropped her cup into a trash can, and together she and Will headed for the auction house.

A bead of sweat trickled down Harriet's spine as they jogged toward the building. The announcer's introduction was loud enough that Harriet could hear him outside. "And now, up for bidding, we have lot number thirty-one. A beautiful, handcrafted brooch dating back to the Victorian era. In near-mint condition, this stunning piece will cap off any vintage collection—"

"That's my brooch!" Harriet cried. Her gait broke from a jog into a full-scale sprint. She reached the doors before Will and

MYSTERIES OF COBBLE HILL FARM

stepped into the cool interior of the auction building. She squinted to see the piece on display up front.

"Excuse me, ma'am." A woman wearing a plastic name tag on a lanyard stopped Harriet just inside the door. "You can't go in right now. The auction is already in progress."

"Y-you don't understand," Harriet stammered. "It's important. I—I need to talk to the auctioneer. It's about the item up for bid."

"I'm afraid I can't let you interrupt the auction." The woman shook her head. "The item has already been authenticated and approved. If you have an issue, you'll need to take it up with someone after the auction concludes."

"No, I'm afraid it can't wait," Harriet protested.

Will appeared behind her, a comforting presence. "Can we get in on the bidding at least?"

"Certainly not." The woman looked at him as if he'd asked if he could plant a bomb in the building. "We can't allow people to cause a distraction during the bidding. The slightest movement could be taken as a bid."

Harriet and Will watched helplessly as the bidding passed by in a flurry of activity. At first, it seemed as though ten or twelve people were raising their paddles all at once. But in just a few seconds, it was obvious that the real battle was between an elderly couple with their heads together, frantically whispering to each other, and a young woman with a long blond ponytail.

The bidding reached a tremendous amount, until, finally, the young woman relented and shook her head at the auctioneer. The elderly woman held her paddle aloft in triumph as the auctioneer's voice threaded through the microphone.

"Sold to bidder 217 for the sum of seven thousand pounds," the auctioneer said. "Bidder 217, please approach the platform to receive your goods."

The woman guarding the door stepped aside, and Harriet shot past her, Will hot on her heels. She hurried to the platform to explain to the auctioneer what had happened. The heat and excitement of the day had muddled her brain though. The right words didn't come easy, especially when the auctioneer wasn't paying any attention to her. Instead, he was trying to usher the couple who'd won the brooch toward an assistant in charge of setting up payment. "You can't sell the brooch," Harriet said breathlessly. "It's all a big misunderstanding. I need to take—"

"I'm sorry, ma'am, but you didn't win the item." The assistant interrupted her with a disapproving look. "I'm afraid you'll need to step aside and, if you'd like, you may bid on something else."

"No, you can't do that!" Harriet was desperate. Her voice rose as the pressure mounted. "You don't understand. The brooch belongs to me. It was stolen this last weekend during my wedding reception."

The assistant narrowed his eyes at her. "Do you know who took it?"

She didn't want to accuse Talia in front of all these people, but it couldn't be helped. There wasn't time to explain. The couple who'd won the brooch were talking to the cashier, and the man was digging into his wallet. She looked around the room. Was Talia even there? Then she saw her, sitting to the side, wearing a straw hat in place of the feathered one she had left behind at the Robin's Nest. With remorse in her gut, Harriet pointed at her. "That's the woman who stole it. Natalia Bishop."

The man got Talia's attention and gestured for her to come to them. "This woman has accused you of selling stolen merchandise," he said to her as she approached.

"Stolen merchandise?" Talia appeared dumbfounded. "Harriet, where would you get an idea like that? And what are you doing in Kirkbymoorside? Don't tell me you came all this way to bid on a piece from my shop?"

"I came to get back my brooch. The one you stole from my wedding reception."

The whole room had grown quiet by this time. The expression "quiet enough to hear a pin drop" really was accurate. It was as if all the sound had been sucked out of the space. Curious onlookers craned their necks to get a view of the drama unfolding on stage, and the couple at the cashier's table stared at Harriet, openmouthed.

Talia stepped forward. "Harriet, it's not your brooch. It's one I bought last month for my shop." She marched to the display stand and snatched up the brooch. Then she whirled around, strode over to Harriet, and thrust it under Harriet's nose.

Harriet looked down at the brooch, fully intending to press forward with her accusation. Except that Talia was right. The brooch wasn't the one Aunt Jinny had loaned to Harriet. There were similarities, but the differences were distinct enough to identify it as another piece of jewelry. "That's not my brooch," she managed to croak out.

"That's what I said." Talia's expression was not one of shock, however. She was angry.

Talia handed the brooch to the auctioneer, grabbed Harriet by the elbow, and steered her outside the auction building. Harriet looked over her shoulder and saw Will speaking to the couple who had won the brooch. Judging from the looks on their faces, she assumed he was apologizing to them for the confusion he and Harriet had caused.

Once outside and before Harriet could say a word, Talia turned, eyes flashing. "Okay, Harriet. Give me one good reason why you'd trash my integrity and my reputation in front of all those people. I thought we were friends."

Tears welled up in Harriet's eyes. How had she gotten everything so wrong? How could she explain this to Talia?

CHAPTER TWENTY-TWO

London, England
Spring 1855

The house was so empty without Mrs. Hosten.

When she had gone, so had the last vestiges of Catherine's old life. She wondered if she was going mad sometimes. Days spun past without reason or purpose. Malaise rested on her like a burial shroud.

Thank goodness for Elizabeth. Her friend had been a saint to drop by for frequent visits.

Catherine glanced at the stately grandfather clock that presided over the hallway. It was nearly noon. Elizabeth was late today.

Catherine wandered from the hallway to the sitting room. She had rationed the nest egg of remaining money as prudently as possible, yet it still wasn't enough. The funds had dwindled in weeks. Helplessly, she had watched as time chipped away at resources. The colonel had assisted her efforts to hawk piece after piece of furniture until she was left with only the bare necessities. All the frills and finery, stripped away. Her jewelry and stylish dresses—tokens of Alexander's optimistic young love—were sold to strangers.

The only item she hadn't yet parted with, aside from her gold filigree wedding ring, was the emerald brooch.

Her face a mask of concern, Mary ran into the sitting room and plopped down on the bare wooden floor. The Persian rug had been sold a fortnight earlier. Mary didn't seem to mind though. Children took things as they came and suffered no worries for tomorrow. How Catherine envied that.

A sob burst from the child's lips, and she looked up quizzically. "Dada gone?"

Her eyes reminded Catherine of Alexander's clear gaze. Catherine reached forward to bundle her daughter into her arms. She pressed her face into her sweet-smelling hair. "Yes, sweetheart. Dada is gone. But dry your tears, my love. He is in heaven, and we shall see him again someday."

Mary snuggled into her mother's embrace then pulled away to take her mother's face between her hands. "Dada gone?" Mary asked again, softer this time.

The doorbell rang in place of Catherine's answer. She pressed a kiss to the top of her daughter's head and set her down. "Someone is at the door. Who might that be?"

Mary's eyes brightened. "Liz-bet?"

"Yes, I think so. Let's go see."

She took Mary's hand and led her into the foyer, where Elizabeth stood outside the door. When Catherine let her

MYSTERIES OF COBBLE HILL FARM

friend in, a cool breeze rippled her skirts. "Let me get Mary settled. Then we can take our tea in the sitting room."

She occupied Mary in the kitchen with a treat. Mrs. Hosten and Nanny might be gone, but Catherine was quite capable of fetching crackers and milk. In fact, there might be a good many things she was capable of. Being alone had forced a certain independence. She carried the tea tray out to the sitting room. She could keep an eye on Mary from there, and she would also have privacy to speak with her friend.

Elizabeth looked expectant as she settled into a chair with her tea. "I may have found a position for you."

How like Elizabeth to try to fix things. It was as much a part of her personality as her caring nature. She was only a few years older than Catherine and treated her like a much-loved younger sister.

Elizabeth continued. "Frederick knows a family in Alton in need of a governess for their two young daughters. They would provide lodging and meals, as well as a small stipend. Their estate is a modest one in the country, but I think you could find happiness there."

"No." Catherine answered quietly but firmly. Certainly, a country estate in Alton would be lovely. But it would be a constant reminder of all she had lost. Her husband. Her home. Her future plans. She would be trapped, never able to aspire to anything higher. It wasn't what she wanted for Mary.

Elizabeth frowned. "Don't be hard on yourself. With your education, you would do well in the position. Mary would be free to learn alongside your other two charges. Language, painting, drawing, archery... All three girls would excel under your tutelage."

Elizabeth misunderstood. She thought Catherine doubted her own abilities. Of course, her friend's reaction made sense. Catherine had always been passive. Letting others take risks while she followed behind on their well-worn path.

But not now. A different dream bloomed in her heart. One where she set aside worry and fear to blaze a new way forward.

"Please consider it," Elizabeth continued. "You would be comfortable. And maybe you could finally let go of your fears about the past."

Catherine set her mouth in a determined line. Elizabeth was right about one thing. She needed to let go of this situation with the brooch. She needed to find a new purpose on which to focus.

What was there for her here in England? Most of her family had migrated to America after the most recent enclosure act swallowed their property. America offered cheaper parcels of land, more freedom, and opportunity for social mobility. Alexander had no brothers or sisters, and his parents had passed years prior in a dreadful cholera outbreak. All he had was a doddering old uncle in Dover given to drink. Aside from the Powells, Catherine had little reason to stay.

An idea had been taking root in her mind for the past few weeks. Maybe America was her path forward too. The thought of remaining in England suffocated her. A fresh start might afford her the best chance for a new life.

"Actually, I've made my own arrangements."

MYSTERIES OF COBBLE HILL FARM

"You have?" Elizabeth's eyebrows shot up. Then surprise turned into admiration. "You have. Good for you. What are your plans then?"

Catherine inhaled deeply to ground herself. "I'm going to America."

"America?" Clearly, this wasn't the arrangement Elizabeth had envisioned.

"Yes, I have some family there. A fresh start will be best for Mary and me."

Elizabeth stared at her. "I don't know what to say. That's a huge undertaking. Have you secured funds for passage?"

Catherine shook her head. "Not yet. But I will."

She still had assets, even if they were meager. A few more pieces of furniture. The house. It would bring a tidy sum. If only she didn't owe so much to the bank. The debt Alexander had taken on in his last few months at home would make a dent in profits. How to manage that?

"Perhaps Frederick could help. We could lend you some money, until you get on your feet. It wouldn't be any trouble, and you could stay here, in London. I can talk to him tonight."

"I can't let you do that." Elizabeth might not understand, but Catherine was determined to find her own solution to her problems.

"Why not?" A puzzled expression crossed Elizabeth's face. "You don't have anything to prove. Why not make it easy on yourself?"

Elizabeth wouldn't let it go. Catherine knew her well enough to be certain. She would keep on with her good-natured

206

prodding until Catherine was tucked away in a country cottage with no space to call her own. She would have no troubles...but also no life. She would become an invisible woman long before her passing.

So she pretended to acquiesce. "Never mind. You may talk to the colonel tonight if you would like."

Elizabeth beamed. "Wonderful. I'm glad you've come around."

In a fit of emotion, Catherine threw her arms around her friend. Were Elizabeth's efforts any less meaningful because they weren't the right option? She would certainly miss her. "You're a good friend, Elizabeth. I won't forget your kindness."

Elizabeth hugged her back before saying goodbye.

Catherine immediately headed to her room to pack her few belongings. She had only a couple of days to get things taken care of before the colonel and Elizabeth pressed about the governess position. It wasn't much time.

When she returned to the sitting room, she saw Elizabeth had left something. The letter that Alexander had dictated in his dying moments.

"Goodbye, my love," she whispered to the empty room. She would leave the letter where it lay.

Elizabeth would find it after Catherine had left.

CHAPTER TWENTY-THREE

Talia crossed her arms over her chest and leveled a glare at Harriet. "Well? You owe me an explanation. Why did you just tell an entire room of buyers that I *stole* the item that my shop had up for bid?"

Harriet exhaled a long breath. "It's a long story. Why don't we sit down?"

Talia agreed, and they navigated a short distance away to a bench in the shade.

"So?" Talia asked again. "Why are you here, Harriet? I thought you were supposed to be on your honeymoon. Somehow, I have a feeling that your original plans didn't include Kirkbymoorside?"

Harriet shook her head. "No, you're right. Will and I followed you here."

"Followed me here?" Talia stared at her as if she had said Big Ben didn't exist. "Why on earth would you do that?"

"I had to. Polly saw you run out of the reception just before the lights went out. When we discovered the brooch had been stolen, we tried to call you…"

Talia pressed a hand to her forehead. "Okay, this is all starting to make sense now. I had to nip out from the reception early, so I missed whatever happened with the brooch. I must've been outside making phone calls when that happened. And I suppose that would also explain the squad cars I passed on my way out of town. I wondered why they were speeding up the road. I assumed there had been an accident."

Was Talia innocent? She had made a good show of acting clueless so far, but that didn't mean Harriet was ready to scratch her name off the suspect list. "So, you really didn't know anything about the brooch disappearing?"

"Of course not. I can't believe you would think I'd steal from you."

Harriet shook her head. "I really am sorry, Talia. I just couldn't think of any other explanation, and you'd just asked about the brooch and told us how much it was worth. Why did you leave the reception so suddenly? When I couldn't reach you afterward, I got suspicious. Then to find out you were selling a vintage brooch at this auction…"

Talia cast her gaze down at her shoes. "You really want to know what's going on?"

"Yes."

Talia sighed. "This is embarrassing to admit, but the shop is in trouble."

"I know. Aunt Jinny mentioned something about a loan?" Harriet rushed to apologize. "I'm sorry if that was private information, but she told me because she was worried about you. She didn't know how much trouble you were in or how desperate you were to get out of it."

"Certainly not desperate enough to steal." Talia hooked her thumb over her shoulder at the auction building behind her. "If you don't believe me, check the rest of my items on the auction block.

MYSTERIES OF COBBLE HILL FARM

They were all sourced ethically. Besides, I'd have to be a fool to try to sell stolen goods at a public auction like this one. The employees at Wensleydale Auction House pride themselves on having a rigorous vetting process. They assess and authenticate every piece. You have to have a paper trail a mile long proving provenance. Trust me, I don't have your brooch."

"So why leave so suddenly then?" Harriet asked.

"Because I was embarrassed! And hurt." Talia's eyes flashed with emotion. "Your aunt had just turned me down for a loan. Do you know how humiliating that was? I was standing at the table at your reception, trying to act like nothing had happened. Finally, I couldn't take it anymore. I had to leave. I ran out to the parking lot and tried to figure out what to do. Then it hit me. I had bought some pieces on a whim at an estate sale, and I remembered this auction in Kirkbymoorside. I called them to ask if they could work my pieces into the lineup, and they said they had a spot."

"But why didn't you come back to the reception to say goodbye?"

"It felt like my last chance to save the business," Talia said. "I didn't know if they'd give the spot to someone else if I didn't show up quick enough. I wasn't going to let that happen. I was determined to sell those items."

Harriet remembered how single-minded Talia had always been with her ambitions. That lined up. But if Talia had headed for the exit before the lights went out, why had Harriet felt the feathers from Talia's hat brush by her face in the dark? The bridal table was in the back of the hall, while the heirloom table and the doors that led into the hallway were on the other side. It was the same puzzling scenario that Harriet had faced with Benedict.

What had happened? Harriet didn't remember anyone else wearing anything feathered. One stray detail, like the sneezing, might be explained away. Two weren't so easy to dismiss. Something wasn't adding up, and all of Harriet's theories over who had stolen the brooch had been proven incorrect.

She must be overlooking some crucial piece of information. Something that would make everything click into place. Every mystery she had solved worked the same way. One clue would lend context to the rest, like a key that unlocked the whole puzzle.

The only question was, would she ever find the key?

Just then, Will approached the bench where Talia and Harriet sat. Talia rose and started to head toward the auction building, but Harriet stopped her.

"Wait, Talia. Please." The enormity of what she might have cost the woman weighed on her. In the thick of a mystery, it was easy to become blind to the needs of others. All that mattered was figuring out whodunnit. Now, she saw beyond that. She might have cost an innocent friend of the family her job. A reputation she had worked tirelessly to establish.

Talia turned to face Harriet. "Yes?"

"I'm really sorry I doubted you. I should've known better. If I can do anything to make things right or to help, please let me know."

"Thanks, Harriet." Talia sighed. "I guess I can understand why you would have been suspicious of me. I've been doing a lot of thinking about how I've been running the business and how that might be creating other kinds of problems for me."

"What do you mean?"

"I've put so much pressure on myself. On the store's success. Worry has cost me more sleepless nights than I care to admit. But I've finally come to the conclusion that if the shop succeeds, wonderful. If for some reason, it doesn't… Well, I gave it my best shot. Maybe it took an incident like this to make me realize how skewed my priorities have been."

Talia told them goodbye and disappeared inside the auction building. Harriet and Will headed for the car and began the trip back to White Church Bay. What were they to do next? What step should they take? Harriet had no idea. Every lead had been exhausted.

But God, You know. You told us not to worry, because You know. Help us figure out what to do. What are we missing?

At her prayer, a heaviness lifted from Harriet. Calm for the first time since the brooch had been taken, she relaxed in the passenger seat as Will drove. How would God answer her prayer? What new revelation would He bring to light?

They were within fifteen minutes of White Church Bay when the car sputtered and died.

One call and a tow to the nearest mechanic later, they had a diagnosis: an overheated engine.

"I guess the warm weather was too much for the cooling system," Will mused as he watched the tow truck leave after unloading the Jaguar. He angled a glance at the mechanic. "Any idea how long the repairs will take?"

"Not long. It's a quick fix. You'll be your way in an hour or two," the mechanic replied. "We'll give you a call when it's ready. You can wait over there." He pointed to some uncomfortable-looking folding chairs sitting in a corner of the stuffy waiting room.

Yikes. A couple of hours spent waiting there would feel like an eternity. Not the way Harriet wanted to spend the afternoon. At this rate, she would be completely worn out before she and Will had a chance to travel around the country together.

The expression on Will's face told her he felt the same way. He peered out the waiting room window to glance down the street. "I think I see a restaurant. Feel like getting a bite to eat instead?"

Harriet looked at her watch. They had already grabbed lunch—take-away fish and chips—on the way home from the auction. Now it was just after one thirty. She wasn't very hungry yet. "I'm not ready for a full meal, but a small pick-me-up would be nice."

After ensuring that a station employee had Will's cell phone number, they left for the restaurant. Amusingly, it turned out to be an American-themed diner. The inside of the building was designed to resemble a 1950s greasy spoon hole-in-the-wall, with checkerboard floors and a jukebox in the corner.

"Is this the equivalent of an English teahouse in the States?" Harriet asked.

"I suppose so." Will appeared similarly entertained.

A server decked out in a poodle skirt and saddle shoes seated them in a corner booth. "What can I get for you?"

"Could I have a slice of blueberry pie, please?" asked Harriet.

"Strawberry rhubarb for me," Will added.

MYSTERIES OF COBBLE HILL FARM

The server hurried off with their order, leaving Will and Harriet alone to talk. Harriet told Will about how she had prayed for guidance as they were leaving Kirkbymoorside. "This wasn't the answer I expected," she said.

"You mean you don't expect to find the thief hanging around in this diner?" Will joked.

Harriet laughed. "Probably not. And I didn't think the car would break down, that's for sure."

Will shrugged. "Then again, we can't always see how things fit together. Sometimes a setback turns out to be a help in hindsight."

"Unless the thief walks through that door or meets us at the mechanic's, I don't see how this is helping," Harriet said. A setback was a step in reverse. Like the suspects list falling through. Like the car breaking down. How could those things turn out to be positive?

"You never know," Will said. "We tend to think of the path we're following as a straight line. But real life is seldom like that. It's often made up of a series of steps that seem random, at least until you step back and take in the whole picture. Maybe the car really did break down for a reason?"

"Maybe." But Harriet harbored a sliver of doubt. "Nothing makes sense, Will. I just can't shake the feeling that we're missing something significant." But what? She had put herself through all the mental paces. She had thought through the details of the reception. She'd pored over the video stills and combed the suspects list. Her last hope was that Polly had dug up some useful information on Alexander and Catherine Taylor and that, miraculously, that information might somehow point to the solution of the stolen brooch.

As she and Will ate their pie, she dialed Polly. Her friend quickly picked up. "Harriet! Where are you?" Polly sounded out of breath. "I just stopped by the hotel, but the woman at the front desk said you were out."

"Will and I are unexpectedly marooned outside of Kirkbymoorside," Harriet answered. She looked around at the empty restaurant. "I'm putting you on speaker so Will can hear." She caught Polly up to speed on all that had happened with Talia over the last few hours. "We were headed back to White Church Bay when the car broke down."

"Oh, no! Are you both okay?" Polly asked.

"We're fine," Harriet assured her. "The car's at the shop right now. The mechanic assured us it's an easy fix, so we shouldn't be gone much longer. We're killing time at a diner. They have the most marvelous blueberry pie."

"I was feeling sorry for you." Polly laughed. "Until you mentioned pie."

"It's a hardship," Harriet said, grinning at Will. "But we'll survive."

Polly sounded amused. "I'm glad to hear that. Do you need anything? Is that why you called?"

"No, we don't need anything, but thanks," Harriet answered. "I phoned you because we're at another dead end with the mystery. Please tell me you found some information on the Taylors? We could really use some help."

"Perfect timing. I'm actually at the library right now and am finding quite a bit." Polly sounded pleased with herself. "It took some digging, but I found an Alexander Taylor who matches up with the dates and information in the letter. I was able to track down his obituary. Do you want to hear what it says?"

"Sure." Harriet scooped up another bite of pie and chewed as Polly read.

"'We regret to announce the death of Alexander Taylor, formerly a respected London banker and a distinguished officer in the Crimean War. Mr. Taylor passed away on February 5, 1855, after a valiant battle with typhoid fever. He spent his last days in the company of fellow wounded soldiers at St. Thomas' Hospital in London. He will be remembered not only for his contributions to the banking industry but also for his courageous service during the recent conflict in Crimea. Mr. Taylor leaves behind a devoted widow, Catherine, and a young daughter, Mary, who deeply mourn his loss.'" Polly stopped reading. "There's more information about his funeral and where it was held, but I think you get the gist."

Harriet did. "So, Catherine was widowed shortly after Alexander wrote the letter we found at my house?"

"It looks that way."

"That must have been so difficult." Being newly married to Will made the thought of Catherine losing her spouse hit hard. How must the poor woman have struggled? "What happened to her afterward? And their daughter? Did you find anything out about them?"

"I did. It turns out that Catherine left England shortly after Alexander's death and started a new life for herself and Mary in New York. She became an author."

Harriet took another bite of pie. The flavors burst in her mouth. She really would have to remember this place. If the rest of the menu was anything like their pie, it might be worth the drive from White Church Bay. "Wow. What did she write?"

"Oh, things for ladies' magazines. Recipes. Short stories. A few mystery novels that achieved some success. She has quite a paper trail professionally, though it was a doozy to link her to her pen name."

"Which is?"

"Kate Tyler."

Harriet nearly choked on her pie.

Polly prattled on, with no awareness of Harriet's reaction. Will, though, was looking at her with alarm. She took a drink of water as Polly said, "At first, I couldn't be sure. I mean, Catherine Taylor and Kate Tyler are fairly similar, but they're also really common first and last names. I wanted to make sure the connection was legitimate. It all came together when I was able to track down her obituary. It linked her right back to Alexander and mentioned her writing success. So bingo! Catherine Taylor…Kate Tyler."

Harriet was still drinking water when Polly said, "Harriet? You still there?"

Harriet coughed a few times to clear her throat. "Yes, I'm here. You're certain that Catherine Taylor is Kate Tyler?"

"Positive." The tone of Polly's voice shifted as she realized something was wrong. "Harriet, you sound shaken. What's going on?"

"Maybe nothing." Or maybe everything. Time would tell. "Will and I helped Florence Pembroke clear some donation boxes from her house, and there was a book inside that caught my eye. It was very old, published in 1871 or 1872. Something like that. It was called *The Jewel of Deception,* and it was a mystery about a woman who suspects her husband is a thief."

"It sounds interesting, but what's the big deal?"

"Polly, this book was in Florence's belongings. As soon as Will and I showed up and started questioning her about the brooch, she acted strange. Suddenly, she wanted us to get rid of items for her, including this book. We've linked the Taylors to the brooch. Now we've linked Florence to the Taylors. It's only a hop, skip, and a jump to assume that maybe—"

"Maybe she knows more about the brooch than she's letting on?" Now Polly was on the same page.

"Exactly." Harriet pushed away her empty plate. "Polly, can you pull up the Taylors on a genealogy database? See if there's any link to Florence Pembroke or her husband?"

"I can do that. Give me a minute…" The tapping of computer keys could be heard on the other end of the line. Then Polly spoke again. "I don't believe it. You're right. Go back four generations in Florence's family line, and you find Catherine Taylor. Florence's great-great-grandmother. You might be onto something, Harriet."

Harriet finished the call with Polly and looked at Will with raised eyebrows.

"I don't know, Harriet. I'm just not convinced," Will replied. "It's a lot of speculation. Florence told us she didn't know anything about the brooch, and I believe her. I've worked with a lot of older people like her in my time in the ministry. She lost her husband. She's struggling. The least we can do is shield her from unnecessary problems."

Still, Harriet was convinced there was something there. More than met the eye. Florence was connected to the mystery somehow.

They just didn't know how yet. She might not be on Will's radar, but Harriet was putting her back on the suspect list.

As the mechanic promised, the Jaguar was fixed by the time they returned to the shop, and Harriet and Will were on the road again. On the way into town, Will stopped by the charity shop to unload Florence's boxes from the trunk and back seat of the car. "Might as well clear these out now. If we leave sometime soon, we'll need the room for our suitcases."

Harriet lifted an eyebrow. "Are we leaving soon?" Van had told them to stay put in White Church Bay until the situation with the brooch was resolved. Yet that hadn't happened, at least, not in her estimation. With the new information she had gained from Polly, Harriet felt confident there was more to explore regarding the mystery.

Will placed a hand on Harriet's shoulder. "I know it's tough to hear, but it might be time to admit we're at an impasse. Maybe the brooch is a loss. What do you think?"

What did she think? It was a good question, and she saw Will's point. They had exhausted their resources and, try as she might, she didn't know what step to take next. Perhaps the authorities would receive a tip while she and Will were on their honeymoon and they would return home to the situation solved. Yet something in her told her to keep pressing forward. "I think I'm not ready to give up yet."

Will studied her face for a moment. Could he tell how serious she was? How important this felt? "Okay. If you're not ready to give up, I'm not ready to give up. We're a team. Still all right with getting rid of these boxes in the meantime?"

It wasn't as if that would affect anything. "Sure. Except for this one. I'd like to hold on to it." She pointed to the box of books containing *The Jewel of Deception*. If Florence had been mistaken and eventually wanted it back, Harriet could give it to her.

Harriet got out to help Will empty the trunk and back seat. She hugged a box to her chest. "I know Florence needed to downsize, but it's a shame to give some of this stuff away. It must've taken her and her husband years to gather all those books and antiques."

"They had quite a collection," Will agreed. They worked together and soon had all the boxes inside the store.

Harriet set down her last box. It was filled to the brim with vintage records, but she stopped as something shiny in a corner caught her eye. "Hold on, Will. I think something fell in that wasn't supposed to."

Will turned to her. "What is it?"

Harriet reached into the box to fish out the stray item. Then she held it up with a shaking hand for Will to see. "I don't believe it. Will, this changes everything. Do you believe me now? Florence knows about the brooch, and she definitely had something to do with the thefts. Nothing was a coincidence. Her uninvited appearance at our wedding. Her family being connected to the Taylors. *The Jewel of Deception*. This is proof."

Will looked perplexed. "I don't get it. What did you find?"

Harriet extended her hand. "This is Aunt Jinny's missing earring. What exactly is it doing in Florence's belongings?"

CHAPTER TWENTY-FOUR

The Atlantic Ocean
Approximately 480 nautical miles
from the Port of London
Spring 1855

Choppy water lurched under the S.S. Victoria. Catherine clamped her hand over her middle as nausea rolled in her stomach. It was nearly the same feeling she'd had when she was pregnant with Mary. This voyage, however, led to a different kind of birth.

Clutching the rail with one hand, she used her other to shade her eyes. Nothing visible showed at the horizon. No land. Only sky and water as far as her eye could see.

Yet she knew without benefit of sight that her future—and Mary's—lay ahead.

"Ain't got your sea legs yet, eh?" A scrawny man with more than a couple days' worth of stubble on his face approached her. Instinctively, Catherine nudged Mary behind her skirts.

"*I suppose not. I haven't traveled by boat before,*" Catherine said. *She took care to remain civil yet detached. She hadn't met anyone on board so far and wasn't eager to form alliances. The crush of people she had boarded along-side formed an unfamiliar chaos she wasn't ready to welcome with open arms. Maybe when this dreadful seasickness lifted she would feel more like conversing.*

"*I might have a cure for what ails you.*" *The man didn't pick up on her reluctance to talk. Instead, he inched closer and took a small, brown glass bottle from his coat pocket. He traced the fancy script on the bottle's label with a craggy fingernail.* "*Professor Bromer's Oceanic Elixir. It'll set you right in less than an hour.*"

The ship hit another wave, making Catherine's stomach drop as though she had fallen from a great height. She didn't trust the man, that much was true. Yet the hope of feeling even marginally better proved alluring. She wasn't up to the chal-lenge of weeks of illness, nor was Mary. According to the cap-tain, early April was usually a safe time to travel, but their journey had already been delayed by storms. Who knew how long it had set them behind their arrival date in New York?

Catherine glanced behind her at Mary. The little girl's dark hair made her wan face appear even more pale. She hadn't been as ill as Catherine but was taking it harder. She had cried more since they set sail than Catherine remem-bered her ever doing before. It broke her heart to see her daughter suffer.

The man extended the bottle to Catherine. "It takes quick effect. Wouldn't it feel good to have a belly full of bread? I'd wager you haven't eaten much since we sailed."

"No, I haven't." He was right. They needed to eat something soon. They must be able to keep down food and drink, or their health would fail rapidly. Perhaps this was an answer to the many prayers she had prayed since they left port. How wonderful steadiness would feel, for her and for Mary…

She reached out to take the bottle and thank the man for his kindness, but he ticked a finger at her. "No, ma'am. Not so fast." He tucked the bottle into his pocket again and held out his hand, palm up.

She frowned and looked at him.

His laugh sounded rusty from disuse. "Aren't you used to paying people for their service? Or are you too high and mighty for that?"

Shame pressed on her. "I'm sorry. Of course I'll pay." She reached in the reticule looped around one wrist and retrieved some money. "How much is it, please?"

The man greedily eyed the coins she held cupped in her palm. Then he snaked his hand toward her. "Oh, for a cure like this, I'd say—"

A woman wearing a straw bonnet stepped between Catherine and the man.

The man immediately burst into protest. "Hey, now. What do you think you're doing? You can't go poking your nose in where it doesn't belong—"

MYSTERIES OF COBBLE HILL FARM

"The lady isn't interested in what you're selling. Leave her be." The woman coolly cut him off. After a bit more pushing, the man wandered off, muttering.

The woman adjusted her bonnet and turned toward Catherine. "You should have asked him what was in that potion instead of its price. Though I doubt he would've been honest about that either."

"Why? What's in it?"

"A large quantity of laudanum and not much else, I imagine."

Catherine gasped. "Laudanum? Why would he give me that?"

"Likely because it'll knock you right out. While you're sleeping—or dying, if you drink too much—he'll pinch your valuables right off your person. I watched him swindle another poor soul last night. I couldn't stop him then, but I'm glad I could now."

Realization dawned on Catherine slowly. The man hadn't been offering a gift or a gesture of friendship. This wasn't a moment of camaraderie among their group of travelers. He sought not only to profit from her but to take advantage of her.

How horrid. Her legs began to tremble violently as reality set in. How close she and Mary had come to danger. If Catherine had drunk the contents of the bottle, she might have fainted or worse. Mary would have had no one to watch over her.

What trouble could befall a small child, left alone on such a ship? Catherine's mind ran roughshod over the *possible calamities. Anyone could snatch her or harm her. What if she wandered off where she shouldn't? Who would feed her or show her where to sleep for the night? What if she fell overboard, to be whisked away by the merciless waves? The final image was too horrifying to bear.*

Catherine pressed a hand over her mouth. Then she grasped Mary's hand. "Thank you. Thank you ever so much."

The woman stuck out an ungloved hand. "Of course. We mothers need to stick together. I'm Jane Carrington." She patted the head of a wide-eyed child partially hidden behind her. He had a tangled mop of curls but looked sweet. "This is my little one, Geoffrey. We're on our way to the continent for a fresh start."

In her former life, rubbing shoulders with upper-crust society, Catherine may not have given Jane a second glance. But things were different now.

She started to extend her own hand but stopped short. The lambskin glove that covered it felt like a silly indulgence. She peeled off the glove before shaking Jane's hand. "Catherine Taylor. And this is my daughter, Mary. I'm looking for a fresh start myself."

"America is a fine place for that. It's a land of second chances. You can be anything there. Do anything. Or so I'm told."

Catherine glanced out at the wild sea beyond the ship. White-capped waves lurched and fell, taking the ship with it. When would the ocean settle? The water was at the mercy of the wind. Nature frightened her. Its strength. Its unpredictability. The future felt the same.

Elizabeth had unknowingly set Catherine on the path to find her own purpose. Who was she, without the trappings of the past? Would she still be Catherine Taylor without the silks and satins? Without the elaborate jewelry or social engagements? Who was she, without Alexander beside her or the Powells around the corner?

"It's a bit much to take in, hmm?"

Catherine's eyes left the swaying ocean to find Jane's understanding face. "Yes, it is. But I might get used to it with time."

"I know what you mean." *Jane smiled kindly.* "Care to hear a real cure for seasickness?"

"Oh, please."

"Visit the cook. Ask if he can spare some caraway seeds to chew. It'll help."

Catherine felt a glimmer of hope as she watched Jane walk away. She clutched Mary close and stared out at the waves.

CHAPTER TWENTY-FIVE

The presence of the earring finally convinced Will that the widow might know more than she had let on. He and Harriet wasted no time rushing to Florence's house, where an unfamiliar car was parked out front.

Harriet and Will exited the Jaguar and navigated to the front door. Will knocked, and the door quickly swung open to reveal Florence's son. Florence appeared behind him and motioned Will and Harriet inside.

As Harriet walked into the living room, her mouth fell open. Florence's home had drastically transformed since her last visit. Surfaces were clear. Boxes were removed. No books or bric-a-brac littered her home. Hercules lay contentedly on the rug, head resting on his paws. "Florence... Your place looks wonderful."

Instead of replying to Harriet, Florence shot a glance at her son. "That's what I've been trying to tell Preston." She smiled. "Preston, I don't think you were formally introduced to my friends at the police station. This is Will and Harriet Knight. They've been helping me straighten up the place."

The man gruffly acknowledged them. "So, you've been helping my mum. I suppose I owe you a thank-you."

MYSTERIES OF COBBLE HILL FARM

Will's eyes were wide as he surveyed the room. "I believe Florence has done more work than we have."

"Oh, no," Florence said. "I've had lots of help. Benedict was a dear to rush through repairs, and that lovely couple from the automobile club helped me sort out Robert's car memorabilia items."

Will continued. "Sounds like Harriet and I got the easy job. All we did was cart away a few boxes."

Boxes! Harriet had been so taken aback by the pristine state of the widow's house that she had forgotten why they'd come in the first place. "Speaking of that, Florence…" She leaned close to the older woman. Even if Florence was the thief, she still deserved a measure of dignity. It wouldn't be right to confront her in front of her son. Especially when he seemed to be in such a foul humor. "Could I speak to you privately for a moment, please?"

"Of course, dear. I need to fill the bird feeders anyway."

Harriet helped Florence lug a bag of birdseed to the garden while Will stayed in the house to carry on a conversation with Preston. Florence poured seed into the feeders, and the birds immediately began to flock in their direction.

Harriet tried not to flinch as they fluttered by her. She cleared her throat. "Florence, I have to talk to you. When Will and I took your boxes to the charity shop, we found one of my aunt Jinny's pearl earrings inside."

Florence looked up with a confused expression. "Jinny who?"

"Jinny Garrett. She's a local physician." Did Florence really not know her aunt? Had she stolen from them all, thinking they were random strangers? "She has a pair of pearl earrings, and one went missing yesterday morning. My father had a watch disappear. And Will's wedding ring was stolen."

She hoped that was enough information to prod Florence into a confession. But she only looked more puzzled. "I don't understand. I don't know any of those people. Other than your husband, of course. How did your aunt's earring get in one of my boxes?"

"Florence, I know who originally owned the brooch. Alexander and Catherine Taylor. I also know that your family line is connected to them. You had a book in your home that Catherine wrote. My friend, Polly, checked a genealogy database to see if there was some familial connection between you and her. I know you're related."

Harriet studied Florence's face but found no signs of deception. Oh no. Had she barked up the wrong tree again? She walked to the car, where she retrieved Kate Tyler's book from the box in the back seat. She returned to show it to Florence.

"See?" She pointed a finger at the book's title page. "Kate Tyler is the same person as Catherine Taylor. Your ancestor."

Florence took the book with a gasp. "This was in the donation items? I didn't mean to give this away. I must've accidentally slipped it in with Robert's books. But the brooch doesn't ring a bell. All I have is Catherine's book and a few pieces of correspondence."

Was she telling the truth? Florence knew about this box of books and had adamantly stated they must be given to charity. Why was she so surprised now? Hercules lay on the front steps, tongue lolling from the heat. He lifted his head to give a half-hearted growl at a passing bird.

Harriet glanced skyward. *Dear Lord, please help me. Every path has led to a dead end. I'm trying not to worry, but the brooch is important. How is this situation going to resolve? I can't figure it out…*

Just then, a dark-colored bird flew close enough to brush by her face. A magpie landed on Florence's arm to nip a sunflower kernel from her open palm.

"Keep an eye on this one." Florence chuckled. "This is Jet. Out of all the birds, he comes around most frequently. I recognize him, and he recognizes me. Or at least he recognizes the food I hold out." The bird tipped his head to one side and then the other as Florence talked. Harriet could detect a glimmer of intelligence in his eyes.

"Jet is smart but a bit feisty," Florence continued. "Likes to dive-bomb if he sees something shiny. You need to watch out."

"Watch out! Watch out!" The bird repeated the words. His voice sounded eerily like Florence's voice, and he punctuated his exclamation with a rusty chortle.

"Magpies are incredibly bright," Florence told Harriet. "They're social, they know how to problem solve, and they're talents at mimicry."

"Watch out!" Jet cried again.

"Wait a minute." Harriet drew in a deep breath as the mystery suddenly zoomed into focus. The brush of feathers by her face at the reception. The sneezing sound. The seemingly random robberies that had taken place near Florence's house. The thief who had vanished into thin air…quite literally.

All this time, she had been searching for the thief in the wrong places! Harriet couldn't believe she hadn't seen the truth before her eyes the whole time.

Without a word, she spun on her heel and began jogging toward the house.

"What are you doing? Is something wrong?" Florence called after her, but Harriet didn't answer. There wasn't time. She owed Florence an apology. But first, she needed to give Will the good news.

She knew where the brooch was.

Harriet hastily explained the situation to Will before making a quick call to Van at the police station.

"I'll meet you at the dower cottage," Van assured them.

Preston remained at his mother's house, but Florence asked if she could ride to the cottage with Will and Harriet. "After all, this is my family we're talking about. I'm invested in the outcome too," she insisted.

"Fine by me," Will agreed. However, he drew the line when Hercules tried to jump in the back seat with Florence.

"Oh no," Will said. "Absolutely not. This is a rental car. She's not built to carry dogs."

"*She*?" Apparently, Florence felt the same way Harriet did about this personification-of-cars business.

"It's a delicate vehicle. The craftsmanship is exquisite," Will continued.

"We could debate this all day, but do we really have time to waste?" Florence raised an eyebrow at him. "Hercules is very neat, I'll have you know. I'll lay a blanket down so he doesn't scratch the seats. Besides, he knows Jet. He's the only bird he consistently barks at. He mostly ignores the others. Maybe he can help track him."

After a bit of hemming and hawing, Will relented, and Hercules got a seat in the back. True to Florence's word, he was no trouble at all. He seemed to really enjoy the lack of a roof. In a few minutes, they arrived at the dower cottage.

"So what are we looking for again?" Will asked as they launched into Aunt Jinny's garden.

"Nests," Harriet replied. "Magpie nests. They're bigger and bulkier than the other birds' nests. And they're high up. Once you know what they look like, they stand out like a sore thumb." She pointed one out so he could see what she was talking about.

After a bit of searching, Will indicated a large, twiggy structure high in one of the trees. "Is that one?"

Harriet exhaled. "Yes, that's one. But how do we know if it's the right one?"

"That's where Hercules comes in." Florence smiled. "See, I knew he'd be a help."

She let the dog off his leash, and he sniffed around on the ground near Aunt Jinny's bird feeder. He ignored the first few birds that came to the garden but broke into a barking frenzy when a magpie swooped down close. The bird immediately flew away...to the nest Will had pointed out.

"Bingo. I think that might be Jet," Harriet said. "Quick, we need to get a ladder."

"I'll ask your aunt for the one we used for the art gallery roof," Will said. "I bet it's tall enough."

Harriet remained outside as Will went into the cottage. The summer party Aunt Jinny had organized was in full swing, and the boisterous cries of children having fun could be heard through the open windows. Harriet hated to take any attention away from the special event, but it couldn't be helped. Maybe they could keep a low profile and wrap things up before anyone inside noticed...

Or not.

Faces pressed against the windows as Aunt Jinny rushed out of the cottage. "Harriet, I'm sorry. You're going to have to explain what's going on. Will tried to tell me, but it was all muddled. He went to the shed to get the ladder. Who stole my earring?"

"No one," Harriet replied. "At least not a person."

"What does that mean?"

"It was a bird." Harriet pointed up at the bulky nest overhead. "All this time, the thief has been a bird."

"And what about the brooch?"

"I don't know. We're going to have to check the nest. Hopefully, we'll find it, and it won't be damaged." Though to find all the missing items in pristine condition would be a miracle.

The commotion had drawn Harriet's parents and Anthony and Olivia from the house, as well as a crowd of curious onlookers attending the party. They all clustered around the tree.

"Why'd we come out here? Is there going to be a magician?" A freckle-faced little boy bounced on his toes next to Sebastian.

His mother put her arm around his shoulders. "No, sweetie."

"When are we having cake? Is it time for cake yet?" another child begged. The adults had their hands full, corralling children

MYSTERIES OF COBBLE HILL FARM

eager for excitement as Will secured the ladder against the trunk of the tree.

"It's no good," he exclaimed after he'd clambered up the ladder and back down again. "The nest is out of reach."

"You need a climber. I can help." Before anyone could stop him, Sebastian shimmied up the tree like a monkey.

"Sebastian, no!" Aunt Jinny tried to stop him, but he was already halfway up the trunk. A phone call and a few heart-stopping moments later, Van arrived, accompanied by a firetruck.

The little boy who had asked about a magician tugged on his mother's arm. "This is way better than a magician, Mum. Can I have a fire engine at my next birthday party?"

Firefighters spilled out of the truck, bringing with them a large safety net that they positioned under the tree.

"I should have stopped him. What if he falls?" Aunt Jinny wrung her hands. "This is such a shot in the dark. Did a bird really fly off with all that jewelry?"

Her question was quickly answered by Sebastian, who gave a celebratory whoop. He had reached the nest and peered inside. "There's all kinds of stuff in this nest. Way more than last time I looked. It's like finding the giant's treasure at the top of the beanstalk."

"Sebastian!" Olivia called to her son. "Be careful. You're terribly high up."

"Just take it slow and steady, Son," Anthony added. "One step at a time coming back down. All right?"

If Sebastian was frightened at being so high up in the tree, he didn't show any indication. He stuffed the items from the nest into

234

his pockets and then slowly began his descent. Halfway down, a small branch broke under his foot.

"Move the net!" the fire chief shouted.

The firefighters readjusted in the nick of time. Instead of hitting the ground, Sebastian bounced safely into the net. Anthony and Olivia, as well as Aunt Jinny, hurried over to make sure the little boy wasn't injured.

Everyone breathed a sigh of relief when Sebastian's head popped up over the edge of the net.

"Wahoo! Can I do that again?" His grin stretched wide. It was the happiest Harriet had seen him the entire week. "This is the best party ever!"

He started to rush toward the tree again, presumably to have another go at jumping, but Olivia held him back. "Uh, no. I hope you won't ever have to do that again. Let me check your pockets?" Sebastian held still as she and Anthony unloaded Sebastian's treasure trove of items.

Harriet smiled as the two of them set the items on a clean blanket Aunt Jinny had spread over the grass. A few strands of beads. Some mismatched cufflinks. Dad's watch. And Will's wedding band.

"Thank goodness." Will slipped off the band he had bought at the event in Kirkbymoorside and replaced it with his original ring. "That's more like it."

As happy as Harriet was to see the missing items restored to their original owners, something significant was missing. The brooch wasn't among the things Sebastian had taken from the nest.

"Did you empty everything from your pockets, Sebastian?" she asked him.

MYSTERIES OF COBBLE HILL FARM

"Yes. You can ask Mum. She and Dad did it."

"Were there any other pieces of jewelry in the nest?"

"No. That was all. I'm sure."

"Where's the brooch then?" Harriet turned to Will. "Do you think it's in another nest somewhere?" Talk about looking for a needle in a haystack. Perhaps all their work and the risk to Sebastian had been for nothing.

Sebastian gasped. "I almost forgot the gift I promised Sophie."

"I don't know if that's going to help us right now," Will said. "But I know you're anxious to get back to your party."

"No," Sebastian said, shaking his head. "I found treasures in the nest yesterday too. I didn't tell, because I didn't want anyone to be mad. I took one of the things to give to Sophie. You know, to make it up to her for breaking her flower girl crown."

Olivia propped her hands on her hips. "Wait a minute, young man. Are you telling me that you've climbed this tree that high before?"

"Sebastian!" Anthony frowned. "It's a wonder you didn't fall and break an arm. What were you thinking?"

Sebastian scurried off with his parents in hot pursuit. Harriet leaned closer to Aunt Jinny. "I take it the twins made up at some point?"

Aunt Jinny shrugged. "At least somewhat. I don't know why, but Sophie changed her tune after you visited yesterday. She didn't even care about her tiara anymore, and I'd glued it back together so it was like new. She kept saying that Sebastian told her he had a special gift for her. It's all she's been talking about the whole party."

Sebastian soon returned to the garden with a shoebox in his hands. The outside was decorated with crayon drawings, and a bow was stuck on top. "Here, Sophie."

He handed her the box, and Sophie looked at her brother with wide eyes. "Is this my present? The special one you told me about?"

"Yeah." Sebastian shoved his hands in his pockets. "I hope you like it. I shouldn't have gotten mad at you because you're better at reading than I am. You're my sister. I'm really proud of you."

Sophie smiled. "You are?"

"I am," Sebastian replied. "Besides, I'm good at other stuff. Like climbing trees. And jumping out of them too."

The twins hugged, fully laying the grievances of the past week to rest.

"Open your gift now?" Sebastian prompted his sister.

Harriet's heart raced as Sophie opened the box. Nestled inside was the emerald brooch.

CHAPTER TWENTY-SIX

Sebastian!" Harriet cried. "You had the brooch the entire time?"

"Why didn't you say anything when we asked if you had it?" Aunt Jinny added.

Sebastian's features crinkled in confusion. "That's a brooch?"

"Of course." Harriet frowned. "What did you think a brooch was?"

"I thought you were asking me about that bunch of flowers you carried at the wedding."

"You mean a bouquet?" Harriet couldn't help but burst into laughter.

The rest of the party went off without a hitch. By evening, the guests had left, and friends and family gathered in Harriet's living room to hear the story of what had happened with the loss and reappearance of the vintage heirloom brooch.

Polly was there, as well as Harriet's parents, Aunt Jinny, and Anthony and Olivia with the twins. Van had some business to finish at the station, but he promised he would check in again as soon as possible. Florence stayed with them, as her family line was an integral part of the story, and Hercules curled up contentedly on the rug. Of course, Will was there too. Whatever adventures her future held, he would be there for all of them.

Mom shook her head. "I can't believe the brooch isn't damaged. It's a miracle."

"Or an answered prayer," Will replied.

"*Definitely* an answered prayer." Harriet leaned against his strong shoulder. What a relief it was to have the mystery wrapped up and to find that none of her loved ones had been at fault. Sebastian taking the brooch from the magpie nest as soon as he did had saved the day. It also helped that the part of the tree that held the nest had been protected by a corner of the dower cottage roof. If the antique piece had been subjected to the elements for long, no doubt it wouldn't be in its current pristine condition.

"So, start from the beginning," Mom said. "This all began when some magpies got into the event hall at Ravenscroft during renovations?"

"It seems that way," Harriet answered. "They got inside at the beginning of the week and started to build nests in the rafters. It took the employees a few days to get the birds out. Everyone thought the problem was taken care of by the time Will and I had our wedding reception."

"But there was still one magpie inside—the bird Florence named Jet," Will continued. "Just before the lights went out, he swooped down from the rafters toward the heirloom table. He was drawn in by the shiny pieces of jewelry and might have been biding his time to grab an object until people had cleared out."

Harriet took charge of the story again. "No one except Sebastian saw him because they were focusing on Will's toast. Florence had already left by that point, and Talia was too upset to notice anything.

MYSTERIES OF COBBLE HILL FARM

Sebastian, on the other hand, was standing guard." Harriet gave Sebastian a squeeze.

Sebastian perked up, eager to chime in. "That's why I dove under the table. I told you I saw a big black dragon."

"You did. You did say that." Harriet laughed. "I wish I'd known what you meant at the time. It would've saved everyone a lot of trouble."

"So let me see if I understand this." Aunt Jinny tipped her head to one side. "This bird swooped down, grabbed the brooch, and flew out of the room? Wasn't he in the hallway then? How did he get out of the hotel?"

"He must have followed Talia," Harriet said. "I can't think of any other explanation. I don't know if he zeroed in on that feathered hat she wore or if he navigated out by instinct, but he got outside before the doors closed behind her. Then he flew with the brooch to his nest."

"Then he did the same thing with the other missing items?" Polly asked. "The watch and the ring you reported to the station?"

"And my earring?" Aunt Jinny added.

"Yes, Jet took those too. They were probably much easier to get back to his nest, since it was right here," Harriet said. "I can't believe I thought someone was trying to break into the art gallery to steal items. All this time, it wasn't even a person. It was a bird."

Dad leaned forward in his chair. "Mike said the damage on that thatching looked intentional. That bird must've been picking at the straw to reinforce his nest after all that heavy loot he had stashed away."

"At least we got everything back," Will said. "It's a miracle Jet didn't drop or damage anything."

"I still say dive-bombing birds are bad luck," Anthony murmured.

"Oh, no." Florence shook her head. "It's all in how you look at it. If we hadn't had the inconvenience of the brooch being stolen, none of us would be sitting here right now. I wouldn't have met the pastor and his wife, and I might not have reconciled with my son. Not to mention we wouldn't know anything about the history of the brooch. I'd say plenty good came out of a bothersome situation."

"It boggles my mind that all this fuss was because of a bird." Will shook his head.

"It boggles my mind that you and your wife thought I had reason to steal that brooch," Florence said with a grin. "Why did you think I was in financial straits, Harriet?"

"Because I connected the wrong dots." Harriet smiled sheepishly. "When Will and I saw the state of your house, we just assumed you were struggling to keep up. Everything seemed out of control. I saw the stacks of unopened mail from the bank, and then you got that phone call that upset you so much. You were talking about not wanting to leave your house, so I imagined you were in danger of foreclosure."

"Oh, my Robert would get a kick out of that if he were still here." Florence's brow wrinkled with mirth. "No, he and I were both very good with money. Those pieces of mail were interest statements. We've always had plenty of investments. How do you think we afforded the Aston Martin?"

Polly made a strangled noise but tried to mask it with a cough.

Florence's eyes darted over to Polly. "Is something wrong?"

Harriet answered for her friend. "This is awkward, Florence, but there were some rumors floating around town that you skimmed

MYSTERIES OF COBBLE HILL FARM

some money from the Gullywash Restaurant so that your husband could purchase that car."

The muscles on the widow's face grew tight. "That bit of gossip still hasn't died down? See, that's precisely why I tend to be a homebody. Better at home with my birds and dog than in the viper pit of public opinion. I'll have you know that I had nothing to do with that. If you don't believe me, there was even an article in the paper naming that fellow who was the headwaiter as the thief. What was his name? Roland something or other?"

"Relax, Florence. We believe you." Will reached over to rest a hand on the woman's shoulder. "You're among friends here."

At that, the tense look on Florence's face eased. Aunt Jinny took advantage of the quiet to pivot the conversation.

"That explains what happened to the brooch after Harriet and Will's wedding reception," she said. "But this brooch has a history that spans decades. Harriet, Polly, you two were doing some research on its origins, weren't you? What did you find out?"

"Florence helped us out some too," Harriet answered. "We found a few more letters and items that referenced the Taylors and helped us fill in a few gaps."

"Including a treasure trove of information in an old journal of Catherine Taylor's closest friend, Elizabeth Powell." Polly looked pleased with herself. "Elizabeth was an ancestor on Harriet's side of the family, you see."

"And Catherine was related to the Pembrokes," Harriet added. "I think Florence is planning to hold off on any more donations until she's sure it's not family history she's giving away."

242

"That's right." Florence smiled at Harriet. She looked as if she felt pleased to be included.

"What I want to know is how Harriet's family came to own the brooch." Olivia sat on the couch with her legs tucked up underneath her. "And why Elizabeth had the letter that Alexander wrote to Catherine. What happened that the Taylors—and Catherine's descendants—didn't have them?"

Harriet smiled. That had taken some figuring out. She had sat down with Florence and Polly and talked for a while after the firefighters and policemen left. They had used every piece of information at their disposal, including the journal with the letters *EP* on the cover that Harriet's mom had found in the art gallery attic, to put together a likely narrative. "As Polly mentioned, Elizabeth was Catherine's closest friend and confidant. She knew Catherine was afraid that her husband had stolen the brooch."

Polly picked up the thread where Harriet left off. "Alexander had written a letter to his wife right before he died. He dictated it to his nurse, and the nurse gave it to Colonel Powell, Elizabeth's husband. But Catherine wouldn't open it. She was convinced that the letter contained her husband's confession of stealing the brooch. So she left Alexander's letter and the brooch behind in England and set sail for America to start a new life."

"We found the letter in the same box as Elizabeth's journal," Harriet continued. "At some point someone must have opened it. We have no way of knowing who it was, but Catherine was wrong about Alexander. He didn't steal the brooch. The secret he kept from Catherine concerned his business failures." Harriet paused to make

MYSTERIES OF COBBLE HILL FARM

sure everybody was keeping up. It was a complex story but an interesting one. "Loan rushes prior to the Great Exhibition of 1851 had destabilized the banks. Alexander was president of one of them. As the family's financial situation grew more desperate, he did everything he could to shield Catherine. But his attempts to prevent her from worrying only intensified her concerns."

Polly carried on. "When the war began in Crimea, Alexander joined the ranks. Colonel Powell assured him that the bounty, or enlistment bonus, would place him back on good financial footing. Not to mention the other enlistment incentives that would have lessened his burden. And it might've all worked out, if not for him dying from typhoid fever not many months into his service."

"That's when Catherine's situation changed," Harriet said. "She had to make some choices about her future, and she wound up making a new life for herself and her daughter, Mary, in America. She lived there for years without connecting with the Powells. They didn't know how to find her, and she was reluctant to contact them because she left without telling them goodbye or even where she was going. She assumed they found the brooch and Alexander's letter that she'd left behind. It wasn't until Elizabeth discovered that Catherine was a writer that she was able to track down a new address and send her a letter."

Polly picked up the story. "Catherine wrote Elizabeth back, expressing a desire to renew their friendship and start fresh. When we looked through Elizabeth's journal, we found Catherine's letter. Soon after Catherine sent it, records show that she passed away from tuberculosis. It appears that Elizabeth tried to contact Catherine again, only to reach Catherine's daughter. Elizabeth offered to send Mary the brooch, but Mary told her to hang on to it. She was getting married and planned to go to Europe for her honeymoon. She told Elizabeth she would arrange to visit her when she passed through England so they could discuss the situation with the brooch, but they weren't able to get together. So Elizabeth kept it, with the hopes that one day she would be able to return it. But by the time Mary finally traveled to the continent and tried to connect with the Powells, they had left London behind and retired to a seaside cottage in White Church Bay."

Harriet allowed Polly to catch her breath. "As the years went by, the families fell out of touch, and the brooch was passed down through the generations…"

"Until it came into my hands, and I gave it to Harriet," Aunt Jinny finished with a sigh.

Everyone was silent for a few minutes as the full story sank in.

"All these years…" Harriet's mother shook her head. "All these years, the two families just missed each other."

"They did, but things finally worked out." Harriet grinned. "I should've known an animal would save the day. How appropriate. Jet stirred up the situation just enough that we all started searching for the truth. All these years after Catherine and Elizabeth's friendship, God was able to help us right what went wrong. Now the brooch can be returned to its real owner."

"But who is the real owner?" Anthony asked. "It may have originally belonged to Florence's family, but it's been with Harriet's longer. She's the one who found it too."

Harriet exchanged a smile with Florence. "Actually, Florence and I have already discussed that, and we settled on a solution."

"Which is?" Polly asked.

"Florence doesn't need the money. And she doesn't want to keep the brooch," Harriet answered. "So she suggested I contact a museum in London and inquire about loaning the piece to them. I think it sounds like a marvelous idea."

"And in exchange, Harriet offered me free veterinary care for Hercules," Florence added.

So everything was taken care of. Catherine's troubles had begun with borrowing trouble…and had ended with a borrowed brooch.

Since the discovery of the brooch, Harriet had been surrounded by nothing but jubilant expressions. Sebastian's miserable little face in the falling summer light stood in stark contrast.

Harriet crossed the garden to meet him. He was slumped with his back against a tree and a scowl on his face. He straightened up when he saw her approach.

"Hey, bud," she called. "All worn out from that amazing party? You were the star of the hour, climbing that tree like you did."

His face brightened temporarily. "The trampoline part was fun. I think everybody was proud of me."

"We were," Harriet assured him. "We *are* proud of you. I hope you're proud of yourself too."

"I don't know." His expression clouded again, and he scuffed one toe of his sneaker at the ground. "I'm still not good at reading, so what difference does it make if I can climb a tree?"

Harriet looked down to see Sebastian's superhero backpack in the grass. Several paperback chapter books had fallen out of it. "Have you been practicing reading some more? You know, the more you practice, the easier it'll be."

Sebastian frowned. "But it's not getting easier. The harder I try, the worse I get. When I found all those things in the bird's nest, I felt really special. Like Jack defeating a giant. Or a dragon. I thought since I climbed the tree and made everybody happy, that suddenly I could do anything."

Oh, her heart. It was painful to watch this precious little boy doubt himself. "You can do anything, Sebastian. You can learn to read. I know you can."

"No, I can't." Sebastian kicked away his backpack and books. He plopped down at the base of the tree and hid his face in his hands.

Harriet picked up one of the discarded books. "Can I sit by you?"

Just then, the back door of Aunt Jinny's cottage opened as Florence let Hercules into the yard. To Harriet's surprise, the big dog bounded toward her and Sebastian. He stopped short of them and sniffed at the backpack.

Harriet nudged Sebastian to get his attention.

"Look. I think Hercules wants to know what happens in the story."

Sebastian raised his head. "That's silly. Dogs can't read. Not even Hercules."

Hercules had continued nosing at Sebastian's backpack, but he stopped when Sebastian said his name. Then he licked Sebastian's face.

"I think he likes you," Harriet said. She exchanged an amused glance with Florence, who was still standing on the back steps. "He's giving you dog kisses. Maybe—"

"Maybe what?" Sebastian reached out and let Hercules sniff his hand. Oh, good. He had stopped thinking about his worries and was distracted by the dog. This might work.

"Maybe... Hercules needs you to read the story to him?"

"I told you already. I can't read."

"Hercules doesn't know that. He just wants to spend time with you. Can you do that?"

Sebastian huffed out a sigh. He seemed ready to protest, but Hercules gave him more dog kisses, and he relented. "Okay. But I'm only reading for Hercules. Not for you or anybody else."

"Right. Just for Hercules," Harriet agreed.

Sebastian moved to one side so the dog could ease in between him and Harriet. Then he took the book that Harriet handed him. He began reading the story, with plenty of starts and stops, the same way he had done when Harriet had listened to him previously. Each time he paused, however, Hercules gave him an encouraging sniff.

After a few minutes, Sebastian started to relax. He held the book in one hand and absentmindedly patted Hercules's head with the other. The more he relaxed, the more the words began to flow. The effort certainly wasn't perfect, but Harriet could tell that just by having the pressure removed, Sebastian's reading was smoother and less halting.

Why hadn't she thought of this before? She'd worked with animals for years. She knew well the therapeutic benefits they had on people. It was well documented that pet owners lived longer, had a higher quality of life, and even had lower blood pressure than people who didn't own animals. Apparently, they also helped reluctant readers find the confidence they needed to forge ahead in learning a new skill.

A sound from the house drew Harriet's attention away from Sebastian. She looked up to see that Florence had left her spot at the door and Sebastian's mother had taken her place. Florence must have fetched Olivia when she saw what was happening.

Harriet quietly left her spot by the tree and crossed the garden to Olivia with a finger held to her lips. "He's reading," she whispered when she got close enough. "With Florence's dog, Hercules."

Olivia stood beside the door as the sounds of Sebastian reading—slowly but steadily—filtered across the yard. She pressed a hand to her heart, and her eyes brimmed with tears. "He's doing it. He's really reading."

"I know." Harriet beamed.

The two women cheered loudly when Sebastian reached the end of the book. He appeared startled, but the expression quickly morphed into pleased. "I finished the book, Mum."

Olivia crossed the garden to scoop him into a hug. "You did, Sebastian. You finished your first book all by yourself. I'm so proud of you for sticking with it."

Harriet hugged Sebastian too. "See? I told you you could do it. And you did. Sebastian, you're reading!"

"I'm reading…" Sebastian said the words slowly, as if to himself. Then he said them louder and clearer. "I'm reading! I did it!"

He ran inside with Hercules to tell everyone his big news. Olivia linked arms with Harriet, and they followed him back inside the house.

"I've been so worried," Olivia said. "This is such a relief."

Harriet had been worried too, but the events of the last week had changed her. Borrowing trouble was an unpayable loan. Worry was difficult to stop, but it changed nothing. She couldn't say she would never worry again. But at the very least, she would try not to let the troubles come home to nest.

CHAPTER TWENTY-SEVEN

New York City, New York
Spring 1869

In the years since leaving London, Catherine's life had changed to be unrecognizable. What she had once thought a tragedy—change—had created her future. She was now Kate Tyler, authoress.

She had spent the time away from England building a new life for herself here in America, busying herself with respectable work. After discovering a talent for scribbling, she began making extra money. The funds accrued from countless articles written for ladies' magazines, as well as quite a few well-received sentimental novels, had propelled Mary and her into the lower reaches of the newly emergent middle class.

A knock at the door made her set aside her pen and paper.

"Mother?" Mary appeared in the doorway. She had grown into a lovely, talented young woman. Sixteen and quite capable. Her days were filled with church events, lessons, and social occasions. Within a few years, she might be married and off on her own to start a family. Though Catherine wasn't rushing anything.

"Yes? Come in, dear."

"You received a letter by post. I thought I'd deliver it to you in case it was important." A pinch of worry creased Mary's pretty porcelain complexion. "It's from a Mrs. Frederick Powell. Wasn't that the name of your close friend back in England?"

Catherine's heart beat fast. She hadn't heard from Elizabeth in years. It was a true regret, leaving England without so much as saying goodbye. At the time, she had worried that the Powells would try to stop her from leaving, and she had made up her mind. She didn't relish any interference. As the years stretched into a decade and beyond, however, she wished she had left a forwarding address. Elizabeth had been a good friend, and she missed her. Once, she had posted a letter to their old address in London, but it was returned to her, undeliverable. She didn't know if they had moved or taken ill.

"Yes, Elizabeth was my friend." Catherine answered her daughter's question. She patted the velvet stool beside the vanity table that she also used as a makeshift writing desk. "Sit with me while I open it?"

Mary obliged. Catherine's hands trembled as she slit the envelope with a letter opener. Elizabeth had sent her a letter...and a newspaper clipping. Catherine turned her attention toward the clipping first.

Her heart leapt in her throat at the headline.

JANUARY 11, 1869
STERLING'S BROOCH FOUND AT LAST! NEARLY TWO
DECADES SINCE EXHIBITION THEFT!

The brooch had been found. Were all her questions finally to be answered? Warring emotions fought within her. How was it that she both longed to know the truth yet also feared opening an old wound she had tried to forget? She had left the brooch behind in her old home, with Alexander's letter. It had no place in her new life. Had it suddenly turned up, and the authorities found it? Would they trace its stolen roots back to Alexander...and to her?

"Sterling? Is that Edward Sterling?" Mary leaned over Catherine's shoulder. "Didn't Daddy know him? I think I've heard you talk of him before. The name sounds so familiar."

"Just a moment, dear," Catherine murmured. Distractedly, she skimmed the rest of the article.

A missing emerald-and-gold brooch, created by the esteemed late jewelry artisan, Edward Sterling, was found last week in an unexpected turn of events. Sterling created the brooch at the request of Her Majesty the Queen for the Great Exhibition of 1851. The brooch, intended to captivate audiences with its intricate design and exquisite workmanship, was stolen before it could be displayed to the public. It has been missing since the opening day of the exhibition.

Authorities from Scotland Yard followed the case until the trail ran cold. They explored several leads without progress. This Thursday past, the brooch was discovered in the flat of the late Mr. Reginald Fairfax, aged fifty-three years. Fairfax was a person under suspicion early on, as he masqueraded as a member of the gentry on the exhibition's opening day. It is believed that he used his faux status to gain access to the royal processional and the palace's exhibit hall before it opened to public citizenry.

The investigation was reopened, and authorities took possession of the stolen brooch shortly after Mr. Fairfax's passing. A relative cleaning out Mr. Fairfax's flat found the item among his possessions and immediately contacted the police. It is unknown why Mr. Fairfax retained the brooch after stealing it, though some who knew him speculate he viewed the brooch more as a trophy than a means of profit. With the permission of Edward Sterling's remaining family members, the brooch will be put on temporary display at the South Kensington Museum before being returned to the family's private collection.

Edward Sterling's eldest son, John, expressed satisfaction upon having his father's creation returned to the public sphere. "My father took immense pride in his work. I'm happy that his workmanship will be enjoyed by the masses again for a brief time."

Lost in memory, Catherine startled when Mary spoke. She had nearly forgotten where she was, much less when.

"Yes, Edward Sterling," Mary insisted again. "I remember you talking about him in stories you've told me about Father. Did Daddy know someone stole from his friend?"

"I'm not sure." Catherine struggled to get the words out. What did this mean? Was Alexander cleared of wrongdoing? Perhaps Elizabeth's letter would clarify the questions swirling in her mind.

She hastily opened Elizabeth's letter. Her friend's familiar curling script greeted her.

Dearest Catherine,

I hope this letter finds its way to you. I have tried reaching out for years with little success. Imagine my surprise when I opened *Godey's Lady's Book* this month and saw your illustrated portrait and the name "Kate Tyler" next to the short story titled "A Winter's Promise." After confirming that the authoress was indeed you, my dear friend, I was able to secure a mailing address from someone at the magazine.

It has been a hardship to be deprived of your presence in our lives. I wish you felt you could have been transparent with Frederick and me, though I think I understand your motivation behind leaving as you did.

I hope you'll forgive me, Catherine, but after many years, Frederick and I decided to open Alexander's letter. I'm so glad we did, because now I can tell you what you've been longing to hear all these years. Alexander didn't take the brooch, Catherine. He had other worries and wanted to tell you about them for so long. When he grew ill with the fever, he knew he must come clean. He confessed all to you. How the bank floundered after the exhibition, pulled low by the weight of unpaid loans accrued by over-eager investors. How he let his worry drive a wedge between you and him. How he joined the fighting in Crimea to provide for you and for Mary. Please know he cared for you deeply and was a man of honor and loyalty. I hope this message provides you with a measure of peace.

I have his letter and the brooch you left behind and will post them to you at your request. Write back at your earliest convenience, dear Catherine. I would love to hear from my friend once more.

Yours affectionately,
Elizabeth

The letter done, Catherine's breath whooshed out. It hadn't been Alexander. All this time, her fear had led her to believe he was the thief. Yet here was the proof, in black and white. She held evidence of Alexander's innocence in her hands. His secret had been that the bank was failing, and with it, his way to provide for his family.

She hadn't needed to leave the brooch. He must have wanted her to avoid wearing it in public because the backlash against the bankers was so strong. She thought of the shouting crowd milling outside the exhibition. How angry they had seemed. How pale and perspiring Alexander had been afterward. It all made sense now. People were angry at him. At people like him, who were the captains of sinking ships that pulled others under with them.

The shock of how wrong she had been—how far astray worry had led her—shook her to her core.

"Mother?" Mary pressed a hand to Catherine's shoulder. Concern was evident in her deep blue eyes. She looked so much like her father, and more so, all the time.

"I'm fine." Catherine turned to embrace her daughter. One day, she would explain the whole story. Everything that had happened and all the circumstances that had led them to the present moment. But not yet.

Catherine had too much to do first.

She coughed into her handkerchief. She needed to answer her dear friend's letter and right the wrongs of the past. Then she needed to sort through her own feelings and make peace with what had happened.

She hadn't written a novel in several years. The magazines had kept her so busy writing sentimental fluff. An idea began to form in her mind. A fictional story based on her own experiences. A woman who loved her husband dearly yet also suspected him of thievery of the crown jewels. It would be a story of love, secrets, and misunderstandings. A cautionary tale to warn against creating problems for oneself out of thin air.

"The Jewel of Deception..." *Catherine whispered.*

"Mother, what are you talking about?" Mary had grown used to her mama's creative mutterings and seemed amused at the outburst.

"Nothing, dear." Catherine broke off a contemplative stare to look at her daughter. *"I'll tell you soon. I promise."*

Satisfied, Mary left the room. With the house quiet and only her thoughts for company, Catherine picked up her pen and began to write.

"All right, we're all set." It was bright and early on Wednesday morning when Will loaded the last bag into the trunk of the Jaguar. He closed the lid and turned to face Harriet. "Ready to finally leave for our honeymoon?"

"You don't even have to ask." Harriet grinned up at him before they shared a lingering kiss. The sentimental moment was interrupted by a loud voice.

"Wait, don't go yet!" Benedict hurried down the steps toward them. "Something's happened."

"Oh no." Will waved his hands in front of him to ward off the young man. "Our plans aren't changing unless the crown jewels have been stolen."

"No, you're misunderstanding me. Nothing's wrong." Harriet looked closer to find that the expression on Benedict's face wasn't one of concern. It was joy.

Lucy rushed down the steps to join Benedict and held out her left hand for Harriet and Will to inspect. A glittering diamond ring rested on her fourth finger.

"It took a lot of talking, but we straightened everything out," she said. "Now we're engaged!"

"Oh, Lucy…" Harriet threw her arms around the young woman. "How wonderful. I'm so happy for you."

"Congratulations, mate." Will slapped Benedict on the back.

"We'd like to ask if you'll marry us, Pastor? Obviously, not right away." Lucy let out a girlish wisp of a giggle. "We're planning to wed next summer. Maybe in June?"

"June sounds perfect," Will replied. "I'd be honored to perform the ceremony for the two of you. And I promise not to say that I knew Benedict from way back when…"

Harriet wasn't sure enough time had passed for the joke to hit its mark. To her relief, however, Benedict laughed. "You can say whatever you like, Pastor. I've made peace with my past. And so has Lucy. It doesn't define me anymore."

"Wonderful." Will's response was genuine and joyful. "I'm happy to hear it, Benedict."

"We should let you two leave." Lucy nudged Benedict back toward the steps of the hotel. "I'm sure you're ready to get going."

Harriet and Will waved goodbye to the newly engaged couple as they climbed into the Jaguar.

Harriet settled into the passenger's seat. Then she turned to Will with a satisfied sigh. The situation with Sebastian and Sophie the day before had clarified some things in her mind. "Will, I think I figured out a way to minister to people."

Will tipped down his sunglasses to look at her. "Oh? Did you decide on the nursery then?"

"No, but I do want to work with children." She took hold of his arm. "Sebastian was having a really hard time learning to read. But when he read to Hercules, it was like all his anxiety over not being good enough faded away."

"So you want to help children learn to read?" Will seemed confused.

"Sort of." Harriet took a deep breath. "I've looked it up, and the idea of pairing reluctant readers with pets is a real thing. A lot of libraries host programs around it, and school districts have seen struggling students make progress when they're reading to an animal instead of fellow students in the classroom. The informality of reading to a pet encourages relaxation. Students learn better when the pressure isn't so high." That was definitely what Harriet had seen happen with Sebastian.

"Wow. Really?" Will seemed intrigued. That was a good sign.

Harriet continued with her spiel. "I'd like to host a program at the church for children who are struggling to read. I won't be teaching them, necessarily. Just providing an encouraging space for them to practice their skills. Every week, I'll bring a trained therapy dog that the children can interact with while they work on reading. Maxwell will be the perfect pup to start with. We'll have a basket of picture books and Bible stories and plenty of kid-friendly seating, like beanbags, so the children feel comfortable. It could really work as outreach into the community. What do you think?"

She held her breath as she waited for his response.

"It sounds like you have it all figured out." Will grinned. "I'll have to get approval from the church board, but I don't anticipate any problems. As far as I'm concerned, you have a green light to start setting things up as soon as we get back to White Church Bay. I think it could be the perfect ministry opportunity for you."

"Thanks, Will. I'm so glad you think it's a good idea." Harriet beamed at her husband.

Will tapped the steering wheel. "I'm pretty sure we've taken care of everything. Is it time to drive off into the sunset now?"

"Here's to happily ever after," Harriet replied. She pressed one more kiss to Will's lips. Then she fastened her seat belt, and, together, they left their worries in the past.

FROM THE AUTHOR

Dear Reader,

Harriet encounters lots of troubles—some small, some significant—in this story. Little inconveniences, such as a broken elevator, pair with larger issues, such as delaying her honeymoon. All these things serve to chip away at her happiness.

It got me thinking... How many exciting moments in life do we allow worry to overshadow? Maybe more than we'd like to admit. Yet we don't have to.

Partway through writing *Borrowed Trouble*, I encountered this theme in a personal way. A concerning medical symptom cropped up out of the blue and required a doctor's appointment. The two weeks waiting for blood work to process felt like an eternity. While writing about Harriet, Will, and the many troubles they encounter, God gently reminded me that I didn't need to embrace worry either. It was tough, but I tried my best to lean into the knowledge that He held my future in His capable hands. When my results revealed a simple vitamin deficiency, I was relieved... and so happy that I hadn't wasted precious hours of my life on stress. Even if I had received negative news, worry still wouldn't have helped.

No matter what trouble you're facing today, remember that worry isn't a requirement.

Signed,
Shaen Layle

ABOUT THE AUTHOR

Shaen Layle is a *USA Today* best-selling author and Carol Award semi-finalist who writes inspirational cozy mystery from her home in the Midwest, where she lives with her artist husband, Danny, their two rambunctious but adorable boys, and their shelter pup, Violet. Trained as a literary novelist and with a decade of librarianship under her belt, Shaen loves discussing all things bookish with her readers on her website and on social media.

TRUTH BEHIND THE FICTION

Endearment Brooches

Endearment brooches, also known as lover's or sweetheart brooches, trace their roots back to the Victorian era. Sentimental jewelry was all the rage in mid-nineteenth century England, and couples exchanged brooches or other pieces of jewelry to express their affection and devotion. These pieces were often intricately crafted, and some even incorporated hairwork, in which strands of a beloved's hair were woven into a design and preserved under glass. Gemstones such as pearls, rubies, and garnets were used to symbolize love, passion, and loyalty. Endearment brooches became treasured keepsakes during times of separation such as war, and valuable holders of history for future generations.

YORKSHIRE YUMMIES

Victoria Sponge Cake

No need to wait for a special post-wedding delivery!

Ingredients:

Cake:

2 cups King Arthur self-rising flour (the brand is important, as this flour already includes baking powder to save you a step!)

¼ teaspoon salt

1 cup unsalted butter, brought to room temperature

1 cup + 2 tablespoons granulated sugar

1 tablespoon milk

1½ teaspoons pure vanilla extract

4 large eggs

Cream Filling:

½ cup heavy cream

½ teaspoon pure vanilla extract

1 tablespoon confectioner's sugar

Fruit Filling:

½ cup strawberry jam

12 oz. strawberries, washed and sliced

1 tablespoon lemon zest

1 tablespoon granulated sugar

Directions:

1. Preheat oven to 350 degrees F. Grease two 8-inch round cake pans, line with parchment paper, and set aside.
2. Sift together flour and salt in a bowl. Set aside.
3. Cream butter and sugar, either by hand or in a stand mixer.
4. Beat in eggs one at a time. Then add milk and vanilla.
5. Slowly beat in flour-and-salt mixture until batter is smooth.
6. Divide batter into cake pans and bake for twenty-five minutes. Cool on wire racks.
7. While cake is cooling, make whipped cream filling by beating heavy cream, vanilla extract, and confectioner's sugar together until stiff peaks form.
8. Next make fruit filling by gently stirring together strawberries, lemon zest, and sugar.
9. Place one cake on serving stand and spread strawberry jam on top. Add strawberry mixture, followed by whipped cream.
10. Set other cake on top of first and sprinkle with powdered sugar. Serve immediately with a cuppa Lady Grey or another favorite tea!

Read on for a sneak peek of another exciting book
in the Mysteries of Cobble Hill Farm *series!*

Lost at Sea

BY BETH ADAMS

Harriett Bailey-Knight leaned back against the fiberglass gunnel of the boat and enjoyed the feel of the wind on her cheeks. Behind her, her husband, Will, and their friend Kyle Manning chatted as Kyle drove his fishing boat north along the coast. Between the roar of the motor and the whipping wind, Harriet couldn't hear what they were talking about, so she decided to just sit back and enjoy the September sunshine. The day was bright and warm, and the newlyweds had been happy to accept Kyle's invitation to join him on a fishing excursion after church. Well, Will was happy to join him for the fishing. Harriet was there for the boat ride, and she enjoyed watching the high, craggy cliffs slide past as they made their way back to the Whitby Marina. Will and Kyle's catch—a large cod and several mackerel—were on ice in a cooler, and Harriet looked forward to fresh fish for dinner.

Gazing out toward the coast, eyeing the burnt ochre color of the high cliffs, Harriet tried to make out the buildings of the small towns they passed. She was pretty sure they'd gone past Ravenscar a few minutes ago, which meant…yes, that was White Church Bay. The adorable little fishing village they called home. There was the spillway where generations ago fisherman launched their vessels into the rough seas. There was the hotel and the pub perched on the hill just above them, and she could barely make out the old lifesaving station building. It was high tide now, which meant the water lapped at the spillway and licked at the buildings above. At low tide, the water receded enough that a person could walk out among the rocks for hundreds of yards, and treasure hunters seeking jet and fossils could explore the wide, flat bay floor.

As they continued north, Harriet could see more familiar landmarks of their small town—the sea wall, Cliffside Chippy, and, beyond them all, the steeple of White Church. Harriet had only lived in Yorkshire for a year and a half, but it already felt like home.

"Look at that."

It was the first thing Harriet had been able to hear Will say for a while, so he must have said it pretty loudly. She turned to see what he was looking at. He pointed at a sailboat bobbing on the waves. Harriet didn't see what was so interesting about it.

"Where are they?" Will asked.

"Maybe below deck?" Kyle shouted to be heard over the sound of the motor. He grabbed a set of binoculars from inside a compartment near the steering wheel and pointed them at the sailboat. "They're for sure not up top." He handed the binoculars to Will.

Harriet still didn't see what was so intriguing about it. It was a big sailboat, for sure. Probably forty or fifty feet long. The white sails were taut against the stiff wind. It was a nice boat, she could tell that. Expensive, for sure. It dwarfed Kyle's little fishing boat. Whoever was sailing in that thing had money to spare. Below deck, there was probably a nice living area. Which was no doubt where the sailors were right now.

"What's wrong?" Harriet pushed herself up and moved over to the driver's seat so she could hear. "What's with that boat?"

"Maybe nothing," Kyle said, but he turned the steering wheel to change direction, heading toward the sailboat. "It's just that we don't see anyone on deck, and it's unusual to see a boat with its sails unfurled like that with no one around. Something about it looks wrong."

"Wrong how?"

"They're too close to shore, for one thing," Kyle said, raising his voice to be heard over the motor and wind. "We're only a few hundred meters out. If they don't turn soon, they'll be headed right for those rocks."

"Plus, this close to port, they need to look out for other boats and fishing lines," Will said. "And no one seems to be doing that."

"But mostly it's the sails," Kyle said. "Boats like that have motors and use those to get where they want to go most of the time."

"So the sails are just for show?" Harriet asked. As they got closer, she could see that the name *Salacia* was written on the back of the boat in a scripty font.

"No, they'll use the sails, of course." Kyle pushed up the throttle to slow the speed of their boat as it got closer. "When it's feasible. They use the motor in tricky spots or when the winds aren't cooperating."

"But that boat has the sails up and no motor going. It's just floating, so it's at the whim of the winds. Which are currently pushing it

MYSTERIES OF COBBLE HILL FARM

toward the rocks at the bottom of that cliff." Will nodded to the shore.

"So we're going to check it out," Harriet said. Of course they were. If someone was in trouble—if someone was sick or hurt, Will would want to help.

"We're going to try the radio first," Kyle said. He lifted the small black handset by the steering wheel. "*Salacia*, this is *Seas the Day*, coming toward you on your port side. Do you copy?"

There was no response. Kyle moved a knob to change the channel he was broadcasting over and then tried again. "*Salacia*, this is *Seas the Day*. We're a hundred meters out from you. Do you copy?"

When there was still no answer, Kyle tried a few more channels, but he didn't get a response. Meanwhile, there was no movement on the deck of the sailboat. No evidence that anyone was on board at all.

"Let's put a bulletin out," Will suggested, and Kyle switched the station again.

"This is *Seas the Day*, location just off the coast of White Church Bay, calling the Coast Guard. Are there any reports of a sailboat in distress in the vicinity?" Kyle paused, and Harriet strained to hear a response.

At first there was nothing but static, but a moment later, the radio buzzed to life. "*Seas the Day*, there are no reports of a boat in distress," came the reply. "Do you need to make a report?"

"Not yet," Kyle said. "Maybe everything is okay. We'll check it out."

"Keep us posted," said the man at the other end of the line.

Kyle replaced the handset and guided them toward the sailboat. As they got closer, Harriet saw how large the vessel truly was. One of the sails swung back and forth across the deck, moving the giant beam—the boom—that held it up as it swayed. At the rear of the boat was a small sitting area with a steering wheel, but no one sat there.

"Hello?" Kyle called as they neared the ship. "Do you need help?" Once again, there was no response.

"What do you think?" Will asked. "Should we go on board, just to make sure everything is okay?"

"I don't know." Kyle hesitated, clearly nervous about the idea of going onto someone else's boat without permission. "Hello!" he shouted, louder this time. "Is everything all right?" He pulled an air horn out of the same compartment the binoculars had been in. "This'll wake them up." He pushed the button, and a loud, high-pitched blast sounded. Both Harriet and Will covered their ears, but there was no movement on the sailboat. Kyle sounded the air horn once again, and then another time. They were only a dozen yards or so from the sailboat. Surely anyone on board would have heard that noise.

Then Harriet heard a frantic barking sound, coming from inside the cabin.

"What's that?" Kyle asked.

"It's a dog," Harriet said. "There's a dog on that boat. And it sounds scared."

"The air horn probably freaked it out," Will said. "But if there's anyone human on board, it didn't get their attention."

"We need to see if the dog is okay," Harriet said. "What if its owner is in trouble and it's trying to let us know?"

"You're right. We should check it out, just to be safe," Kyle said reluctantly. Will edged past Kyle to climb, on his hands and knees, onto the front of Kyle's boat. He made his way carefully across the sheet of molded fiberglass that topped the enclosed storage area. While Will grabbed a rope tied to the thin metal railing, Kyle slowly and carefully steered his boat toward the back of the sailboat. When they were close enough that Will could lean over and reach the sailboat, he called out, "Hello! Requesting permission to board your boat!"

Kyle sounded the air horn one more time, and the only response was more frantic barking. Will slipped the rope from Kyle's boat around a railing on the sailboat, and then he pushed himself up and jumped from one boat to the other. Kyle's boat dipped, and Will landed softly on the deck of the sailboat, which barely swayed under his weight.

"My name is Will Knight," Will called out. "I'm a vicar in White Church Bay. I just want to see if you need help."

Again, no sound or movement from inside. As a wave tossed the boat, the boom swung toward Will, whipping the sail around.

"Watch out!" Harriet called. Will ducked just in time.

"Something is definitely not right," Kyle said quietly. "The hatch is wide open."

"I'm going to check inside," Will called out. He started toward the hatch, which led to a small set of stairs. "Hello," he called again, starting down the steps. "Is anyone here?"

The barking grew more frantic as Will descended, and then went quiet. What had happened? Harriet had no idea what Will would find in the cabin, but all signs pointed to it not being good. Were the sailors hurt, or worse? Was there something illegal or dangerous down there? Long moments passed, and Harriet started praying.

And then, when she was starting to get truly scared, Will popped back up above the deck. He climbed the steps, clutching the metal handrail with one hand. In his other arm he cradled a small, brown, shivering Yorkie.

"They're gone," he called out. "There was only the dog."

"What do you mean, they're gone?" Kyle yelled back. "Why would they leave their dog?"

"I have no idea," Will said, coming closer. "It looks like—well, it looks like something happened. Stuff is spilled, and it's a mess inside." He looked dazed, like he was trying to make sense of what he'd seen. "But I can tell you there's definitely no one here. Except for the dog, this boat is sailing with no one on board."

A NOTE FROM THE EDITORS

We hope you enjoyed another exciting volume in the Mysteries of Cobble Hill Farm series, published by Guideposts. For over seventy-five years, Guideposts, a nonprofit organization, has been driven by a vision of a world filled with hope. We aspire to be the voice of a trusted friend, a friend who makes you feel more hopeful and connected.

By making a purchase from Guideposts, you join our community in touching millions of lives, inspiring them to believe that all things are possible through faith, hope, and prayer. Your continued support allows us to provide uplifting resources to those in need. Whether through our communities, websites, apps, or publications, we inspire our audiences, bring them together, and comfort, uplift, entertain, and guide them. Visit us at guideposts.org to learn more.

We would love to hear from you. Write us at Guideposts, P.O. Box 5815, Harlan, Iowa 51593 or call us at (800) 932-2145. Did you love *Borrowed Trouble*? Leave a review for this product on guideposts.org/shop. Your feedback helps others in our community find relevant products.

Find inspiration, find faith, find Guideposts.
Shop our best sellers and favorites at
guideposts.org/shop

Or scan the QR code to go directly to our Shop.

Printed in the United States
by Baker & Taylor Publisher Services

Therefore do not worry about tomorrow,
for tomorrow will worry about itself.
Each day has enough trouble of its own.

—Matthew 6:34 (NIV)

MYSTERIES OF COBBLE HILL FARM

Digging Up Secrets
Hide and Seek
Into Thin Air
Three Dog Knight
Show Stopper
A Little Bird Told Me
The Christmas Camel Caper
On the Right Track
Wolves in Sheep's Clothing
Snake in the Grass
A Will and a Way
Caught in a Trap
Of Bats and Belfries
Stray from the Fold
Borrowed Trouble